INTRODUCING
C. B. GREENFIELD

"HILARIOUS!"
—*ALA Booklist*

"KALLEN HAS A BRIGHT, BLITHE STYLE, a pleasant way of turning a funny line and a genuine affection for small-town life—without sentimentalizing it."
—*The New York Times*

"AN INTERESTING AND SUSPENSEFUL STORY WITH LIVELY AND WITTY DIALOGUE."
—*Houston Chronicle*

"KALLEN COMBINES THE TANGLED WEB OF SUSPENSE fiction with the best qualities of a novel: careful character delineation, fast-paced dialogue, stylish details."
—*Publishers Weekly*

INTRODUCING

C. B. GREENFIELD

LUCILLE KALLEN

BALLANTINE BOOKS • NEW YORK

Library of Congress Catalog Card Number: 78-22100

ISBN 0-345-32159-6

This edition published by arrangement with Crown Publishers,
Inc.

Printed in Canada

First Ballantine Books Edition: August 1980
Sixth Printing: June 1984

First Canadian Printing: August 1980
Second Canadian Printing: July 1981

◘ 1

It was a Tuesday afternoon toward the end of February. By that night we would have put the weekly *Sloan's Ford Reporter* to bed—not a monumental task, since the *Reporter*'s circulation had never topped six thousand and its bulk and importance were correspondingly minor. Nevertheless, the dozen-odd of us involved in its content, layout, and printing had a certain emotional stake in producing a paper worth reading, and we tended to feel a distinct loosening of the shoulder muscles on Wednesdays.

I had barely met the deadline with my stunning article on the proposed countywide garbage-disposal plan and it was lying beside me in a manila envelope on the seat of my very used mustard-colored Honda Civic as I drove in low gear down Poplar Avenue. There'd been a heavy snowfall the night before and more snow late that morning, which had melted on the plowed streets but stuck to the two or three inches already accumulated on lawns, foliage, and various inanimate objects. Now a wintry sun was pushing through departing clouds, and I hoped fervently we'd had the last storm of the year. I hated driving on winter-wet roads, even plowed; you never knew when you might hit a patch they'd missed.

I pulled up to the curb in front of the old white mansard-roofed house which harbored the *Reporter*'s offices, picked up my envelope, and made my way up the path to the long, narrow porch attached like a well-worn apron to the deceptively domestic facade. The rent for this establishment with its slightly derelict charm was paid by my boss and occasional friend,

Charles Benjamin Greenfield, who used the top floor as his living quarters.

C.B. Greenfield had spent twenty-five years as a staff writer for NBC News, but he had grown increasingly annoyed with the news, the network, the city, and the state of the world, and, turning his few simple investments into cash, he discovered he had saved enough to indulge his romantic image of himself as a journalistic gadfly. Now he owned, edited, and was king of the *Sloan's Ford Reporter,* with which he intended to vanquish corruption, greed, injustice, disease, and inferior English teachers in the school system.

Whether he accomplished this or not, he made a good gadfly; he was irritating, relentless, stubborn, and waspish—although very few people were aware of these traits, since he walked around in the guise of an immensely calm and soft-spoken man. He also played the cello, and from the moment I first set eyes on him, sawing away earnestly at a Beethoven trio in Gordon Oliver's living room, where I'd come to play some chamber music, I knew my life was going to be a lot more colorful.

His office was on the second floor, with the second-best stereo in the world, the best being ensconced in his living room on the floor above, and the passionate strains of Wagner's Overture to *The Flying Dutchman* swept down the narrow staircase to greet me as I opened the front door and stamped the February slush from my chic new Bonwit Teller boots. (I had sprayed the boots to make them water-repellent, so although my lungs were damaged, the boots were not.)

I turned left into the rooms where the hard labor was done. Helen Deutsch sat at a desk near the door, transferring the words from the eleven-by-fourteen sheets on her right onto a ticker tape of inch-wide columns via the keys of the Justo-writer. She was a chunky middle-aged lady wearing two sweaters, fleece-lined, flat-heeled boots, and the determinedly optimistic expression of a hospital nurse.

"Ah! And how is Maggie?" she asked brightly, as though we were discussing some third person not present.

I countered by putting the manila envelope on her desk. "Read all about it: 'Solid Waste into Energy.' The story of the century. Woodward and Bernstein will eat their hearts out. Is the coffee hot?"

A familiar wail issued from the room beyond, followed by the appearance of Calli Dohanis, tall, skinny, with black hair coiled around her head and at least six long arms in purple wool all moving in different directions. "Baggie!" she cried. "Could you believe there is dough coffee id this place?" It was her seventh head cold since November. She waved a pair of scissors in one hand, a "cut" in the other. "All day I ab dying for a cup of coffee!"

"Tea?" I suggested.

"Dough tea!"

Helen held up a jar of some powdered health food mixture. "You're welcome to some of this."

Calli made a retching sound.

"Oh, pooh, pooh," Helen said. "It's better for you than all that caffeine."

"I *love* caffeine!" Calli shouted, dabbing at her red nose with a damp Kleenex.

"You have to admit," I said to Helen, "that stuff of yours does taste a lot like boiled detergent."

"Ha! That's giving it a *copplibet!*" Calli said, cropping her picture of the Sloan's Ford high school orchestra winning a statewide contest.

I went into the alcove where the kettle, hot plate, small refrigerator, toaster, Ritz crackers, and Girl Scout calendar lived, and searched vainly in the cupboard for a stray tea bag or a quarter inch of overlooked Nescafé in the bottom of a jar.

"You have dough idea," Calli called after me, "what I have to put up with. At hobe I have a leak id by dishwasher, by brother-id-law is cobing to stay for two weeks, Felicia had a report card so bad, wed her father fides out he will burder her, add dow Charlie is driving be crazy with the layout. I told hib this is the last tibe I chadge it—he duzzit like it, tough od hib! Right, Baggie?"

"Right," I said, trying to decide if a very old lump of Ovaltine could make you sick.

"On a newspaper, Calli," Helen said in her third-grade teacher's voice, "you can never say, 'It's finished and that's it.' What if we get some legals before tonight?"

"Thed I quit! I retire! I will be a big-tibe hooker add get rich." She teetered into the far room on her three-inch heels. Legal notices had to be printed, whether you had room or not. Many a perfect layout had been ravaged to accommodate the legals.

I waited for the water to boil and carried my cup of dubious Ovaltine over to the layout table and offered it to Calli, who looked at it, wrinkled her nose, and shook her head. I sipped. It wasn't bad.

"Look!" she commanded, "here I leave roob for your story—six huddred words, right? Is that a beautiful layout? I ask you."

I looked, "NEW ZONING FOR MIDWAY AVENUE," I read. "DOG ORDINANCE PASSED," "YOUTH CENTER PLANS REVIVED."

I had to remind myself severely that society did not live by matters of world-shaking import alone, and that in any case, if I were involved daily with the matters that were currently shaking the world, I would likely never sleep again. But I did long for something a little more piquant, more provocative, more . . . dangerous . . . than garbage disposal.

Above our heads the floor creaked, Wagner ended, and from the top of the stairs a mild voice summoned me. It was a voice that walked softly and carried a big stick.

"Maggie?"

I went up the narrow musty stairs. The second-floor room ran the depth of the house and was crammed with books, records, wall maps, file cabinets, odd discarded armchairs piled high with newspapers and magazines, and a huge old oak desk covered with clippings, correspondence, and note pads bearing indecipherable scribbles. The desk was pushed up against the windows overlooking the street and by the time I got up there, Greenfield, in the noisiest swivel chair known to man, was leaning back, gazing out at the black-and-white branches of a large and ancient maple making patterns against the clearing sky.

"What's the Greek yelling about?" he asked without turning.

"You know Calli, she loves to yell. Nothing important."

"I wish," he said thoughtfully, "she would stop spreading germs."

He swiveled slowly around, to an accompaniment of associated squeals and groans, and regarded me from behind his large horn-rimmed glasses. He was a long, slope-shouldered, mournful-looking man, with wispy gray hair and the face of a dignified basset hound. His movements were supremely deliberate and his pronouncements infinitely calculated; he moved through life like a man who found himself crossing a gorge on a high wire without a net. His expression suggested he was resigned to this unaccountable infamy of fate, but, as I've said, the expression of benign and gentle melancholy was totally deceptive. He had been known to cut an ego to ribbons while giving a perfect impersonation of a kindly old country doctor handing out lollipops.

"Sit down," he said gravely.

I looked around pointedly, but he merely waited until I had shoved a stack of newpapers to the back of an armchair and perched on the rim.

"What are you drinking?"

Happily, I offered it to him. He sniffed it.

"My God." He handed it back. "Nice boots," he said.

"Whatever it is, Charlie, just tell me." This was one of Greenfield's more endearing little rituals; when he had something specific on his mind he walked as far away from it as possible and approached it by the most circuitous route he could devise.

"Do you know the Bruckner Opus Zero?"

"Opus *Zero*?"

"Don't you find your ignorance alarming?" he asked sadly. "There's one movement in this Bruckner that's worth any ten symphonies you care to name, and you haven't even heard of it." He shook his head and gazed into the distance. "Ignorance," He went on in his leisurely fashion, "is unimportant in a fashion model. It's irrelevant in a television comedienne. Among the bubbleheads who inhabit charity balls, it's mandatory. But in an intelligent woman of mature years—"

"Forty-two!"

"Forty-five. And one who, furthermore, chooses to make the dissemination of facts her profession—"

"Will you just tell me what you want me to do before I'm too old to do it!"

"—it's unforgivable. What *do* you know? Do you know, for instance, anything about the history of the village in which you have now lived for—what—fifteen years?"

I changed tactics. "Very little," I said. "As a matter of fact, I've been realizing lately how little I know about anything. Just the other day, for instance, I saw an ad for the Singhalese Ballet and it occurred to me that I hadn't really been aware the Singhalese even *had* a ballet. And then last week I came across—"

"Maggie. This is a business office, not a tea shoppe. I really don't have time for idle chitchat—"

Infuriating. Fortunately, beakers of Ovaltine do not snap under pressure as the stems of wineglasses are wont to do.

He reached to the desk top, picked up one of his numerous note pads, tore off the top sheet and held it out.

I took it and read—with difficulty—"Hollis Farm. Traprock Road."

"Farm?" I said. "I didn't think there were any farms left in Sloan's Ford. Or is this just wishful thinking on the part of some hotshot in the real estate office?"

He sighed. "You prove my point. This is a farm— what's left of a farm—that goes back to the seventeenth century, to the time of the Dutch patroons. The land and most of the house that stands there were once the dwelling place of an Englishman who liberated them from the Dutch. Having survived past the year of our bicentennial, the house has achieved sanctity and the Heritage Committee has put up a plaque and designated the place as a landmark house. Now this woman—Hollis—has set aside an acre of land, divided into plots, for local children and senior citizens to use to grow vegetables and flowers. A laudable project which deserves recognition. In the Sloan's Ford library there is a minihistory of the area which may add something to your meager fund of knowledge, and, when you've absorbed that, you can go to the farm, look around, and do a piece. With color, point, and economy."

"And pictures?"

"It would help."

"How come they didn't let us know in time for the plaque ceremony?"

He shrugged. "Sloppy thinking," he said, which meant they *had* let us know and he'd ignored it because it wasn't a controversial issue, but the vegetable plots had captured his imagination.

"Right," I said, and stood up.

"What's your rush?"

"Well, you know how it is, I really don't have time to hang around in tearooms."

He looked at me with bottomless sorrow. "I don't mind your being acerbic, or even sardonic. But don't be petty."

"Mr. Greenfield!"

The front door downstairs had opened and a young male voice was calling up the stairway.

"Mr. Greenfield!"

He got to his feet and went to look, and I followed. It was young Peter Kittell, our one remaining delivery boy, most of our subscribers having long since been receiving their copies by mail. Peter was grinning up at us from under a mop of brown hair topped by a ski cap.

"Got something to show you!" he said, gesturing for us to come down, and disappeared out the door.

At the open front door we were joined by Helen and Calli. On the slushy sidewalk the twelve-year-old Peter stood proudly clutching a glittering new blue bicycle.

"Byootiful!" Calli shouted.

"So that's the famous French bike," Greenfield said.

"Yep! Ten speeds! I finally made it."

"You shouldn't ride when the roads are wet, Peter," Helen crooned.

"Why don't you save it for the spring," I suggested.

"I'm not riding it where there's any snow. I walked it most of the way down here."

"Does this mean," Greenfield asked, "that the *Reporter* is losing your services?" And it suddenly became clear why Peter had been allowed to keep his route while all about him were losing theirs.

"Oh," Peter said, dropping his grin. "Do I have to give it up now?"

"That depends." Greenfield looked like a Supreme Court judge struggling with a tricky decision. "If an important percentage of our delivery is going to depend on that vehicle, it will have to be used and cared for in a mature and adult fashion."

Peter nodded maturely. "Listen," he said, "I'm a very responsible person. Besides, you think I want anything to happen to it after all I went through to get it? Trust me, okay?" Greenfield nodded. "So I'll pick up the papers tomorrow?" He grinned again and turned the bike around. "See you!" he called triumphantly, and went off, literally into the sunset, as it was now five o'clock and all that was left of the sun were three strips of apricot along the gray horizon.

I turned and caught Greenfield looking after Peter with an odd expression—not fond or sentimental or even wistful, but involved. Greenfield was a widower with three grown daughters at various stages of Lib.

"I ab goig to catch doobodia," Calli moaned, rushing back into the office. Helen, in Calli's wake, murmured something about wet streets.

"The library is open late today," Greenfield announced over his shoulder as he started up the stairs.

"It's nice how you can make a command sound like a news bulletin," I said to his back. "I'll be in constant touch."

"I expect you to."

He had to have the last word.

▣ 2

At the library I learned a great deal about Sloan's Ford.

I learned that in the days when the Mohican Indian was hunting deer, bear, and wildcat in its vicinity, the main street of Sloan's Ford had been the beginning of a trail which led from the Hudson River to Long Island Sound. In the seventeenth century, when the Dutch patroons (patroon: owner of a manorial estate who had certain privileges under the former Dutch government of New York) first colonized the Hudson Valley and later, when the English took it over, the trail became a dirt road, fairly messy and useless in winter and spring. During the Revolution, when Washington's men camped on the surrounding hills, it resounded with the clatter and clomp of raiding parties scurrying along its rutted surface. By 1850 it was providing a tranquil farming community with a blacksmith shop, a post office, a pickle factory, a four-room schoolhouse, a grain-and-feed store, and Pinkney's Market, where the canned goods lined up on the varnished wooden shelves like a regiment of toy soldiers.

I learned that the twentieth century brought a railroad station to the far bank of the Sloan River, and the main street (which had once been a dirt road which had once been a trail) was named Poplar Avenue, and a large brick schoolhouse appeared halfway along its south side from which the first high school graduating class consisted of nine persons. And naturally, with the railroad linking countryside and city, a land boom followed and the village street blossomed with carpenters, plumbers, hardware merchants, barbers, druggists, and firemen, whose small houses clustered on tiny plots close to the village center, leaving the wooded hills farther away for the eventual invaders from the city—the doctors, lawyers, and executives of various persuasions whose expensive homes now stood gleaming amidst their manicured lawns and cookie-cutter bushes.

I also learned that there was a place called the Hollis Farm, formerly the Mayfield Farm, boasting a house with seven fireplaces on two chimneys and a Dutch oven in the main living-room fireplace. At one time corn, potatoes, and rutabaga turnips had been raised on this farm. Period.

And finally, I learned that it was not too terrible to have a husband whose work as a consulting engineer kept him traveling around the country a great deal of the time—one could not stay at the library until seven and also have dinner on the table by six-thirty.

I had previously stopped off at Food of the Sea and Sam's Supermarket for fresh brook trout and Fig Newtons—a delicious combination—figuring that a temperature of thirty-seven degrees would keep them from spoiling in the back of the Honda while I acquired knowledge, and now I started for home, going the back way, up Hawthorn Road, where doubtless two hundred years ago the British stopped for tea before marching on White Plains. Now, however, it was merely a wide, tree-lined road where the hundred-thousand-dollar houses are set so far back from their split-rail fences that a minor skirmish on the road between the Redcoats and the Colonists might very well go unheard behind those lamplit windows.

I was thinking about writing to my two boys, Matt and Alan, who were in different years at the same college upstate, growing moustaches and hunting females, when my headlights picked up what at first appeared to be a bundle of clothes dropped from an open-ended truck. Then I saw the twisted bike wheel and braked.

Peter hadn't been able to resist trying out the seductive new ten-speeder. He lay several feet from the wrecked bicycle as though he'd been tossed there, carelessly, by a giant hand. His mop of brown hair was blood-streaked and his twelve-year-old face was white and still. I fought down the sick feeling that rose in my throat and ran to him. A faint pulse was beating in the hollow between his shoulder and his neck. My own pulse was racing and I felt clammy and dizzy. I am generally struck stupid in emergencies, but this time I managed to switch on the blinkers on my car, grab the rug from the back seat, cover him, and run what seemed like a quarter of a mile to the front door of a large fieldstone house. A frowning fifty-year-old man in a thirty-year-old's leisure suit listened to me, and agreed, somewhat cautiously, to call the ambulance, the police, and Greenfield.

I ran back to stand guard over Peter and found another car pulled up facing mine and a man and a woman climbing out of it. I waved a hand toward the house behind me.

"They're calling the ambulance," I told them through chattering teeth.

"Oh, my God," the woman said, shivering.

"How did it happen?" the man asked me. "You skid?"

"Me?" I gaped at the man. "*Me?* Are you crazy?"

"I'm sorry—"

"I just *found* him!"

"Oh." He took a few steps toward Peter and leaned over, carefully.

"My God," the woman said, "it looks like Jerry de Santis. Is it Jerry de Santis, Bill?"

"No, no, it's not anybody we know."

"*I* know him" I said.

"I'm sorry. What happened, you think? You think *he* skidded?"

"He didn't skid," I chattered. "Look at the bicycle. Something ran into that bicycle."

"That's what I thought." We all looked at the ruin of the "byootiful" blue ten-speed French bicycle. "Then that's what it was," he said slowly, "hit and run."

The poisonous words hung in the air. What kind of incredible nonhuman had struck down a twelve-year-old, left him unconscious by the side of a dark road, and driven off?

We heard the ambulance siren coming in our direction from the village, but before it arrived I saw Greenfield's tan Plymouth tearing up the road toward us. He screeched to a stop, slammed out of the car, crossed to Peter, kneeled on the ground, and put a hand carefully on his cheek. The ambulance came screaming up, and then the police car, and lights flashed and a stern young officer began asking questions, and the volunteers carried Peter into the ambulance and took off.

The police officer wanted to know who had found him, whether any of us had passed any speeding vehicles, whether I had seen a vehicle leaving the area at any speed in any direction, whether anyone knew the boy, his name and address, our names and addresses, and finally, having established that no one present had actually witnessed the accident, he prepared to leave. Greenfield stepped forward and put a gentle hand on the patrolman's sleeve.

"Officer," he said quietly, "I imagine the chances of finding this . . . offender . . . are fairly small, since the car may have been merely passing through. But I think you should know"—he took a deep breath—"the *Reporter* would like to be able to say that our police were making a *massive* effort. You understand me. I mean a *tremendous* . . . a *gigantic* . . . effort."

The patrolman nodded, with considerably less stern authority than he had previously displayed, got behind the wheel of the patrol car, and took off. The man and woman who had arrived while I was getting help backed slowly away from Greenfield as though he could be expected to pounce at any moment, and, once in their car, drove quickly away. We were alone on the cold dark road.

"Do you think I should go see the Kittells?" I mumbled.

"By the time you get to their house they'll be at the hospital."

"Then I'll go to the hospital."

No answer. He stared up into the trees, breathing audibly. Suddenly he turned, glowering at me. "Are you shocked?" he demanded.

"Of course!"

"Well, you shouldn't be! Angry. But not shocked. Monstrous behavior is the order of the day. I'll tell you when to be shocked. When something human and decent happens!" He shambled off toward the tan Plymouth, hands in pockets, the sloping shoulders looking lost in the loud plaid hunting jacket. "Call me!" he barked over his shoulder. It was the first time I'd ever heard him raise his voice.

I got into the Honda, made an illegal U turn, and headed back toward the village, tense and nervous, with the classic need to turn the clock back and have this terrible thing not have happened. I would drive up Hawthorn Road and there would be no bundle lying there, no broken bike, nothing but trees and lamplit houses. I would turn down Chatham Drive, curve around the circle, peel off into Putney Lane, pull into the driveway at the sprawling old gray house with the white shutters that needed a paint job, walk into my warm kitchen. . . .

I drove on, past the shopping center that had probably once been a pickle factory, past the beauty parlor that stood where once had been a blacksmith shop, past the pizza parlor and Victor's Garage, which had replaced the grain-and-feed store, past the real estate office haunted by the ghost of Pinkney's emporium, over the bridge to Gorham Road, turned right, and went on past the village limits and tacky motel, which probably had the blacksmith and Mr. Pinkney turning in their graves.

The hospital was seven minutes away, in Gorham. It had recenly been acquired by a group of doctors, revamped and equipped with sophisticated instruments for detecting and treating almost every ill known to man, except monstrous behavior. I pulled into the hospital parking lot, where as usual all the empty spaces were reserved for doctors, but as I maneuvered around trying to get back onto the street to look for a place there, two woman emerged from under the glaring light of the emergency entrance and got into a station wagon and pulled out, and I pulled in.

The revamping had not extended to the emergency waiting room. This one was done up in the standard inspirational decor of sick green walls with fluorescent tubes for lighting and madly gay mud-colored vinyl and aluminum sofas. On one of these sat Mr. and Mrs. Kittell, he looking straight ahead, sunken-cheeked, and stricken, she looking at the clenched hands in her lap, trying vainly to stop shaking. They were in their late forties, a blue-collar family. Mr. Kittel was a house painter, his wife the kind of mother who had timidly but faithfully attended every Parents' Day, Christmas concert, P.T.A. meeting, graduation play, orientation, festival of the arts, and what-have-you since the first of her four bright, hard-working children had entered the school system. Peter was their youngest.

I went over to them and told them as much as I knew of what had happened. Mr. Kittell told me Peter was being X-rayed, he was in a coma, their own doctor was on the way over. I sat with them, trying to be comforting and not knowing how, until a lanky man with a long thin nose and a heavy overcoat appeared. He was their family physician, Dr. Walsh, and he was going to find out what was what. He disappeared through a depressing green door and after a century or two he returned, looking neither sad nor glad.

"They have taken a skull film," he said, "and there are no evident fractures, but they will have to do an arteriogram—a brain scan—before they can rule out any subdural or epidural hemorrhage. If there is hemorrhaging, that could be serious. But if not, if it's only an edema—a swelling in the brain stem—that is reversible, curable. It can be treated with medication to absorb the fluid. Cortisone. I've called in Dr. Jennet—he is a neurosurgeon, a very good one."

In other words, Peter was a very sick boy, and he might make it and he might not. But I had been so afraid Dr. Walsh would come back and tell us it was all over that I actually felt grateful. There was hope.

To the Kittells I said, "I'll come and see you whenever it's convenient. Mr. Greenfield said you must call on him for any kind of help you may need." He hadn't, only because he didn't have to.

"Thank you," Mr. Kittell murmured. "thank you very much. Thank you."

Mrs. Kittell never looked up and never stopped shaking.

Feeling as though I'd just been given leave from World War Two, I left the hospital and drove home. It was very late for me to be getting home, and as my lights hit the driveway, George, our golden retriever, came rushing up to the fence to complain. He'd been named after that literary nonagenarian vegetarian, not to save on meat, but in the hope that he would live that long; we just couldn't go through that training process again.

"Sorry, kid," I said, "I'll be right with you." I got the trout out of the back of the car, told George to meet me at the back door, went into the house, switched on lights, cleaned George off in the mud room off the kitchen, let him in, called Greenfield at the *Reporter* office, and reported.

His voice was back to quiet. After a short silence he said, "I'm going to get my hands on that humanoid."

"The odds are not good."

"They weren't good for Truman in forty-eight."

"Are we going to do a story on it?" I asked. "I could have it to you in half an hour."

"I've already done it. It's going on the front page."

"Oh." I thought briefly of Calli, and then realized she would have been the first to tear her layout apart when she heard. "Well, if there's anything—"

"Did you go to the library?"

"Yes. My fund of knowledge is limitless."

"You'd better call Mrs. What's-her-name and make an appointment."

"I was just going to."

"Are you in one piece?"

"I think so."

"Good night."

I picked up the phone book, looked up Hollis, Victoria, Traprock Road, and dialed the number. The ringing was answered by a female voice, clear as a bell and quivering with goodwill and energy.

"Yes! Hello!"

"Mrs. Hollis?"

"No, this is Mrs. Trager! Can I help you? Mrs. Hollis is at the dinner table! This is her daughter!"

"Oh, sorry, I'll call later." Trager. The name was vaguely familiar.

"No, it's all right, if you don't mind talking with me instead! Mother doesn't like being disturbed, but I don't mind. There's only the three of us tonight— mother, myself, and my daughter Elizabeth—so a little interruption won't matter. Besides, we've reached dessert and I seldom have it." (A girlish laugh) "I talk too much, I know, everyone tells me that. What can I do for you?"

"This is Maggie Rome. I work for the *Sloan's Ford Reporter* and I—"

"Oh yes! I've seen your name! Very good articles! Bright, snappy, and to the point! It must be very interesting to work for a newspaper. Have you been writing long?"

Marvelous how she grabbed the ball and ran a mile a minute in the wrong direction. *I* was supposed to be the reporter.

"Well, yes and no. The reason I'm calling is that we'd like to do a story on the farm and the vegetable gardens and the plaque the Heritage Committee put up, and I was wondering if it would be convenient if I came down tomorrow morning with—um—a photographer—to see the house and ask a few questions."

"How exciting! We'd be delighted! Come anytime— Why don't you come for lunch?"

"Well—no—thank you—but I hope to be there sometime before noon."

"Mother will be thrilled to death! And if you change your mind about lunch just speak up, we don't stand on ceremony here, and it's going to be quiche tomorrow, which I really do make very well, it's one of my few accomplishments—"

"Thank you, I'll see you tomorrow then. Goodbye."

I hung up quickly to avoid a possible suggestion that I pack a bag and spend the night.

Trager . . . Trager . . . the name nagged at me. And what a strange lady. A Niagara of hospitality and personal information at the first ring of a telephone bell.

I dialed Arthur's number. Conversationally, I was going from a plethora to a vacuum. Arthur was a non-talking, sleepy-eyed high school senior with a lot of wavy red hair who liked to photograph telephone poles wrapped in tinfoil, garbage cans draped in billowing chiffon, and things like that. He was also very good with uninteresting subjects like people, storefronts, bridges, and so on, and since he had very few classes to take in his senior year, he was generally available, at a price. I explained the assignment to him.

"How long?" he asked.

"Will it take?" I supplied. "Oh—half an hour, forty-five minutes. What's your free time?"

"After first period."

"Then I'll pick you up at the high school at—what—ten o'clock?"

"That's cool."

I started to say goodbye but he had already hung up.

In the kitchen I tuned in some Vivaldi on the radio while George sat staring at me, tongue lolling to remind me I was being cruel to a dumb animal. I fixed his meal while he watched every move, then I finally decided I was hungry enough to eat something, broiled my trout with lemon butter and parsley, tossed a salad, and sat down.

The unopened mail still sat on the big round walnut dining room table where I had dropped it earlier while in the heat of creativity with the garbage disposal piece. I looked through it between forkfuls of food: several requests for donations from organizations to which I'd already sent donations, a spring catalog from B. Altman, a bill from Bonwit Teller (for the boots), a letter from Elliot, a letter from Matt, no letter from Alan. Of course no letter from Alan. The day Alan writes a letter the telephone company will declare bankruptcy.

Elliot said San Francisco was mild and sunny, the work was going as well as could be expected, he had been accosted seventeen times in the Berkeley area by members of various cults, selling, yelling, proselytizing, chanting, and generally behaving like fanatics have always behaved, from Savonarola to Hitler. He had had a letter from Matt and a phone call from Alan, and he had been witness to an accident on the street as he was hailing a cab—a loaded shopping cart had rolled off the curb beside him and run smack into a moving Alfa Romeo, and the driver, a vociferous blonde, had threatened to sue Elliot because she assumed he was responsible for the scratches on her baby-blue fender. He expected to be home in a couple of weeks and please don't forget to make the mortgage payment and had I called the garage about the malfunctioning automatic clutch in the Chevy, and take care of myself.

Matt said he had a new roommate because the old one couldn't put up with Matt always being in the room studying when he wanted to use it for an orgy, and Alan had a girl at Cobb and was always hitching back and forth so he didn't see much of him, and he wasn't too impressed with the Renaissance literature professor, and he was thinking of taking a public speaking course next semester, and had I seen his red sweater, maybe he'd left it home during Christmas vacation, and if so could I send it and also his French dictionary, which might be on the shelf in his closet, and if it wasn't too much trouble a couple of pomegranates, and give his best to George.

I had my coffee quietly in an armchair in the living room with George dozing not at, but on, my feet, and in my hand an old Graham Greene, which I preferred to a new almost anything, but I couldn't concentrate. My mind was worrying at something in Elliot's letter. Scratches on her baby-blue fender. And that was just from a shopping cart. A car that had collided with a bike would have something to show for it—maybe even a dent—which would have to be fixed—perhaps at a local garage.

I dialed a number I had memorized long ago, when Elliot had made his first out-of-town trip, and gave

Sergeant Walchek the benefit of my fine deductive mind.

"Yes, ma'am," he said, "we'll be looking into that."

I'll never know whether or not the police had really thought of it before I called.

◙ 3

Wednesday morning the sun was out and the sky was Mediterranean blue. From the horizon up it was summer. From the horizon down it was cold. I called the hospital, but all I got out of them was "There has been no change."At Dr. Walsh's office he was with a patient and couldn't come to the phone. I asked when he was likely to be free. Never, apparently. I left the office number and requested that he give any information on Peter to anyone who answered.

At a quarter to ten I backed the Honda out of the driveway and proceeded to the high school. I hadn't been that way recently, and as I passed a stretch of road which last summer had been an untouched area of wild trees and bushes, I saw that bulldozers had been at work sometime in the fall, trees and bushes uprooted, and mud and rocks and gaping holes preparing the ground for the works of man. An example of man's work had gone up last spring on a large plot of land adjoining this ravaged ground—a solid pink-brick house of a style of architecture my friend Barbara Drexler called Early Sicilian, with a half-circle driveway punctuated at entrance and exit by stone lions, and a sweep of white roll-up doors hiding a three-car garage. All it needed was a bank of black limousines lining the drive.

I staved off depression by concentrating on the unexpected gift of beautiful weather, and turned left up Brookfield Road and right onto Hillcrest, and up to the high school. Another beauty. I was certain it had been designed by someone who specialized in penal institutions. Still, it did stand on a rise of land surrounded by stretches of tree-dotted lawn and playing fields, and the sun shone all over it.

Arthur's long, thin arms in a scruffy, unzipped ski jacket drooped over a No Parking sign at the curb, supporting his equally long, thin body. At sight of me he slowly disengaged himself from his prop, picked up his camera case and tripod from the ground beside him, and got in beside me.

"Hi," he said.

I responded in kind. When I first started hiring Arthur I'd made a conscientious attempt to keep the conversation going, but I finally realized he was neither shy nor insecure—he just liked to be quiet—and I no longer forced banalities on him. We drove, in more or less companionable silence, out the far end of the high school grounds, down a steep street to Chase Road, past the park where all the Little League nonsense would soon be going on, and up Butterworth Drive to Cliff Road, which actually ran along the edge of a cliff—well, only a steep hill, really, but I wouldn't care to go over the edge. When Cliff Road made a turn and stopped being a cliff, there was an occasional street running off to the left or right, and one of these, on the left, proved to be Traprock Road.

It was a kind of lane of overgrown trees and hedges, with only three modest houses scattered along its length. At the end of the lane the road curved sharply to the right to disappear behind a wall of evergreens, and we followed it and found, suddenly, that we were in true countryside. I stopped the car and got out.

Facing us was a white wooden gate flanked on either side by a dry-wall fence of gray stones carefully fitted into each other's contours so that they made a solid wall two feet thick and four feet high, stretching out east and west as far as you could see. Beyond the wall a snow-packed field reached westward in sunny serenity to the edge of an orchard. To the east a small wood sloped gently upward to the horizon. Between the two a gravel road curved away to a distant rise of land on which stood a white clapboard house with dark green shutters and two brick chimneys from which streamers of pale gray smoke curled quietly into the sky. Beyond

the house was a rust-colored barn and beyond that a
fenced-in pasture where two horses, a black and a
chestnut, were moving dreamily about. Dotting the
land around the house and barn were old, old dogwoods, firs, and oak trees. The entire scene was bathed
in a profound and peaceful silence, emphasized by the
brief, repeated call of a bird, and then, far away, the
short echoing bark of a dog. And I knew how it felt to
step out of a time capsule and find yourself back in
1938.

I turned to Arthur, who had climbed out and was
standing beside me. "Heavens to Betsy," I said, "what
have we here?"

Arthur's response to the scene was predictably cryptic.

"Man!" he said.

"On the contrary"—I gave him a grin—"nature." I
went back to the car. "You open the gate," I told him,
"and I'll drive through." He did, and I did, and he got
back into the car, and we drove up the gravel road
leading to the house.

Halfway to the house I had an impulse and pulled
the car to one side of the road. "Let's walk the rest," I
said.

We walked. I wondered why people were always
calling winter landscapes "bleak." True, this was no
riot of autumn foliage, but what was there, as Jimmy
Durante would say, was cherce. The wood on the right
stood in a bed of fallen leaves the color of walnut
shells. The trunks of trees ranged in shade and texture
from satiny pewter to elephant-hide gray, some with a
patina of mossy green like a long brushstroke along
one side. A stand of barren birches silvered the hillside
like an illustration from a fairy tale. A winter willow
hung over the road in a mist of antique gold. A clump
of dormant forsythia was a heathery haze against the
snow, the bare black branches of a beech made an inky
scrawl against the blue sky, there was a brook that
meandered in and out of the wood, bordered by
tangled bushes the colors of driftwood, nutmeg, cinna-
mon, olive, and beet. Hardly bleak.

I suddenly realized I was alone and looked back to see Arthur taking pictures with great abandon.

"Save some film for the job," I called to him.

"Color," he called back, meaning he was using the color camera, and since the paper could only use black-and-white he was not jeopardizing our mission.

There was the crunching sound of someone stomping through underbrush and I turned toward it. Emerging from the wood with an armful of branches was a tall, angular woman in shapeless slacks and a loden coat. Her hair was a white mass coiled into a knot at the nape of her neck, her face and hands were weathered as by sun and wind, and she might have been the wife of some Iowa farmer or Wisconsin lumberjack, except that she moved like an aristocrat and spoke with the voice of a Mount Holyoke dean.

"Mrs. Rome from the *Reporter*," she told me, "I'm Victoria Hollis." She shifted her burden of branches so that she could grasp my hand firmly in her woolly mitten. She spoke in the same clear, clipped tones that her daughter had projected over the telephone, but without the exclamation points. And, Mrs. Trager to the contrary, she didn't look as though she were anywhere near being thrilled to death by my interest in her farm. Polite and civilized was about all.

"Can I help you with those branches?" I asked.

"They're not weighty, only cumbersome. I like to clear out the dead things before spring arrives."

Arthur came up and I introduced him and she repeated the handshake and started up toward the house with a good long stride. I discovered later that she was seventy-two.

"As soon as the snow is gone," she was saying, "we'll have to get busy cleaning out the dead leaves— not from the wood, of course, but around the house. It takes a month—there are a great many of them. My husband used to call it nonsense. 'The new growth will cover them,' he said. But I don't like dead things covering up the young shoots. I like to see the new green things from the very beginning."

"I've been to the library," I told her, "to do a little homework on the history of Sloan's Ford. They mention the farm but don't tell much about it. Have you been here long?"

"I came to Sloan's Ford as a bride, from Massachusetts, but we didn't get the farm until Catherine was about ten—my daughter—you spoke with her on the phone."

"And how much of the family lives here now?"

"There never was much of a family. Catherine is an only child. She has a husband. And I have a granddaughter, Elizabeth. My husband died a few years ago. The four of us live here." There was something a little chill about that last announcement.

We had climbed the hill on which the low white house sat among its firs and dogwoods and the bare bushes which would eventually blossom, Mrs. Hollis said, with lilac and wisteria. There was a brick walkway leading to a set of fan-shaped brick steps and a low, wide Dutch door. Beside the door, shiny and obtrusive, was a brass plaque which established the building as The Van den Hoorst Farmhouse, built 1659, and now officially pronounced a landmark house by the Hudson Heritage Committee.

Arthur took a few close-ups of the plaque and a few long shots of the house with Victoria Hollis and the plaque in evidence.

"If you don't mind, we'll go in through the back," Mrs. Hollis said, "and I can leave my brushwood on the porch for Andrew to get rid of."

We followed her around the side of the house, passing by the huge spread of a majestic oak, which cast its shade on a white shed evidently doing service as a one-car garage. There were a brown Chevy station wagon and a four-year-old green VW standing in the snow to one side of a cleared driveway leading to the shed, and I peeked through the window in the shed door to see what privileged species was resting inside: it was a dove-gray Mercedes two-seater, twenty thousand dollars' worth of automobile.

Arthur called, "Look!" and I turned and he snapped a picture of me and grinned. A most unusual display of humor for Arthur, I thought, I must take him to old farms more often.

Mrs. Hollis was disappearing around the back of the house. We caught up with her and proceeded to the back porch by way of an old stone covered well with a chain and bucket. The bucket rested on a circular slab of wood, which fitted into the well opening and had to be pried out through a groove in its side.

"That's been here for two hundred years," Mrs. Hollis said. "During the Civil War they constructed a platform about eight feet down. This place was a stop on the underground railway. They hid people in there."

I made notes. Arthur took a shot of it. We followed Victoria Hollis onto the wide, pillared back porch, where she put her brushwood in a corner and turned back to look out past her barn and her horse pasture down to the tranquil meadow and orchard beyond, and beyond them to a valley of miniature houses, and beyond that to the winding thread of the Sloan River. Her sharp gray eyes were narrowed against the sun and her profile would have looked well on a coin.

"I would have Andrew show you the land where we're putting the vegetable gardens," she said, "but it's a little too mucky out there today." And she anticipated my question: "Andrew is my resident help. He has a room over the barn. We decided one day—Andrew and my granddaughter and I—that there were people in the area who would benefit from a chance to cultivate the earth—youngsters and retired people who live in apartments—and we roped off an acre—you can see it out there, between the pasture and the woods. Andrew is going to fence it in as soon as the ground thaws, and divide it into plots. There's a short track beside the woods which leads back to the River Road park, so that cars or bicycles or whatever transportation brings people here can be left in the park lot, and we won't have traffic going by the house. Lots will be assigned by the season, in order of application, and the only stipulation is that they be used and cared for properly. The produce, of course, will belong to the people who grow it."

"What do you think the response will be?"

She turned to me with an expression compounded of irony and regret. "What do *you* think? People are starved for natural sights and sounds and smells. The surface of the earth is being laid waste with asphalt. Every chance to plant a seed may be the last one." She turned back to scan the horizon.

"Open space," she went on, "is becoming a luxury. When the small farms finally go, there'll be nothing but human jungle. That will be fine, I suppose, for the human lions and hyenas. But what about the rest of us?"

Since it wasn't a question, I didn't answer. A man emerged from the barn with an axe in his hand, wearing a red wool jacket and a hat with ear flaps. He looked to be about thirty, dark haired and swarthy. He sauntered toward the wood and out of sight.

"Andrew," she explained, and opened the back door and invited us in.

The house was warm and dry and smelled of baking. The ceilings were low and beamed, the floorboards pegged, the doorways unusually wide. "For hoopskirts, I was told," she said.

She led us across a kind of sun porch, not part of the original house, down two wooden steps, through a sunny dining room papered in a faint china-blue pattern and boasting a small fireplace, and into a hall with a stairway along one side, down which floated the muted sound of a male voice in a bad temper. Victoria Hollis ignored the sound and took us into a large, low apple-green room full of white-curtained windows with deep window seats, mellow paneling, bookshelves, and comfortable armchairs. There was a fire in the fireplace, a worn, chintz-covered sofa in front of the fire, books lying about on chairs and tables, a Baldwin baby grand in one corner, and in another a small glass-fronted cabinet containing a viola.

"Musicians in the family?" I asked.

"The viola is mine," she said. "I play poorly, but that's a good instrument. The cabinet is thermostatically controlled to take care of heat and humidity and so on. Elizabeth plays the piano."

"You have two-thirds of a trio."

She took a deep breath. "I haven't played chamber music for years."

"Why not?"

She hesitated and gave me an answer, but not the one she had in mind. "There don't seem to be many amateur musicians around with the time for it. I'm sure you've realized they didn't build rooms this large in seventeenth-century farmhouses. I assume this is the result of two smaller rooms having been combined, probably in the mid-eighteen hundreds." Her subject-changing was not so much smooth as determined. She went on, pointing out the Dutch oven built into one end of the fireplace, a small, curtained recess, which she understood was a "prayer corner," and the slope of the floor, which, if you looked carefully, was a half-inch closer to the ground at one side than at the other. Then from an antique English desk she took what looked like a rolled-up calendar but proved to be a chart showing the farm's line of descent: from Willem Van den Hoorst, who owned it and a great deal more until his death in 1660, to Edward Druce in 1665 as part of a Manor granted him by royal charter which included most of the county, to a Major Brandywine of the Colonial army in 1780, to Homer Gibbons, a wealthy merchant, by which time it had been reduced to three hundred and sixty acres, and on down to Simon Mayfield, whose family, one way and another, held on to twenty acres until one of them sold out to George Everett Hollis.

Arthur took a few pictures of the interior with a flash, and then sidled over to me and mumbled something that sounded like "Math class." I stood up.

"I'll try to do the farm justice," I said, "and thank you very much, Mrs. Hollis. I hope we haven't been—"

At that moment a door was flung open at the top of the stairway, releasing the full force of the bad-tempered voice announcing, "I want those goddamn shirts and I want them today!" This was followed by a heavy clatter of feet on the stairs with a flutelike counterpoint from the floor above which I recognized as the inimitable voice of Mrs. Trager.

"That's impossible, Julian! The laundry doesn't have them! They send them *out!*"

Julian. That's why the name had nagged at me. Julian Trager, who regularly, every seven years, landed in the pages of the Sunday *Times Book Review*. In the late forties he'd been one of those bright and bitter young men who wrote antiwar novels, telling it like it was—not gallant, romantic, and full of heroes, but dirty, cowardly, and full of four-letter words. Far from deglamorizing war, however, cowardice and obscenity proved to be just as intoxicating to boys of all ages as the phony glamour of previous eras, and the movies bought Trager's novel and catapulted him to temporary fame. All that, though, had been many years ago.

He prowled into the room chewing on a piece of doughnut, with the nervous arrogance of a delivery boy in the lobby of the St. Regis. At sight of us he stopped short and spent a moment deciding what face to use in the circumstances.

Victoria Hollis gave him his cue. "This is Mrs. Rome from the *Reporter*, and Mr. Brofman, photographer."

He decided on unpretentious. "Hi," he said, downed the rest of the doughnut, and grabbed a pipe from a rack of forty of fifty standing on one of the bookshelves. "This must be what Cathy was babbling about, right? The Heritage Committee going around enshrining the past with their little pieces of brass and a basketful of nails? You going to do a nice little story on what it's like to own a piece of American history?" He gave me what he thought was a boyish smile but looked more like the grimace of a man hiding a hangover.

He was a chunky man with graying brown curls, small, restless eyes, and the kind of loose-lipped mouth I had last seen on a Breughel peasant who was gorging himself on something. He was wearing an expensive Irish fisherman's sweater with suede elbow patches, rust-colored Dior slacks, and Gucci loafers. No queston who owned the safely stabled Mercedes.

"Should make interesting reading," he went on, filling the pipe from a humidor and spilling considerable tobacco on the rug, "all about Mr. Van den Hoorst, who screwed the Indians out of a thousand acres more or less, and got screwed out of them in turn by one of Her Majesty's empire builders. For which Lady Bountiful makes amends by allowing the peasants to grow a few things in the north forty."

"I'm sure there's a lot of historical culpability lying around," I said, "but I don't see how this house or the land out there can be held accountable."

A corner of Victoria Hollis's mouth twitched. Julian Trager lit a match, puffed on his pipe, and squinted at me through the smoke, while he debated how best to put me down.

"Lady," he said, smirking, "enjoy yourself. You can't do much harm."

Very good. In only eight words he managed to sneer at my sex, my job, and my general insignificance in the scheme of things.

"Oh! You're here! You came!" A tall, thin, pale woman with limp dark blonde hair pulled back and secured at the nape with a thin dark ribbon appeared in the doorway. She looked to be within a stone's throw of forty, and wore a loose pullover and jeans of an indeterminate grayish-greenish-bluish beige, the kind of noncolor worn by women who would like to call as little attention as possible to their physical being and hope to make it on spirit. Mrs. Trager had plenty of spirit, or nervous determination, or something.

"I'm afraid lunch is going to be a little late! We're off-kilter this morning! Julian usually goes off to the city much earlier than this but he had to work late last night and he took the morning off and I haven't started my quiche! It *is* Mrs. Rome, isn't it? I'm Catherine Trager!" She shook my hand with great energy. "And this is—" I introduced Arthur. "The photographer! Arthur, how marvelous! I would love to see some of your work! It's a great art, I believe. I do some photography myself! Oh, nothing much, but I work, work, work! Have you seen the exhibit at the—"

"For God's sake, Cathy, don't babble!" The look Julian Trager gave his wife was one not so much of contempt as dismissal. Catherine's face flushed and her large gray eyes widened and her chin went up, and for a moment she looked pretty. But she crumpled quickly.

"I *do* talk too much!" She gave him a small, propitiating smile. Victoria Hollis turned away, presumably to inspect a begonia blooming on the windowsill.

There are several things you can do when you've committed a gross social rudeness. You can apologize. You can leave the room. Or, if you have a painfully large ego and the sensitivity of a rhinoceros, you can run the subject into the ground in an effort to prove your rudeness was justified.

"Talk is not what you do," Julian went on, gathering papers from a tabletop. "Your endless monologue is not talk. Talk is Hamlet. Talk is an Eskimo inviting a stranger to partake of his wife. Talk is Einstein telling the world that E equals MC squared. Talk is my friend Ziggy explaining the joys of shoplifting in Woolworth's. Talk is either illuminating, entertaining, or dirty. What you do is lady-babble."

"I think you've made your point, Julian." Mrs. Hollis still wasn't looking at anyone, but her voice flew across the room at Julian like a well-aimed dagger. He made a noise like a chuckle and tried to imitate an Elizabethan courtier bowing.

"Your Majesty," he said, and left the room.

"We really have to get back," I said quickly, "Arthur—"

"Oh! But you're staying for lunch!" Catherine insisted. "We're expecting you!"

"I wish we could, but I'm afraid Arthur has to be back at the high school—"

"Oh, of course! Well, Julian can drop him off on his way, how's that! And you can talk to Mother while I make the quiche! Julian—" She stopped him as he passed the doorway wearing a fur-lined duffel coat.

"I'm going to miss my goddamn appointment!" he muttered, and stomped out the front door, slamming it.

"No problem!" Catherine, undaunted, smiled brightly. "I'm sure Mother would be glad to drive Arthur—"

"Catherine. You know I don't drive during the winter."

"Then I'll dig out the station wagon and take him! Elizabeth takes the bus to school," she said to me, "and I can't drive mother's VW, it's a stick shift. I know I should learn, but I never get around to it!"

"Look," I said, "I have a car, and getting Arthur back to school *is* my responsibility—" This problem of Arthur was beginning to sound like the arrangements for an international summit meeting.

"But once you leave, you won't feel like coming back, and we did want you to stay for—"

"Perhaps Mrs. Rome could make it another time." Victoria Hollis was beginning to sound a bit strained. I looked at Catherine's painfully eager face and realized that company was in very short supply at that house.

"I'll be glad to," I said, "and I'll definitely come. I love quiche."

"Tomorrow, then!"

"Fine." It wasn't fine, but I'd manage. We said goodbye to Mrs. Hollis, and in the hallway Catherine pushed her feet into boots, grabbed a coat, and walked back down to the car with us. The Mercedes was ahead of us, zooming past the open gate and leaving it open.

Catherine tried to persuade me that her husband was really a man of great charm, but was under a terrible strain at the moment, working very hard on his new book, and that in any case one had to make allowances for gifted people, they contributed so much to the quality of life, and they were subject to pressures which we lesser mortals were spared.

Even if I'd agreed with the premise, I wasn't all that certain Julian Trager belonged in that illustrious category, but I made amiable noises. Catherine said Arthur must let her see some of his work sometime, and then she stood waving as we got the car turned around.

We went down the road and through the open gateway, and Arthur went back to close it, and we were heading back toward the village when Arthur took a deep breath and gave his one-word commentary.

"Weird!" he said.

I wouldn't have put it that strongly. But odd, yes. Definitely odd.

◉ 4

As I dropped Arthur at the front entrance to the high school, I saw Calli come out through the double doors and mince carefully down the slushy walk clutching her huge brown leather bag against her soft wooly burnt-orange coat with the big raccoon collar. I tooted the horn and rolled down the window. She saw me, but she wasn't about to negotiate the distance between us since her car was in the other direction. She stood still and yelled at me that she had been to see the guidance counselor about Felicia's report card, that all guidance counselors were stupid and she couldn't understand how they kept their jobs or even got them in the first place.

"Did you get a call from Dr. Walsh?" I asked, knowing that even though Calli and Helen went into the office only on Wednesdays to clear away, pick up the copies, and mail them at the post office, they were sometimes there until noon.

"About Peter? Dough!" she yelled. "By God, Baggie, I hope that whoever did it breaks his deck and dies! If I could fide hib I would *shoot* hib! I *bead* it!"

"Is Charlie at the office?"

"Who does? All bordig he's beed ruddig id ad out." She shivered. "Po po ti crio! It's code! See you, Baggie!" She waved a goodbye and picked her way to her spattered white Dodge.

I swung around the parking island and headed for the village center. I thought briefly of dropping in at the office, but if Greenfield was running in and out there was only a fifty percent chance of finding him there and a phone call would do as well. If I didn't get him by phone I would see him at seven—he'd been coming to our house for dinner every Wednesday for a year or more. The ritual had begun as a kind of celebration that yet another edition of the *Reporter* had actually gone to press, and continued because he was alone most evenings except for weekends, when he saw his various daughters.

Just past the shopping center I pulled into Victor's Garage, Body Shop, and Service Station and left Billy to fill the tank while I went in search of Victor.

I found him in the smelly, cavernous garage standing with Frank, the mechanic, both of them scowling down at the insides of a sick Buick. The mechanic was scrawny and he coughed like Mimi in the last act of *Bohème.* Victor was a big, swarthy, barrel-chested man with long, dark, curling eyelashes, which should, if there were any justice in the world, have belonged to me. He looked up and gave me a brilliant Neapolitan smile.

"Hello there, Miz Rome."

"Hello, Victor, Frank. What's the trouble, inflammation of the carburetor?"

"Agh!" Victor made a gesture of disgust at the machinery under the hood. "I tell you, Miz Rome, this time of year everything falls apart. We can't keep up with it. This morning we got calls for six stalled cars. And everybody expects you to be there in five minutes."

"Listen," I said, "about the automatic clutch for the Chevy—"

"We got the order in, Miz Rome. Nothing we can do about it until the part comes."

"Give them another call."

He shrugged. "Wouldn't do any good."

"Try." I gave him my brilliant Hungarian smile and turned to go (I should mention here that the name Maggie in no way indicates my ancestry. My mother, in the grip of some Transylvanian fantasy, called me Magda, which I, at a tender age, rejected.) Turning back, in an offhand manner, I said, "By the way, did anyone bring in a car with dents or scratches on it since yesterday?"

Victor and Frank exchanged a look.

"You mean that hit-and-run? You're the third person came asking about dented cars."

"Oh, yes? Who else?"

"First Mr. Greenfield, then one of the cops—"

Greenfield. And I hadn't even mentioned it to him. Two minds with but a single obsession.

"And did you have any?" I asked. "Cars with dents?"

"We got a Pinto out there," Frank croaked between coughs. He slouched past me and through the open side door of the garage, and pointed to a shiny little number with a mauled fender and snow covering its windshield.

"Nah," Victor said, "they're lookin for somethin' that came in since last night. That Pinto's been there since Monday. Gotta get around to that fender, Frank. The lady's been buggin' me."

"Yeah, well, I'm backed up solid."

"And that's the only one?" I asked.

"The only one with dents. We've got one that's totaled, but that was in a three-car collision. Jeez, the things people do. How's that kid, all right?"

"I don't know."

"Jeez!' He stood there shaking his head.

"Well, thanks anyway. You'll let somebody know if anything turns up?"

"Oh, sure!"

I went back to the car, collected my credit card from Billy, and took off, wondering what it was about the Pinto that bothered me.

At the supermarket I bought an eggplant—one of Greenfield's favorites—tomatoes, apples, a French bread, lamb chops, and a packaged cheese strudel. On my way to the checkout counter I bethought myself of my friend Barbara Drexler, incarcerated in her bedroom, slogging away at torts and contracts and civil procedures, and asked the manager if I could use his phone. With all the charm for which the managers of chain supermarkets are famous, he growled, grunted, and sulked, turned away from me to listen to a long-winded story from one of the two listless checkout girls who were dawdling their way through the purchases of fifty-odd customers while the three other checkout counters remained uninhabited by personnel of any kind, and finally moved away from the phone, which I chose to interpret as a sign that I could use it.

Barbara's weary voice said she needed milk, lettuce, a roasting chicken, and probably a hundred other things but she was too tired to look. I added those items to the shopping cart, waited my twenty minutes in the checkout line, and on my way home detoured to Dunstan Hill, where Barbara lived.

Dunstan Hill was a craggy, wooded area of about twenty-five acres at the northern limit of Sloan's Ford, inhabited mostly by people who worked in television, publishing, advertising, and similar high-risk professions, and who lived in very expensive contemporary homes built to look like they were growing out of the rocks. Barbara called it Dunsinane and the small forest behind it Birnam Wood, because, she said, most of the inhabitants reminded her of Macbeth and his lady.

"And someday," she said, "great Birnam Wood to High Dunsinane will come, and there won't be enough shrinks around to cope with it."

Her own barn-red house was an exception; it sat firmly on a level piece of ground and somehow resembled a pioneer cabin in its setting of white snow and dark green pines. She opened the door to my ring and stood there staring at me with a glazed look.

"Maggie Rome," I said helpfully, "the lady from the supermarket."

She nodded dumbly and took the brown paper grocery bag. "I almost forgot. I think very soon I'll be certifiable." I followed her into the kitchen. "I don't know, I don't know," she went on, shaking her head, "what am I doing, will you tell me? A middle-aged jerk, knocking myself out with this—horrendous—" She waved an arm toward the bedroom where she studied. "I'm swamped! I'm inundated! I'm still working on *last* week's assignments; I read and I read, and I still don't know what they're talking about. I had some dumb idea that the law was a noble profession. It's a business. A dull, boring business. I'm going to quit."

"No you're not."

"If I were *smart* I'd quit." She pushed a hand through chestnut-colored hair. "I don't think I had lunch. Sit down and have lunch with me." She opened the refrigerator. "I don't have anything here for lunch. How about bread and cheese and tea?"

I watched her fill the kettle and put the groceries I'd bought into the refrigerator. She was an unremarkable-looking woman, with only a few qualities to recommend her, like warmth, honesty, humor, and intelligence. She had four children, half of them in college and half on the way, and an ex-husband with whom she had stayed, locked in unalterably conflicting points of view, until two years ago when she'd decided that "lonely" and "being alone" were not necessarily synonymous. Now she was juggling guilt, anxiety, relief, the various problems of her various children, and a freshman year in law school.

"I mean," she said, slicing bread, "I couldn't pick something easier, right? I couldn't sell real estate or take up interior decorating, because what would that prove? No, I have to take on the world. Only by achieving the impossible can I convince myself that I'm capable of surviving at all."

"Why don't you start a new kind of S-M club, for psychological flagellation—no whips required."

"I'm going to flunk, you know."

"Mm-hmm."

"Because I'm fighting it. It's lousy law. It's one part justice to nine parts expediency. Who needs it. Especially when it's so goddamn hard to learn! It's agony. It's torture."

"Tor-ture?" I murmured.

"That's a sickness," she said. "Puns are a sickness."

"Pour the tea."

"Anyway, it's taken care of my social problems, because I don't have *time* for social problems."

"Just as well. I can't see you in those places for married singles or whatever they call it."

"Oh, those places are only for serious mate-hunters. If all you want is temporary diversion, you can do very nicely right around here. The extracurricular activity in this neighborhood is legend—or will be, someday."

"Surely you're joshing."

"You wouldn't know, you live down in that respectable section with all those doctors. All they have time for is saving lives and becoming private corporations. But up here with the media people there is considerable hanky and a terrific amount of panky."

"From what I've seen of your neighbors I don't see that any one of them would be gaining anything by switching to any one of the others."

"It's the novelty, the novelty."

"As in cases of arrested development?"

"Res ipsa loquitur. How's that for legalese?" She sliced off a hunk of Edam and offered it to me. "But we have a new entry now. Walter Gipfel sold his house to some people called Seberg. Marshall Seberg. He's an agent with Creative Talent International. And *her* name"—for the first time in a month Barbara actually grinned—"is Sidonie. Sidonie Seberg."

I thought about it. "I would say a Sidonie Seberg is good for forty thousand a year."

"Close. She's only about thirty-five and she just got promoted to managing editor, with Curtin-Driscoll. Sickening?"

"There's nothing 'only' about it, Barbara. If you told me she was *fifty*-five and just landed a big job with a publisher, I might be impressed. But at thirty-five— unless one leg is shorter than the other or she's gone bald—almost any woman can get almost any job she wants. You know that, for God's sake."

"I thought that kind of thing was restricted to show biz."

"You've been cloistered too long. As the man said, life imitates bad art."

"Doesn't it, though. For all I know she may be a good editor. But according to the grapevine she has an open marriage all by herself. His side is closed, but hers has swinging doors."

"Why not? She belongs to the 'me too' generation. Ah!"

"What?"

"I need somebody for a 'Local Profiles' column. Do you think she would scorn being interviewed for a small-town paper? I wouldn't ask about the swinging doors, only about the job."

"As long as you're going to talk about *her*, scorn doesn't come into it. She'd be happy to talk about herself to a ninety-year-old Eskimo with a hearing problem."

"I'm going to call her."

We finished our Spartan lunch and I left Barbara to her legal agony and drove home. I found I couldn't wait until seven, and a call to the office got me the information, from a strangely abstracted Greenfield, via Dr. Walsh, that the brain scan showed no hemorrhaging, but that there had also been no change in Peter's condition. He was still in a coma.

"What does that mean?" I asked.

"Don't ask foolish questions," he said. "Medicine is in its infancy. Just make a good dinner."

"You shouldn't have sent all those roses," I said, "I don't know where to put them all."

"What are you talking about?"

"Be on time." I hung up and set to work mapping out my story on the Hollis farm. As I expanded my notes on the description of the land and the exterior of the house, something elusive nagged at the edge of my memory—something I'd seen that didn't fit the picture, but I didn't know what or why. It slowed me down a bit, but I finally completed a reasonable outline, and that done, I sliced, buttered, sprinkled, and baked the eggplant, marinated the lamb chops, prepared the tomatoes for grilling, filled a bowl with Boston lettuce, green peppers, and scallions, and put it in the refrigerator to chill.

I took a lovely hot shower, brushed my hair into a nice brown halo, dressed in my burgundy velvet pants and pale blue angora tunic, put Borodin, Chabrier, Saint-Saëns, and Ravel on the record changer, set the table, looked up Seberg, Marshall or Sidonie, in the phone book and dialed the number.

"Jess?" said a female voice.

"Mrs. Seberg?"

"She not home. Who is calling?"

I hesitated. "Maggie Rome" would probably get me nowhere. "A reporter from the newspaper," I said. "I want to write a story about her."

"Oh, yes? I see maybe she is home. Esscuse me."

After a minute or so a velvet voice came on the line. "Sidonie Seberg here." Fancy that.

I explained my mission.

"Oh, yes, the local paper." As one would say, "The wastebasket."

"Hold on a minute, would you," she said sweetly, "I just got in and I'm parched." There was a pause during which I heard bottles clinking. She came back. "Now—about this interview—I don't mind, if it won't take too long. I'm up to my eyebrows in work."

"I'd appreciate a half hour whenever it's convenient."

"Well—" She swallowed whatever she was drinking. "I suppose I can manage that. Damn! Sorry, I was trying to light a cigarette. Well, let's see. This is what? Wednesday. Good. I don't see how—hold on a minute—" At a distance I heard her voice change. Through a rip in the velvet there was a glimpse of steel. "Jennifer—" Quietly: "God *damn* it—*sit* down—and *eat—your—dinner*." A pause and she returned, all soft and plushy. "Look, dear—I'm in the city all week and the evenings are out, so it'll have to be the weekend. Saturday. No, wait a minute. Oh, all right, Saturday."

"Morning, or—"

A soft, husky laugh. "God, no. I have to get *some* sleep. Sometime in the afternoon."

"Two? Three?"

"Three. Make it three. Now—I'm so bad about names—what did you say your name was?" I was about to tell her when we had another interruption in a contralto register. "Carmelita, are you going to take care of that *child?*"

We finally got my name disposed of, also my references, the name of my paper, and the date this interview would appear, provided, after I'd written it, she read it and approved. Then she quickly said there was a call waiting on her other phone and I said goodbye.

I let George in the back door, fed him, lit a fire in the fireplace, and was taking the sherry out of the cabinet when there were three ponderous knocks at the front door. I got into the hall just behind George, whose tail was going as fast as his legs, and opened the door. Greenfield was standing there clutching a flowerpot of bronze chrysanthemums.

"Why, Mr. Greenfield," I said sweetly, "how thoughtful."

"I don't usually succumb to blackmail." He handed it to me brusquely.

"And what do you have against doorbells?" I asked, as he removed the rubbers covering his shoes and left them on the mat.

"The other day I pushed one and nothing happened. Electricity is unpredictable. When my knuckles make contact with wood, I know a sound will result." He came in and scratched George's inquiring nose. "This animal is dirty."

"Just around the mouth. He's been eating."

"Can't you teach him to use a napkin?"

"Napkins are unpredictable. When his jaw makes contact with a man's coat, he knows—"

Greenfield handed me his coat and went into the living room.

When we were settled by the fire, Greenfield in the big honey-colored armchair holding a glass of bourbon, me on the walnut-colored sofa with sherry on ice, George on the hearth with his tail about to catch fire, I told him about the Hollis farm, the whole thing, beginning to end, because I knew it relaxed him to listen to trivia. When I stopped he got up, turned over the records on the record changer, reset it, and sat down again.

"You haven't heard a word," I accused him. "You've been listening to the bloody music."

"I heard," he said mildly, and looked into the distance. "A viola," he mused, "in a thermostatically controlled cabinet."

"Oh, of course. *That* you heard."

"We could do the Hunt quartet."

"I told you, she brushed me off when I asked about chamber music. She's not interested."

"Rubbish. That's because of him. Trager. That's the only reason she doesn't play."

I stared at him. "*Tell* me about these psychic powers of yours."

"Maggie, you just described a destructive man. He insults his wife in public, patronizes you, mocks the old lady. She's not likely to expose something she cares about to his verbal meat cleaver."

"She let him verbally cleave her daughter!" I protested. "Although I must admit she finally ran him through with a small verbal stiletto. You know, it surprises me that she puts up with him. It's not in character."

"Age sometimes demands compromise."

"She doesn't strike me as a compromiser."

"Does she seem to be well heeled?"

"What? Oh, no, Victoria Hollis sell her dignity for money? Never. Besides, *he* couldn't support that place."

He thought about it. "You may be right, he hasn't made any big money for about twenty years."

"I think everything but the first book could be collected under the title *An Author in Search of Six Plots*."

"Well, he was one of those boys who found the war a hard act to follow. . . . But he drives a Mercedes?"

"Maybe he won it in a poker game. It's the kind of thing he would do. Or it's a gift from Catherine. He seems to be the world and all to her. God knows why."

"Ah! So the *daughter* has money."

"Who said that? Did I say that? How could I possibly know who has what in that family after a half-hour visit?"

Greenfield, as he often did when it suited him, ignored me. "The daughter has money. That makes sense. Why else would that kind of man marry that kind of girl—apparently no beauty, apparently no wit, and almost certainly neurotic."

"Come on, Charlie, how many times have you seen the most unlikely people married to each other?"

"That's what I'm saying. They're an unlikely couple, therefore she must have something he needs. I admit I'm working on marginal knowledge, but I can't think of anything a man like Trager would need from that setup—except money."

"Well, I'll tell you, that place didn't look—I mean, the carpets were worn, the wallpaper was patched in a couple of places, the station wagon is shabby, the VW is a good four years old—it just doesn't have the feel of a money house."

As I spoke, that fugitive memory teased me again, like an ache in the teeth that you can't pin down to one spot. Then my subconscious made a connection I didn't understand. "By the way, I understand you were at the garage asking about dents and scratches?"

Greenfield's bushy eyebrows rose and then knit. "Are you trying to tell me you had the same idea?"

"I had it first! I called the police last night, after I got home, and suggested it."

He regarded me quizzically for the count of ten. "You suggested it to the police, but not to me?"

"I didn't think of it until after I'd spoken to you."

He looked down at his glass. "Maggie, if I weren't a guest in your house—"

"Well, *you* thought of it, and you didn't tell *me*."

He uttered a profound sigh, got up, holding the bourbon, walked slowly around the room back to this chair, and sat again.

"*You*," he said, "work for *me*. Any information you acquire in connection with our mutual interests, whether by the use of your eyes, ears, or instinct, you are morally obligated to pass on to me. The reverse is not true."

"Then I hereby tender my resignation."

"Accepted."

"Fine."

"You have an underdeveloped sense of loyalty."

"I'm surprised you don't practice droit du seigneur."

One of his cheeks twitched, which was his version of a smile. "That sounds like an oblique invitation."

"Not bloody likely."

"Your loss. One of these days you might finally succeed in your obvious attempts to pair me up with your friend Barbara. Then it'll be too late."

"No danger. My friend Barbara doesn't like the feudal arrangement any better than I do."

"Your friend Barbara has more than *that* count against her. Namely, she doesn't respond to *music*. I take it as a signal example of your latent hostility that you suggest I take up with a woman who—"

I stood up. "Excuse me. The lamb chops."

I went into the kitchen to shut off the oven before the pink left the lamb chops and to put the dinner plates in to warm. Greenfield went to the dining room table and sat; he never helped in the kitchen. I put the bowl of salad, the warm French bread, the platter of chops, grilled tomatoes, and sautéed eggplant on a tray and carried them in, and returned for the warmed dinner plates while Greenfield poured the Portuguese rosé.

No one said anything for a while. We ate. Saint-Saëns filled the air. It was a comfortable silence. We'd had our daily fencing match and we were content. It was Greenfield who spoke first.

"None of the other body shops," he said, "had anything either. I practically covered the county. Nothing in Gorham. Nothing in Chester. I even went to Pinecliff."

"It may be too early. People don't necessarily rush out the morning after an accident to have a car repaired."

"Unless the accident has implications they can't face. Think of driving around with the stigmata of that act constantly before your eyes."

"Maybe he—or she—isn't driving it around. Maybe the car is stashed somewhere."

"And the driver is using what form of transportation?"

"The other car. Most families around here have two cars."

"You've just eliminated an entire economic bracket."

"In the bracket you're talking about it's usually a truck, and after five P.M. it sits in the driveway. Unless junior gets to drive it, and that's only on Saturday night."

Greenfield took another helping of eggplant while he reflected.

"Most people," he said, "given that kind of accident, would have a moment of panic. Then reason would take over and they'd deal with it. Poorly or well, depending on character, but they'd deal with it. What kind of person"—he chewed ruminatively—"would sustain a degree of panic that would prevent him from dealing with it at all?"

"What the psychologists call an emotionally disturbed person."

"That could apply to anyone these days."

"All right, forget that—how about a coward?"

"What would he be afraid of?"

"Blame. Maybe a charge of criminal negligence, or manslaughter if the boy—if he didn't recover."

"Rubbish. Couldn't be proved. He could say the boy rode out of the shadows into the path of the car before he had time to brake."

"No matter what, he'd have to take blame. He might be one of those people who are incapable of accepting blame. Something in them refuses to be responsible. They can't grow up."

"Or possibly they are *not* grown up. What if you were sixteen and driving at night without a full license? Driving someone else's car?"

"I could panic to the point of no return."

"If I had money I'd bet on it. What's the name of that place in the village where the kids hang out?"

"Dodie's."

"I think I'll check it out."

"All the action there is on the weekend. There won't be much happening tonight."

"Tonight! You think I'd go there tonight? The Boston Symphony is on." He took a third helping of eggplant. "With a little more practice you should be able to prepare a fairly good eggplant," he conceded.

And after I'd stacked the dishes in the dishwasher I joined him in front of the television set, where the one-and-only Ozawa was fluttering his hands and sucking in his cheeks and giving Mozart a pretty good run for his money.

▣ 5

I was sitting at the dining room table, my left hand resting on the keys of the typewriter, my right hand cradling a cup of Sanka, and my eyes following George outside the window, ambling around the yard looking up and down the street for a stray dog or cat or sanitation truck to bark at, when the telephone rang. It was Greenfield.

"Maggie."

"Oh, Mr. Greenfield, there was no need to call and tell me how much you appreciated last night's dinner." He ignored it.

"Arthur dropped off the prints of those pictures he took yesterday," he said. "There seems to be one of you."

"Is it any good?"

"It's irrelevant. What was the point of it?"

"Arthur had a sudden attack of the giddies."

Silence. Then: "Well, as it happens, it's not without interest. Come in and look at it."

"I'm working. And then I have to go up to the farm for lunch."

"For lunch?"

"I told you last night. I got trapped by my sense of compassion."

"Oh, yes. Good. On your way there, drop in." *Click.*

The weather was holding. Clear, cold, and sunny. It was thirty seconds past noon when I parked in front of the office. The horrendous shriek of the whistle which, for some reason I've never discovered, blasts from the loudspeaker of the firehouse every so often at noon was only just fading away as I got out of the Honda

46

with a paper bag containing a pound each of coffee and tea. Helen was at her usual post.

"Good morning, good morning," she said in a singsong.

"The morning is no more," I replied," the whistle killed it. Calli!" I raised my voice to reach the source of the mouselike noises in the layout room. "I brought coffee and tea!" I went into the alcove to put them away.

"Oh, Thank you." Calli's voice from afar lacked the enthusiasm I'd anticipated. I opened the cupboard. Standing on the shelves were three cans of coffee, one of Earl Grey tea, one of Tetley tea bags, one of Lipton's, and one of instant chocolate.

"It's really depressing," I said, "to find you're superfluous."

"Don't be silly," Helen protested, "the more the merrier. Now we don't have to worry about running out."

I tried to point out that useful was different from unique, but there are some subtleties that escape Helen.

"Any news about Peter?" I asked.

"No change." Helen sighed. "That poor family. The brother picked up the papers yesterday to deliver them. He looked so miserable."

"And what are the police doing about it?" Calli shrilled from her room. "Haddig out parkig tickets! Forget it!"

I went up the stairs. Greenfield was leaning back perilously in the aged swivel chair, the telephone receiver at his ear.

"I don't like the man," he was saying slowly and pleasantly to the mouthpiece. "He has as much right to be making educational decisions as the mechanic at Victor's garage. Possibly less. He has consistently vetoed every intelligent course of action proposed by the other members of the board. He is incompetent, arrogant, pernicious, and corrosive." He looked at me to make sure I was appreciating his vocabulary. "And I'm afraid this paper's going to say so whether you give us your advertising or not. Yes, that's my position. Yes, sir. Whatever you say." He replaced the receiver, swiveling toward the desk and back again.

When the creaks and groans stopped, I said, "Does this enterprise run to severance pay?"

"You really *are* resigning?"

"Not yet, but I have a feeling we're all going to be out on the street pretty soon anyway. I mean paper costs money, ink costs money, printers cost money, Helen and Calli and Stewart and Mr. Becker cost money. Presumably I'd work for the glory of it, but even so someone has to underwrite those other expenses—"

"Are you suggesting I put my good or bad opinion up for grabs?"

"Your opinion may not reach too many people unless it's in print."

"We're not about to go under for lack of the Villa Appia ads. The restaurant should be condemned anyway. Twenty-four dollars for lukewarm veal and fettuccine that was prepared sometime during the wars with Sparta."

"Six months ago it was that manufacturer in Chester—"

"The man was using the Hudson River as a sewer and getting away with it."

"And last year you carried the flag for the committee to limit Christmas decorations—that won you a lot of friends."

"Someone had to get the fools to recognize an energy problem. And someone has to stop that cretin up the street."

It was true. There was a house on Poplar which still, at the end of February, had an enormous plastic Santa and reindeer riding across its roof, another Santa (a rival firm?) riding a red plastic train across the lawn, a three-foot-high group of plastic, white-smocked choristers with round mouths presumably singing hymns, also on the lawn, an obscene four-foot red plastic candle with a bulb on top representing a flame, which went on and off perpetually, next to the driveway, a string of red-and-green colored lights that looped across the porch and circled an enemic pine tree, six wreaths laced

with twinkling blue lights in various windows and doorways, and an assortment of plastic elves frolicking
hither and yon. The only thing that could be more obtrusive on that street would be a Coney Island roller
coaster powered by a rock band.

But it was dangerous to give an inch on this issue. I
liked this job and I wasn't sure I could get another
one.

"By all means," I said, "let's fight the good fight and
let the bills fall where they may. The bankruptcy courts
are full of idealists."

"Maggie. Be quiet and sit down."

I stood. He stared up at me.

"Whatever you may think you're gaining in self-as-
sertion," he assured me softly, "you can be sure you're
losing in charm."

He knows just where to hit a woman who isn't quite
sure how far liberation should go. I carefully, and with
obvious distaste, removed the debris from an armchair
and sat.

"When," he began, "did we have our last snowfall?"

"Charlie," I said, "I really don't have time for here-
we-go-round-the-mulberry-bush."

"Just answer the question."

The answer came through clenched teeth. "Monday
night."

He nodded. "When you were giving me that account
of your visit with Mrs. Hollis, you said Trager drives a
Mercedes, the daughter can't drive a stick shift, and
Mrs. Hollis won't drive in the winter."

His memory is flexible—absent or phenomenal, depending on his whim.

"Very good," I said, "total recall. Does this have
anything to do with anything, or is it just a sequel to
Bruckner's Opus Zero?"

He swiveled back to the desk, picked up a black-
and-white print, and handed it to me. It was a very
nice picture of a rather startled woman with windblown
hair and expensive boots standing next to a shed: me.
To one side, in the foreground, were two automobiles.
I stared at them and then whooped with relief.

"Ha-ha! *That's* what it was! *That's* what I was trying

to remember while I was writing the piece—and then at the garage, when Victor said the Pinto had been there since Monday! *That's* what it was!"

"Tell me," Greenfield suggested patiently.

"The snow! At the garage this banged-up Pinto that Victor said had been there since Monday—it was covered with snow, the windshield and everything, because it obviously hadn't been moved since the snowfall. And at the farm, the station wagon was covered with snow too. But the VW—"

Greenfield uttered a gently inquisitive sound.

"Well, it's right here in black and white," I said flatly. "The VW was cleared off—the windshield, the windows. I suppose the discrepancy got stuck in my subconscious."

"Mm. It isn't likely anyone would clear the snow off the windshield of a car that wasn't going to be driven until the spring."

"Of course, someone else might have driven it."

"Not the daughter, evidently. And why would Trager choose a VW that doesn't belong to him over a Mercedes that does?"

"So Mrs. Hollis told a white lie," I said. "She didn't want to be bothered driving Arthur back to school. What's so terrible about that?"

"Or the daughter lied."

"No, because she offered to drive Arthur back in the station wagon."

"It's not Arthur I'm thinking about."

"Then what?"

Greenfield swiveled to the desk, looked out the window for a long moment, and swiveled back. He seemed, to my amazement, to be slightly embarrassed.

"There was snow falling on and off until Tuesday afternoon. This picture was taken on Wednesday around noon. Some time between Tuesday afternoon and Wednesday morning, someone was driving that car."

"So?"

"And someone lied about it. By implication, if nothing else."

"Well, Charlie, I'm impressed and all that. You obviously have hidden talents as a sleuth, but—"

"I'd like you to do something when you go up there for lunch."

I stared at him. He was perfectly serious. I began to sense what this was all about. "If you're thinking—" I spluttered.

"See if there are any scratches on the VW."

For the first time since I'd met Greenfield, I felt sorry for him. Peter's accident had obviously unhinged his mind.

"Charlie, we can't go looking for burglars under every bed. There could be a dozen innocent reasons for Mrs. Hollis or Catherine to avoid driving that car. Neither of them actually said it *hadn't* been out sometime on Tuesday. They weren't necessarily *hiding* anything. Besides, if you lined up a hundred suspects, they'd be the first two I'd eliminate."

"On what grounds?"

"Victoria Hollis has the moral fiber of six Christian martyrs and her daughter is incapable of keeping anything to herself—if she'd been involved in an accident she'd be stopping people in the street to confess it."

"People with moral fiber have been known to use it in the service of strange convictions. And people who seem to be spilling their life history at the drop of a hat are sometimes merely laying a smoke screen."

"It's ridiculous. Ridiculous. If you'd ever met them you'd know how ridiculous it is."

"Ridiculous, maybe. Not impossible."

We stared at each other like two statues representing Obstinacy and Monomania.

"You're asking me to abuse someone's hospitality."

"I'm asking you to use your head and your eyes and get the information on the sly."

When did I ever win?

I stood up and walked to the stairway. "I'll try," I said, determined to have the last word. "It may not be possible," I added, starting down the stairs.

The last word floated down after me.

"Everything's possible."

▣ 6

This time I drove all the way up to the house, hoping to have a few minutes alone near the shed before anyone realized I was there, but as I took the keys from the ignition I saw a figure coming across the field toward me from the direction of the barn. It was a girl of fourteen or fifteen in jeans and a peacoat, tall, angular, with straight blonde hair, accompanied by a small brown-and-white dog of uncertain lineage. She walked—not loping or lurching or slouching or sidling or propelling herself forward by any of the methods common to girls of her age—she just covered the ground in a straightforward, calmly proprietary way, as though she were responsible for everything in the immediate vicinity and equal to the obligation.

"Victoria," I thought, "you've managed to pass it on, in spite of Catherine and Trager." Because this, of course, had to be the granddaughter, Elizabeth.

She came up with a small smile and an outstretched red mitten.

"Hello, Mrs. Rome." The gray eyes regarded me steadily. "I'm Elizabeth Trager. My grandmother said I should watch out for you. Lunch won't be ready for half an hour and she said the ground is harder today and I should ask if you'd like me to show you around the land."

The way she said "the land" suggested a personal continent. "I'd like it," I said, patting the dog who was investigating traces of George on my coat.

The gray eyes lit up. "Where would you like to start?"

How about the Volkswagen? "Your choice," I said,

and she said "Come on, Alice" to the dog, gave me a swift grin, and we started out.

"There's a teachers' conference today," she confided, "so we only had a half day of school. Would you like to see the barn?"

"Why not."

"It's partly a stable and partly for Andrew's things. Andrew does everything around here. He's the farmhand and the gardener and he takes care of the horses."

As we approached I noted an outside stairway leading to the second story, and two windows up there, the sills lined with what looked like potted herbs.

She opened the barn door and we went in. It was large and dim inside, and smelled of hay and horses and machine oil. The front half seemed to be a combined toolshed and potting shed, and a small tractor stood against one wall surrounded by various attachments for plowing and digging post holes. The far end consisted of two horse stalls, and a space to stack hay. It was all very neat and clean. I followed Elizabeth to where a dark-haired man was cleaning out one of the two horse stalls. It was the man I'd seen the day before crossing toward the wood.

"Andrew," Elizabeth said, "this is Mrs. Rome."

Andrew, who was bent over his work, slowly straightened up and looked, with equanimity, straight into my eyes, and I felt a sensation I hadn't felt for many a year. There are some men who possess a quality which goes way beyond romantic or even sexual appeal, a quality which literally enslaves. It has very little to do with looks and nothing at all to do with youth, because there are some quite mature and unathletic specimens who have it. It's an expression in the eyes, or an aura of being in control, and responsible, or something easy and powerful in the stance, or who knows. Anyway, Andrew had it, and I felt distinctly uncomfortable, because I was about fifteen years too late. I wondered how Catherine handled it. Obviously it went right past Elizabeth, and probably would for a few years.

He nodded briefly and made an inarticulate sound,

which was all he needed to do, since the rest of him was eloquent enough. I couldn't think of a single sensible thing to say to him.

"I saw the horses yesterday," I mumbled, "from a distance. They're beautiful."

"Andrew's teaching me to groom properly," Elizabeth said. "I've been doing it for years, but not properly, he says."

I cleared my throat. "Where did you develop all these skills, Andrew?" I asked. "Did you grow up on a farm?"

"Liking it," he said in a voice like the young Walter Huston, "is all you need."

Which is one way to answer a question without answering it.

"Well, we only have about twenty minutes," Elizabeth said, "and I want to show Mrs. Rome the rest of the place."

"Nice meeting you," I understated.

A corner of his mouth went up and he nodded.

We left the barn and started across to the pasture.

"He's not terribly social," Elizabeth said. "He comes from out West somewhere. He just walked up to the door one day and asked for a job, and my grandmother hired him. That was five years ago. We had old Mr. McClure then, but he had arthritis and wanted to go to live with his daughter in Jacksonville, and after he got Andrew broken in, he did. He doesn't get along with my father."

"Mr. McClure?"

"No, Andrew."

That was hardly surprising. What man would want Andrew around?

"My father," she went on, "once knocked out his pipe in one of the horse stalls and walked out, and the horses were in there, and Andrew was in a rage. He said the ashes could have started a fire in the hay and the horses would have been trapped. He called my father some names. My father told Grandmother to fire him, but she said Andrew was wrong to say what he did, but he was right about the ashes, and she wouldn't fire him."

"I gather your grandmother makes the decisions around here."

There was a moment's hesitation.

"Usually," she said, and then took a deep satisfied breath and sent her eyes to the horizon. "Someday I'll have to make them. When I'm twenty-one, the farm belongs to me."

And a good choice, I thought, watching Elizabeth's strong, quiet face as she planted her hands on a split-rail fence and swung her long legs over. I followed, less gracefully.

She introduced me to the horses, whose names were Hawkeye and Radar ("I named them," she added unnecessarily), and in the adjoining field showed me how the vegetable plots were going to be laid out, and we tramped across the fields, through the orchard, along the crests of hillocks and the ridges of gulleys, squelched across soggy turf and scrambled over boulders, tripped over the surfacing roots of trees older than the Union, followed the snowy banks of the stream through the wood to where it passed under a small bridge and out of sight, and all this to the accompaniment of Elizabeth discoursing on the merits and disadvantages of the surrounding flora and fauna. A certain field had miraculously rich soil, it would grow anything. There was a blight on a windbreak of poplars and Andrew would have to cut them down and plant evergreens. There were sometimes partridges walking around in the woods, and Alice had once trapped a terrified groundhog in the well bucket.

"And look!" she exclaimed as we came out of the woods, pointing her red mitten at a solitary figure moving at what seemed to be a steady crawl along the far perimeter of the field. It appeared to be an old, bent man in a too-large overcoat, a cap with ear muffs, and a series of mufflers of various patterns and colors, all of which were blowing like pennants in the wind. "That's our walker, Mr. Chanin. He's eighty-five years old. He got my grandmother's permission to walk around the edge of our land because he loves to walk and he can't walk where there's traffic. He comes every day, usually about this time, because it's the warmest part of the day."

We walked to meet him, and when she introduced me, Mr. Chanin's sharp little eyes gleamed at me from their wrinkled folds, but that was all I could see of his face because a glen-plaid woolen scarf was covering everything else. Below it a blue-and-yellow paisley was wound around his neck, and the cerise object that was presumably meant to be folded over his chest had escaped and flailed around with the rest. He pulled down two inches of the glen plaid to greet me and comment on the weather.

"Not bad," he said, in a surprisingly strong voice. "Cold, but dry. Hope we don't have a rainy spring. Spring is the best time for the outdoors. The outdoors, the great outdoors! That's all there is, you know. All the rest is garbage. Concrete. Automobiles. Fumes. Lung cancer. Factories. Politics. War. What do they expect? Destroy the land, you destroy life. Airplanes crashing into houses. If I had my way I'd wipe 'em all out. *There's* your enemy. Money and power. Curse of the world. Have a nice walk, now." He replaced the wool plaid, waggled his fingers, and went off, banners flying.

By the time we arrived back at the house I was ravenous and could hardly wait for the quiche, but I'd made Greenfield a promise and there might not be another opportunity, so I resisted the impulse to rush into the house and told Elizabeth I wanted to get something from my car and I'd be right in. For a moment I thought she would offer to wait for me, but her good manners must have sensed a desire for privacy. She went in.

For appearance's sake I opened the door of the Honda and reached inside, then shut the door and quickly covered the half-dozen feet to the green Volkswagen. I circled it, scanning it carefully, trying to look as though I were considering buying one, in case anyone happened to see me.

And there, on the right front fender, was a gash about five inches long and vivid white against the green. And in the white were flecks of blue.

I don't know how long I would have stayed there with my mouth open if I hadn't suddenly felt something cold and wet against my knee. It was Alice, a good hostess, waiting to see me into the house.

I took a few deep breaths, telling myself not to be caught up in Greenfield's insanity—there must be another explanation for that scrape. Or maybe *Andrew* had taken the car that night. (Andrew? Who became violently incensed at the mere *possibility* that harm might come to two innocent equine creatures? Use your head.) I resolved to steel myself and refuse to think about it for the next few hours, and made my way to the house, wishing I'd been invited for drinks instead of lunch. Resolve or not, in the circumstances light social conversation would have been much easier with an alcoholic glass in the hand. And just to top off the misery, my appetite had disappeared.

When I stepped into the sunny dining room with its blue-and-white wallpaper, Elizabeth was placing napkins on the large round fruitwood table standing in the windowed bay that overlooked a sweep of snow-patched lawn and a number of leafless lilac bushes. She smiled at me, and then a delicious aroma reached me as Catherine came in carrying a buttercup-yellow quiche pan on a tray with a basket of hot rolls. Almost, you expected the scene to freeze and become a Norman Rockwell illustration. It was grotesque to think of monstrous behavior in this setting.

"Hurry, hurry," Catherine said, "it's at its peak *right now!* How are you, Mrs. Rome? You look marvelously windswept! Did you enjoy the walk! Mother!"

There was the sound of feet descending the stairway. Where had she been? At an upstairs window watching me examine her car? She came in wearing a kind of mandarin jacket of turquoise wool over black slacks, the sun from the window lighting up her elegant white hair. Beside her, Catherine faded into obscurity. Elizabeth, of course, could hold her own even in a potato sack, which her golden orange sweater was not. I occupied myself quite successfully with all this trivia while Mrs. Hollis greeted me and we all sat down and passed salad and hot rolls and butter and Catherine dished out the quiche. I evidently missed some of the conversation because when I tuned in again Victoria Hollis was talking about the city.

"I'm too old to put up with the noise, the crowds, the hostility, and the constant threat of unprovoked attack. Also, the tragedy of it depresses me—that what used to be the mountaintop to which the most creative and most original minds in the world aspired has become a giant slop trough, where pigs fight each other for a chance to guzzle."

"That's not *strictly* true, Mother! Not *strictly!* There are still a great many—"

"Yes, I know. If the Metropolitan were robbed of all but one Rembrandt, one El Greco, and half a dozen Watteaus, Holbeins, Manets, and so on, and turned over to the populace to use for their graffiti, you could truthfully say, 'There is still something of great value at the Metropolitan.' But 'still' is a very sad word."

"Do you never go into the city then, Mrs. Hollis?" I asked.

"I went in some years ago, to hear Casals. I felt I could suffer some discomfort for that privilege. Nothing less important would take me in again."

"It's such a shame!" Catherine cried, "such a waste! You might as well be living in Tennessee!"

"You're slouching, Elizabeth," Mrs. Hollis said gently, and lightly touched Elizabeth's shoulder, which looked straight enough to me.

"Sometimes," Catherine said, turning to me, "I feel we're a nineteenth-century family! Sitting at the table with backs like ramrods! Such formality!"

"I've never had anything to do with formality," Mrs. Hollis said, "only with health and manners. A straight back and good manners can cure a lot of ills. Psychologists keep harping on our insides and ignoring our outsides. That's a mistake. People tend to live up to the image they create."

"Now, Mother!" Catherine protested. "Surely a person's image is the *result* of what they are, not the *foundation!*"

"To a degree. And to a degree the reverse. I don't

deny the importance of one, I wish people wouldn't deny the other."

"It's true," Elizabeth put in, "that when Hawkeye and Radar have just been groomed, their behavior is much better than when they're all scrungy."

Catherine began to shrink and I tottered to the rescue.

"This quiche is superb!" I told her, and immediately she glowed.

"Have some more," she insisted. Thus are the virtuous rewarded, with forced feeding.

"How was your walk, Mrs. Rome?" Victoria asked me, and I tried to think back to how I was feeling before the discovery of the scratch.

"Marvelous," I said, "I was completely renewed, inside and out. I'd like to replace all the tranquilizers and pep pills in the world with trees, brooks, and meadows, and force people to take three a day, before meals. Like Mr. Chanin."

"Oh, you met Mr. Chanin!" Catherine crowed. "Isn't he splendid? He never fails, better than the postman, rain, hail, or snow! He has gear for any kind of weather!"

"I worry about him in the winter," Victoria said. "He could so easily have an accident—slip on an icy patch—"

"I wish there were no such things as accidents!" Elizabeth said with sudden heat. We all looked at her. "One minute everybody's happy, and the next—" She got busy with her fork.

"What's all this?" Catherine asked. "Did you have an accident?"

"No. But there's a girl in my class—Marjorie Kittell—"

My throat closed and the quiche stayed in my mouth.

"She has a brother Peter," she went on. "He was riding his bike the other night and some car came speeding along and knocked him over and drove away and left him there!"

Did I imagine it, or had Victoria's face suddenly gone pale?

"And now he's in the hospital, in a coma," Elizabeth concluded, "and whoever knocked him down—" She jabbed viciously at her salad.

There was a pause and then Victoria asked quietly, "When did this happen?"

"Tuesday," Elizabeth said, "Tuesday night."

I swallowed the quiche. "As a matter of fact, I know the boy. I was the one who found him."

"You? Really?" Elizabeth looked as though she were going right out to have a medal struck.

"You found him?" Catherine repeated breathlessly. "How did you—I mean, it must have been awful for you! Was he—? Did you—? What happened?"

Victoria looked at me blankly.

I went through the story quickly, bringing them up to date, then as tactfully as I could segued to a discussion of doctors. This, I find, is always a topic of mutual interest, no matter what the company. There is no one on the face of the earth who doesn't have an opinion about the medical profession.

From there the conversation veered to my work on the *Reporter,* and I answered questions about its background, progress, stresses, and rewards, while I silently longed for lunch to be over so that I could go away by myself and put some pieces together. But when we'd had coffee and some wafer-thin pastry, Victoria suggested Catherine show me some of her work while she and Elizabeth washed up.

I followed Catherine up the steep stairway and along an upper hallway lined with old prints into a room at the back of the house which must at one time have been an extremely large closet. It was inhabited by a workbench, a high stool, an enlarger, a developing tank, several types of trays, some brown plastic bottles, and all the usual darkroom equipment. The walls were cork, and covered in mounted enlargements of photographs.

Surprise.

Catherine Trager was an extraordinarily good photographer. She had captured the essence of everything on which she had turned the lens of her camera—a lone duckling gamely paddling through ice floes in the stream, the two horses exuberantly racing each other in the snow, Andrew perspiring in rolled-up shirt sleeves and squinting at something in the distance, the tiny, silhouetted figure of Mr. Chanin crossing a seemingly vast expanse of meadow at sunset, six white petals scattered on the grass below a blossoming apple tree, Andrew seen through a curtain of rain, poised in the open barn door, Elizabeth sitting tall in the saddle on Hawkeye, laughing. Victoria in an old sweater weeding a flower bed, Julian asleep in a hammock, Andrew again. . . .

I spent twenty wordless minutes admiring the collection while Catherine pretended to fuss with her flatbed dryer and paper tongs and safelight and fixer and all the rest of her paraphernalia.

"I don't really know," I said finally, "but I think this is art."

Catherine laughed nervously and looked frightened. "Oh, no!" she said. "No, no! Art! Just sentimental little pictures, I'm afraid."

"Who told you that?"

I could swear she opened her mouth to say "Julian," but she only laughed again. "No one has to *tell* me! I only have to look at Ansel Adams, and Bodine and Steichen and Bourke-White and Cartier-Bresson! Art! Good Lord! I have a long way to go!"

"Have you shown these to anyone?"

"A friend or two—"

"I mean professionals. People who can evaluate them."

"Oh no! Jul— I'm not ready. Not ready for that! I'd be embarrassed!"

"The ex-husband of a friend of mine," I said, "is a professional photographer who's had a couple of one-man shows. If I set up an appointment, would you take these down to the city and let him look at them? He's a very nice, sympathetic guy, even if he was a lousy husband, and I have a strong feeling he'd be impressed."

She shook her head rapidly. "I really couldn't. Jul—It would be such an imposition!"

"Rubbish," I said, sounding like Greenfield. "I'm going to do it and you'd better be ready. Where's the bathroom?"

Elated and fearful, she showed me the bathroom and said she'd see me downstairs.

On my way back to the stairs, I passed the open door of a room in which I could see shelves of books, a man's sweater thrown over the back of a chair next to a desk, a pipe rack, a tin of tobacco—Julian Trager's study? I have to admit I am not really well bred, because my feet carried me into the room with hardly a moment's hesitation.

It was a small, low-ceilinged room, and it told me a few more things about Mr. Trager. For one, he ate Milky Ways between meals—the crumpled wrappers dotted the blotter on his desk. For another, he had either a grown son by a previous marriage or a nephew he was crazy about—there was a framed snapshot of a long-haired eighteen-year-old slouching against a palm tree. Also, he had a correspondent in some faraway place, because there was a pale blue envelope lying next to the Olivetti with an exotic Polynesian-looking stamp on it and the postmark "Apia." And he had a motto. It was scrawled on a sheet from a lined writing pad and pinned to the wall with a thumbtack: "One chapter in the bedroom is worth a hundred anywhere else."

That seemed a little simplistic for a man of letters. Perhaps he had a better one on the wall of wherever he did his writing in the city.

I went downstairs with that edgy feeling in the fingernails I get when the weather turns bad, and sure enough, when I left the farm a quarter of an hour later, a mass of purple-gray cloud was moving across the sky like a battleship. I greeted it with a short, pungent word, and thought about moving permanently to Apia, wherever that was.

◙ 7

It was Friday morning before I saw Greenfield. I had deliberately stayed away from my own house the previous afternoon in case he should call. I was simply not ready for whatever consequences might result from my report of the damaged VW. When I left the farm I headed into White Plains, took care of some long-postponed shopping for the boys, and when I got home wrote letters to Elliot and Matt, and even one to Alan, since forgiveness is a mother's divinity, all the while waiting for the phone to ring. But there was no call from Greenfield, and that in itself made me nervous—a condition hardly remedied by the persistent and furious rain that lashed the house all night.

I slept badly, and the next morning, just to give myself something to live for, I called the beauty parlor immediately after breakfast and made an appointment to have my hair shampooed and "shaped." It was a gray morning, but at least the rain had washed all the snow away, and when I opened the front door, there, visible for the first time in months all up and down the street, were the lovely old, brownish, winter-worn lawns. It was a start.

On my way to the hairdresser I stopped in at the office, shouted hello to the girls, and went up the stairs to Greenfield. Halfway up I paused, because I heard a strange female voice.

"I will never forget," it was saying in a strong contralto, "and I thank you very much. And my husband. And we are going to pay it back as fast as we can."

"We've got to do something," I heard Greenfield say, "about the health insurance plan in this state."

63

"Yes," she agreed, "it's not very good. I have to go now. Goodbye, Mr. Greenfield."

I continued up the stairs and met Mrs. Kittell at the top in her dark blue cloth coat and knitted hat. There was a harsh, besieged look about her face, which didn't change much when she recognized me and tried to smile. I asked after Peter and she said he was the same, thank you, and started down the stairs.

Greenfield was regarding me with the grave disappointment of one betrayed. "I've been waiting," he said in measured tones, "almost twenty-four hours for the simple courtesy of a phone call. Did you or did you not find evidence that the Volkswagen could have been in collision with a bicycle?"

I looked past him out the window. "If you're going to put it like that, I'm not talking."

He actually leaned forward. "You found something. I knew it. What did you find?"

"No one will ever convince me that Victoria Hollis drove that car into Peter's bike. Or Catherine."

"What did you find?"

"And Julian Trager wasn't even home that night. Remember when I called to make an appointment? Catherine volunteered the information that only she and her mother and Elizabeth were at dinner. And the next morning she mentioned that Trager had been working late the night before, in the city."

"She mentioned that? Why would she mention that?"

"Because she mentions everything."

"Working late." He nodded portentously. "The oldest lie in the history of fabrication."

I groaned. "Charlie, this is sheer, groundless speculation. I could probably find you six hundred cars in Sloan's Ford with scratches on them."

"Scratches." He pursed his mouth. "Tell me about the scratches."

I paused, and in the pause I heard the front door open and close. Mrs. Kittell, I took time to reflect, couldn't have taken that long to get downstairs. Most likely she'd been intercepted by Helen, who lost no opportunity to commiserate.

"Scratches," Greenfield repeated.

"Yes! All right! One horizontal scratch. Six inches long. Could have been made by a careless neighbor in a parking lot. Could have happened by backing out of a tight space. Could have been put there by vandals—"

"What color is the car?"

"Green. Why?"

"I'll check out the bicycle. If there are any signs of green—"

I tossed the end of my scarf over one shoulder and tried to look unconcerned. I hadn't told him about the flecks of blue in the scratch. I hadn't told him of Andrew's existence. I was definitely bipartisan.

"I'm going to get my hair done," I said. "Are we playing tonight?"

"Yes. At Gordon's. By the way, it's the end of the month. Are you going to have one of those profile things for next week?"

"I hope so. I'm interviewing some lady editor tomorrow."

"If not, I'd like to do something on the sloppiness of the highway department. They fill those potholes every February with useless cold gook, which has a built-in obsolescence, because the hot asphalt is not available until the spring. Forty-eight hours later the potholes are back, and if they had repaved the bad spots six years ago it would have cost the taxpayer half the amount."

"It looks good for the profile, but I'll let you know." I turned to go and stepped on something soft. A woman's glove. I picked it up. "Must be Mrs. Kittell's," I said, showing it to Greenfield. "I'll drop it off later."

"We'll do the Beethoven tonight."

"I know." I started down the stairs. "We decided last week."

"I could have changed my mind."

Formidable!

Downstairs I poked my head into the workroom, told the girls I was late for an appointment, congratulated Calli on the improvement in her cold, and left.

Since I'd learned something of the history of that

block of old brick buildings in the village square, and could justifiably imagine there had once been a black-smith shop on that particular piece of ground, Francine's Beauty Parlor had achieved an added distinction in my mind. It already had attributes which set it apart from other such institutions. It was nothing like what the affluent middle class expects from a "hair salon"; it was more like an old rural general store or an old urban candy store, where the gossip and the hanging around are equal in importance to the business transacted. The place, in spite of its name, was owned and operated by an unequivocally virile middle-aged man with Italy in his background called Anthony, who, during his shampooing and coloring and setting and snipping, conducted seminars on politics, nutrition, history, crime in the streets, jazz, and football. He and his single assistent, Janice, who had her own specialties (soap operas, medical bulletins, and local scandals), were both exceedingly warm and friendly people, and I wouldn't have traded Francine's with its chipped sinks and uncertain water pressure for any glossy perfumed coif palace you could name.

When I walked in, Anthony was applying what looked like blue glue to the ash-blonde hair of a plump lady with a baby-doll face, and Janice was belatedly taking down her Valentine decorations. No holiday went unrecognized at Francine's. In October there were paper pumpkins and witches scotch-taped to the mirrors, in November paper turkeys and Pilgrim hats took their place, in December a tree with ornaments made by Janice out of clothespins dipped in red and gold paint, cotton balls dipped in something sparkly, and so on. For New Year's we had balloons and streamers strung along the framed photographs of plastic-faced models with perfect hairdos, and now, even as she removed the red paper hearts, I glimpsed a batch of bright green craft paper in a far corner, from which she would painstakingly fashion her shamrocks. Janice was the stuff of which Hallmark dividends are made.

I greeted and was greeted, and hung up my coat, and was just lowering myself into the chair in the last

booth, the partitions of which were only shoulder high
when seated, ensuring a continuous flow of conversation throughout the shop, when the front door opened
again and Zena walked in. Zena was a tall, broad,
handsome woman in her fifties who lived in rooms
above the needlework shop next door, and did, so far
as I could tell, absolutely nothing from morning to night
but cruise about the village like a stately ship in full
sail, and drop anchor at Francine's every hour or two
to take a cup of coffee from the urn and impart the
latest communiqués from her ports of call.

The subject of the morning was Mrs. Bierback's
daughter's wedding.

"They decided on the Roundelay Club for after the
church," Zena announced, "and she's having four
bridesmaids."

"She's lucky she's got a groom, never mind bridesmaids," Janice said darkly, "after that mess she was
in."

"Janice." Anhony said, in a voice that despaired of
her rehabilitation, "you make remarks like that when
you don't know all the facts of the situation—"

"I know plenty! Carl told me. And he works there.
He's the night clerk. He's at the desk there all night."

"Hearsay."

"Anthoneee! Didn't I drive Mrs. Washinsky to the
hospital when her husband was having his operation?
She knows that family for years, the Bierbacks." She
turned to Zena. "He died, you know, Mr. Washinsky."

"When!" Zena all but produced a notebook to
record the information.

"Wednesday. It was gastric colitis."

"Huh!" Anthony removed his rubber gloves with
scorn. "Do you know what you're talking about?
There's no such thing! Gastric colitis!"

"The son came down from Rochester," Janice went
on imperturbably. "Thank God. Somebody had to take
over, make the arrangements. She was in no condition,
believe me. Anyway, she told me plenty about Andrea
Bierback. when I used to drive her to the hospital.
How wild she was and everything. Well everybody
knew that. Personally, I think Donnie's crazy, marrying

a girl like that, after she was mixed up in such a mess at that motel."

"Which motel?" Zena believed in getting her facts straight.

"Right up here, the end of town—you know, on Sixty-four? They should really close that place down, the things that go on there. Except then Carl would lose his job, and I got nothing against him."

"Besides, he wouldn't be able to tell you about the orgies, right, Janice?" Anthony taunted, tying a plastic cape around me.

"Andrea was in an orgy?" Zena was ready for anything.

"I wouldn't be surprised. But she was there in a room with a married man, all right, and the wife came banging on the door, screaming. If they put it on TV you wouldn't believe it."

Anthony tipped the chair back and the hiss of water in my hair screened out further revelation. By the time I was right side up again Janice had progressed to a dissection of the characters in her favorite soap opera, and Anthony was giving me his considered opinion on how the President should manage the energy crisis.

Thirty minutes later I was digging for my wallet to pay his comparatively modest fee, when I came up with Mrs. Kittell's single navy-blue glove. I asked Anthony for the phone book and change of a quarter, looked up the number, and dialed it on the pay phone. An old woman's voice answered in minimal English that Mrs. Kittell was at the hospital. I thanked her, replaced the receiver, and considered. If she'd had an emergency call, it would hardly be wise to seek her out at the hospital simply to return a glove. On the other hand, I might be able to help, or it might be a routine visit, and in any case the hospital was closer than the Kittell house and by going there I would avoid trying to explain the glove to the old woman.

I said goodbye and left Anthony shampooing the blue glue out of Baby Doll's hair and Janice explaining to Zena why it would be disastrous for Mark to adopt Jennifer's daughter who'd just had an abortion while he was still in a wheelchair and had to appear in court on behalf of his ex-wife Beverly who was on trial for a crime actually committed by her gambler brother Roger.

At the hospital I ran into the same parking problem I'd had the last time, but I noticed that the occupant of one space was the local taxi, with the driver at the wheel, and on the theory that no one was going to keep a taxi standing around very long, I waited. Three minutes later someone emerged from the hospital entrance and headed for the taxi.

The someone was not anonymous. The someone was tall and angular and had a crown of white hair. I quickly bent sideways and down, as though looking for something on the floor of the car, and stayed there until I heard the cab start up. Even as I asked myself what Victoria Hollis was doing here, it was obvious I had come to a conclusion, or I couldn't have risked a slipped disc to keep her from seeing me. Greenfield had done it. He'd trapped me in his cops-and-robbers fantasy. I was furious.

I zipped into the parking space, slammed out of the car, and marched into the hospital telling myself that Victoria Hollis was there to see a doctor, to get an X-ray, to visit a friend. . . .

"How do I find a patient here?" I demanded of a woman behind a desk.

She looked at me with dull indifference, asked which patient I was looking for, and directed me to the second floor. I took the elevator, and when it stopped I stepped out and found myself facing Mrs. Kittell, who was waiting for it. She eyed me carefully; in her present state two accidental meetings in one morning could not be coincidental. I explained about the glove and gave it to her, and a dull flush crept over her cheeks as she took it and thanked me, which was an unaccountable reaction. Why be embarrassed about losing a glove?

"Is Peter—is everything all right?" I asked.

"The same," she said. She had stepped into the elevator and was holding the door open with one hand, so I stepped back in and we went down.

"Is Peter allowed to have visitors?" I asked.

"No. Just me and my husband. He is . . . never awake anyway."

"I wondered, because a nurse told me he'd had a visitor," I lied, "I mean a stranger."

The elevator stopped and we stepped out into the lobby. She turned to me, her face wary.

"The nurse said a lady came and wanted to go in and see him," she said, "and the nurse told her no. What kind of lady wants to see him? Who is she?"

"I have no idea." At this rate I'd be an accomplished liar before the day was out. As I looked candidly into Mrs. Kittell's eyes I saw that hers were as cold and bleak as an arctic night.

"Some lady," she repeated. "Why does she come? Is she afraid God will punish her? She can be sure of that. Whoever did such a thing to a boy can be sure God will punish. And I will help Him."

I believed her. This small, frail woman was one-third timid and two-thirds steel.

As we reached the door I offered her a lift, but she said a neighbor brought her there each day and would pick her up shortly. I left her standing just inside the front doors, looking unseeingly out at the gray day, and when I was back in the car heading home, the questions sprang at me like jungle animals from an ambush.

Question: Why did Victoria Hollis make a trip to the hospital to see Peter Kittell? Answer: Her morality is outraged by the incident and Peter's sister is a friend of Elizabeth's. She wanted to help. Question: Then why didn't she speak to Mrs. Kittell at the hospital? Answer: She didn't know Mrs. Kittell was there. Question: Why didn't she just call her on the phone instead of going to the hospital? Answer: That's *her* business. Question: A taxi? Why a taxi? Why not Catherine, driving the station wagon? Answer: She didn't want Catherine to know she was going. Question: *Didn't want Catherine to know?*

I arrived home with a headache, took an Excedrin, skipped lunch, and gave George his heart's eternal desire—a long walk.

It was not a great day for walking; although the gray sky had broken up into patches of blue and dirty white, there was a chill wind, and I had a choice of squashing my nice bouncy hair under a scarf, or having it torn to shreds by the wind. I squashed it.

As George led me along one street and then another, and a seemingly endless stream of cars went whipping by, spraying us with carbon monoxide fumes, I thought how clever of Mr. Chanin to get himself a carless route to walk, and then immediately visualized the farm and Victoria arriving back there in a taxi, and how would she explain *that* to Catherine, or was Catherine away somewhere, and why, anyway, would she want to keep it from Catherine, unless she harbored guilt, which was impossible, or Catherine harbored guilt and she didn't want Catherine to know she suspected, also impossible. . . .

"Stop!" I said aloud, and George stopped and looked at me with a pained expression. "Not you," I said, and we continued.

I forced my mind to concentrate on the scenery: a child's lost muffler, green and white, by the side of the road, a rock garden where I remembered the man replying to my question last summer that the tiny flowers he was growing there were portulaca, a lovely old tulip tree going bad at the base of the trunk, a moving van with the doors open and someone's belongings coming in or going out.

Walking, even in a chill wind, is the best way I know to get rid of tension. After forty-five minutes of up hill and down dale, the iron rod running the length of my back had once again become a normal collection of vertebrae and I got back to the house feeling well enough to sit down and practice the Beethoven trio for an hour, attend to the laundry, stew some chicken with onions and white wine and cook some wild rice to go with it, change into a gray flannel skirt, white cowl-collared sweater, and chocolate-brown belt, feed a ravenous George and then myself, leave lights burning upstairs and down and tell George if anyone showed up to bark his head off, put the music in the back seat of the car, and take off for Gordon Oliver's house.

The Olivers lived in the Dunstan Hill section, a few houses down from Barbara and up from the place I would be visiting the next day to interview Sidonie Seberg. As I passed the Seberg house I slowed to see what I could see, which proved to be about forty feet of floor-to-ceiling window framing a living room which featured a great deal of chrome and a seven-year-old girl leaping feet first onto a white sofa, followed frantically by a small, plump woman in a white uniform. Home, evidently, is where you hang your kid.

I continued up the street and turned left into a tortuous driveway that wound up a steep hill to the Oliver's aerie, built of expensive rough-textured wood and barely discernible through the surrounding vegetation. Greenfield's tan Plymouth stood at the side of the pebbled drive and a faint sound of tuning came from where a warm glow of light seeped through the boughs of a blue spruce.

Shirley opened the door. A very beautiful woman with sleek black hair, almond eyes, skin the color of cappucino, and a body of awesome perfection, hidden at the moment by a long, loose scarlet robe splashed with three huge black poppies.

"Hi, Mag," she said, "they're in the studio. Oh! Sensational! I've been looking for a pair of boots just like that."

"Bonwit's," I supplied.

"The trouble is, I hate shopping. I mean I *hate* it. But maybe I'll go. I hope it's warm enough in the studio—there always seems to be a draft in there. If Gordon had designed this house there wouldn't be any draft, that's for sure. I'll have some Irish coffee ready when you want it."

She went off to the kitchen, letting loose the sounds of Kibby and Gordon, Jr., doing the dishes as she went through the swinging door, and I went into the studio, which was a combination music room and workroom for Gordon. It was a pleasantly austere room, paneled in a dark wood, with a wall of books, a good Oriental rug on the floor, a long, narrow red-lacquered table along one wall holding several rolled-up blueprints, a Steinway upright against a third wall, a fourth wall of built-in cabinets, and above the table and the piano two large framed sketches of a church and a community center Gordon had designed, both very spare and elegant buildings.

Gordon and Greenfield were seated on straight-backed ebony chairs behind music stands. Gordon, an exceedingly tall, thin man with a small, refined Vandyke beard and an air of quiet self-confidence, stood up and gave me a long, thin brown hand to shake. Greenfield gave me his usual doleful look and struggled with an E string.

"I thought we should concentrate on the last movement," Gordon said, "since we pretty well butchered it last time. But Charlie wants to start from the top."

"You have to start at the beginning," Greenfield explained patiently, "to get a sense of the *structure*. It's no good just playing notes."

"Especially wrong notes," Gordon said dryly.

"Wrong notes," Greenfield pronounced, "are unimportant. We're here to make music."

"Yes, I read that Rubinstein interview too, but I don't think even he would consider fifty percent an acceptable average. However, I don't mind starting with the first movement, if you insist."

Greenfield looked at him over the black rims of his glasses. "I never insist," he insisted.

I sat down at the piano, stretched my fingers, and gave them an A. They tuned for a minute or two and said they were ready.

"Allegro," Greenfield reminded us. "That means lively but not eighty miles an hour." He stomped his foot on the rug, indicating the tempo.

We played. The first trio is a very satisfactory piece of music to play. It lies nicely and predictably under the fingers and gives the pianist several exhilarating and showy passages. We got through the first movement with no breakdowns, but in the andante—my favorite—Greenfield kept missing his entrance, and just as I'd be swept up in the lyrical flow of it, we'd have to go back to letter *N* or letter *O* or letter *P*. The scherzo was easy and fun, but the last movement was a back-breaker—we took turns falling apart and there was a great deal of "Wait a minute, those are sixteenths!" "That's what I was playing." "Someone missed the change in the key signature!" "What's going on here? Maggie, where are you? What are you doing at the double bars? We hit the double bars ten minutes ago!" "Look, this is the tempo, da, da, dee dee dum—" And so forth.

By eleven o'clock we were exhausted and inordinately pleased with our performance; we'd made a staggering improvement of about five percent over the week before. Shirley called us into the kitchen for our reward. We had a choice of Irish coffee or plain, or tea, and hot bagels, an assortment of cheeses, honey, and strawberry jam. We sat on high stools with low backs around a butcher-block counter which projected like a peninsula into the middle of the room from the work area, where copper pots hung against a real brick wall, and Shirley and Gordon discussed a play they'd seen recently at Lincoln Center.

"I think he was just using the kind of language and imagery those kind of people would normally use," Shirley said.

"He used that language and that imagery," Gordon replied, "because they are normal to *him*. He's a lazy thinker, he has a poverty-stricken imagination, and he substitutes shock and titillation for literacy and invention."

"You're a prude, Oliver, that's your trouble." Shirley bit hugely into a buttered bagel.

"It's a matter of aesthetics," Greenfield observed. "Gordon isn't prudish, merely chaste."

"As a friend of mine once said," Shirley managed to articulate through the bagel, "a little vulgarity is what makes the flowers grow."

"There's entirely too much vulgarity running rampant these days," Gordon said decisively, "vulgarity, hostility, and violence. They feed on each other. I deplore all three."

"Thus speaks the man"—Shirley made a sweeping gesture—"who threatened to beat up one of the guests at a dinner party!"

Gordon frowned. "That's a gross exaggeration."

I paused in my careful spreading of strawberry jam. Abstract discussions are all very well, but a good concrete social crisis is more fun. "What happened?" I asked.

"There was this huge party up the street a couple of months ago"—Shirley grinned teasingly at her husband—"buffet style, you know, everybody standing around holding plates of stroganoff and jellied salad. And Gordon and I were talking to a few people—"

"We were discussing the business of the magazines at that place where the high school kids gather on weekends—"

"Dodie's," Greenfield put in knowledgeably.

"Those porno magazines," Shirley elaborated, "that the man displays—racks of them—which of course is what makes the place so popular—"

"And I voiced the opinion," Gordon went on, "that the man should either be forced to remove them, or bar the place to teenagers—"

"And this guy joined the group," Shirley interrupted, "just as Gordon said that, and started blasting away about censorship and civil rights and Henry Miller, as though Gordon was the head of the D.A.R.—"

"I said anyone who could confuse Henry Miller with this sewer slop was badly in need of remedial education—"

"And he gave out with that hit song, 'If you start by suppressing porn you end by suppressing Dostoevski'—or is it Shostakovich?"

"I pointed out," Gordon continued, "that I hadn't mentioned suppressing these magazines—though, by God, that amendment could use a rider—but that we had an obligation to maintain a few small pockets of civilization in the encroaching slime—"

"It was like this man didn't hear a word!" Shirley gestured with a piece of bagel. "More stuff about the right of the storekeeper to display what he wants and the right of kids to read whatever they like—"

"I asked him if civil rights applied only to those who corrupt, degrade, and exploit—"

"Gordon said, 'What about the rights of the antismut citizen? We're being ghettoized. We were forced out of prime areas in the city, now we're being pushed out of parts of our own villages. We're in constant retreat!

What about our rights?' And this bird yelled, 'You talk about ghettos! When was the last time you walked around the East Bronx?' And Gordon said 'Last week, as a matter of fact. Are you implying that by surrounding the teenagers in Sloan's Ford with salacious material we're somehow rectifying the inequities of society?' "

"And the man said," Gordon managed to interject, "that there were evils a hell of a lot more pressing than a few dirty magazines. And I said they're all the same evil, smut and dehumanization and hostility and violence, they escalate each other. And he said kids have read dirty magazines since the beginning of time and in his opinion it was just another facet of education. Education!"

"What he said was, 'You want to create a precious little group of effete kids who think the world is all opera and ballet, so they can perpetuate all the elitist institutions.' "

"I have no patience with black-and-white thinking!"

"That's when Gordon said, 'Don't be an ass!' and that man got purple in the face—he was practically spitting—and he said, 'There's nothing more reactionary than a black man who's made it to a hundred-thousand-dollar house!'

"At which point I became angry"—

"And if I hadn't taken your plate away that idiot would've had stroganoff all over his face!"

"I had no intention of throwing that plate. I was going to put it down and take him outside. There was no violent emotion involved. I made a calm, rational decision that this man had to be taught a lesson. I don't say I'm not capable of doing damage to such a man, but it wouldn't be an act of violence in that sense. It would be judicious. Because a man like that is dangerous."

"And what *happened?*" I demanded.

"Oh, he sneered and walked away," Shirley said, "and a little while later he left the party. Only now, before we accept a local invitation, I always ask if Julian Trager's going to be there."

My cup stayed suspended in midair and Greenfield's

eyes swung slowly in my direction and locked with mine.

"So," he said to Gordon, "you think Mr. Trager's a dangerous person?"

"All those men," Gordon asserted, "who believe the end justifies the means, freedom being the end, pornography the means, and can't be made to see that the means eventually become a way of life."

"He might say the same of you," Greenfield suggested, "censorship of a kind."

"Possibly. But he's more dangerous. He's a writer, he can influence too many people."

"To hell with him," Shirley said. "How about some more tea, Charlie?"

Greenfield said no thanks, he had to get home, and I said me too, and we got our coats and arranged to play again in two weeks because the Olivers were going to Boston the following weekend, and went out into the cold night.

"Well, that was nice," I said breezily, trying to avert the inevitable discussion. "That was a good session, didn't you think? Well, have a good weekend, Charlie."

"This man Trager," he said, standing under the greenish driveway light clutching his cello. "Consider all the aspects of his character that have come to light. Vain, contemptuous, opinionated, self-indulgent, resentful, angry . . . a bully . . . and a coward."

"That's quite a list, considering you've never met the man."

"I never met Genghis Khan either. Or Francis of Assisi. The deductive faculty was given to us for a reason."

"Well, my faculty doesn't work too well after eleven P.M. I'm going to go home and get some sleep. Good night."

"The end justifies the means . . ." he murmured, as though it were a newly coined phrase.

I shut my ears, went to the Honda, opened the door, got in, put the key in the ignition, and drove off, leaving Greenfield standing there under the light posing for a portrait of a pensive musician.

I was suddenly feeling cranky, and I knew it was because I'd postponed telling Greenfield about Victoria's visit to the hospital. I was never comfortable putting off something unpleasant. Some people, hearing strange noises in the night, immediately pull the covers over their heads so they can't see whatever's coming. I would die of fear if I did that. I have to go out and meet it, get it over with. This business of delaying troublesome encounters was highly uncharacteristic. I decided I was behaving this way because I wasn't sure whose side I was on. With strange noises in the night there was no *question* whose side I was on.

Facing the fact that I wouldn't be able to get to sleep with that chore undone, I turned into someone's driveway, backed out, and started up the street again. I met Greenfield halfway, blinked my lights and touched the horn, and he stopped. I pulled off the road, shut off the motor, went over to the tan Plymouth, and got in beside him.

"I forgot," I said. "I have something to tell you."

He looked at me with raised eyebrows, clearly skeptical of my poor memory.

I told him about seeing Victoria at the hospital and discovering that she'd asked to see Peter. When I was through, he sat staring out the windshield with his chin pushing his mouth into an inverted U. Then he heaved a profound sigh and quietly said, *"Merde!"* Delicacy prevented him from cursing in English.

I stared at him. Of all possible responses, this was one I had not even contemplated.

"Merde?" I asked.

"This only confuses the issue."

"What issue? Confuses what?"

"I was beginning to work on another theory. Never mind. I'll have to ponder it. This incident with Mrs. Hollis happened this morning."

"Is that a question? Yes, this morning."

"Why did you wait until"—he looked at the dashboard clock—"seven minutes past midnight to tell me?"

"I don't know. I suppose I just don't want to believe that Victoria Hollis is involved in this thing."

"Why?"

I thought about it.

"Because," I said finally, "if she is, then I have to face the fact that my judgment is totally unreliable. And I still have a few years left during which I'll have to keep making judgments. This could destroy my self-confidence."

"Mm," he said, "I doubt it."

"In any case, I finally did tell you, which is a good indication that I prefer lack of self-confidence to life as an ostrich."

"More likely your curiosity is getting the upper hand."

"That too. In a taxi, Charlie. She went there in a *taxi*. Isn't that a little peculiar?"

No answer. He stared out the windshield.

"I know you're not obliged to tell me, me being just an employee and all. But this theory you were working on—"

"A theory with holes in it is worse than no theory at all. You said you were tired. Go home." He started the motor.

I opened the door and got out. There was no use pressing him—he was unpressable.

"Sweet dreams," I said, just to get in the last word for once.

"I don't dream."

◙ 8

I dreamed that Victoria Hollis drove a delivery van to the motel on Route Sixty-four to drag Andrea Bierback from the clutches of her married lover, and was prevented at the last minute by Gordon Oliver, who said she had to come back immediately because he'd smashed his violin over Trager's head and she had to fill in and take the andante from letter *N*.

I woke feeling dispirited, turned on the radio, and showered to the bells of Bizet's "L'Arlésienne," which improved my mood somewhat, and as I was dressing the radio said we were going to hit a high of fifty degrees, which improved it even more. By the time I'd breakfasted on orange juice, hot oatmeal with honey, and two mugs of decaffeinated coffee, I decided I was going to have a good day and the rest of the world could take care of itself for a while.

I called Barbara and made a date to have dinner with her at a chic new restaurant in Connecticut called Parsley and Sage, got her ex-husband's phone number, explaining what it was for, and called him and told him about Catherine. He said sure, send her along, and we made an appointment for Monday, because I knew I had to present her with a fait accompli or she'd back out.

When I called Catherine and told her, she was, as expected, flustered and nervous, but didn't ramble on for once, because she was just leaving to drive her mother to the station to catch the train to the city. A lot of running around Mrs. Hollis was doing these days, and to the city, which she disliked so much! I told myself to forget it and sat down at the typewriter and finished off the article on the farm with estimable detachment, got the car out of the garage, and drove to the village.

My first stop was the hardware store, and I actually found a free parking space in front of it, and went in, hoping that just for once Mr. Farnham wouldn't be tied up with another customer, because none of his transactions seemed to take less than twenty minutes and the hired help seldom knew where anything was. Sure enough, he was at the back of the store engaged in one of his lengthy discussions with a customer. I turned to a young man in a blue sweatshirt who was opening cartons to one side of the door and asked him where I could find the metal baskets that fit into the holes of kitchen sinks. He pointed vaguely to a spot halfway down the center aisle.

As I moved toward the rear of the store I realized that the voice of Mr. Farnham's customer was one I'd heard before—an unmistakable, mesmerizing baritone. I took another look at his back. Red wool jacket, hat with earflaps, loose-limbed stance. Andrew.

". . . bought them here last week," he was saying, "two dozen angle irons, a hundred fifty feet of wire mesh. Left them tied up in a corner of the barn. This morning I cut the cord on the angle irons and counted them out. Twenty-three. Counted them several times."

"I don't understand that. Unless you dropped one in the truck. Did you look in the truck?"

"I would've heard it drop," Andrew said patiently. "Angle irons don't exactly fall like rose petals."

"Well—" Mr. Farnham was caught between natural stinginess and the consideration that the Hollis farm was a good customer. "I don't understand it—"

The young man in the sweatshirt appeared at my elbow. "Find it?" he asked.

"Oh—yes." I slipped a plastic-covered card containing a sink basket from its rod, handed it to him, and followed him back to the cash register. Waiting for my change, I glanced back and saw Andrew accepting a five-foot length of iron from Farnham's reluctant hand.

I dawdled a little at the front of the store, pretending to examine the various Pyrex bowls and kitchen utensils on display there, unable to leave the arena while the gladiator was still there to be seen, and moved to the door as I heard his casual step approaching. I opened the door, held it, looking back as I normally would to make sure it didn't close on whoever was following, and said, "Oh—hello!"

He looked polite, then placed me and smiled his devastating corner-of-the-mouth smile.

"Hello," he said, and held the door until we were both outside. "Seems to be warming up." He glanced at the blue sky, momentarily reproducing one of Catherine's photographs.

"It has a long way to go."

"Can't hurry it up. It'll come in its own time." He paused beside an old gray slat-sided truck.

"Is that yours? I don't remember seeing it at the farm."

"It belongs to Mrs. Hollis. I probably had it at the far side of the wood. I've been clearing some dead trees and carting them up for firewood."

I nodded, smiling. He smiled back. We had used up all the innocuous conversation possible between strangers, but he stood there. I realized he would not make the first move to leave; it was instinctive with him to make a woman feel she was too important to be treated lightly—an instinct totally unrelated to the degree of his interest, but it had the effect of a pint of vodka, taken neat.

"I have to be going," I said.

"Have a good day."

I got back in the Honda hoping I wouldn't be apprehended driving while intoxicated and headed for the supermarket.

It was my day for catching sight of familiar figures. As I passed the garage, there was Greenfield in earnest conversation with Victor, but I was on the wrong side of the road and couldn't pull in to find out what theory he was currently exploring. (I couldn't believe he was there for any personal reason; nothing *ever* went wrong with Greenfield's car, he drove—except for the night of Peter's accident—at a stately thirty miles an hour, triumphant but alert, eyes flicking left and right, like an

Allied general entering a newly liberated town. No vehicle he drove would dare to break down.)

I bought my groceries, deposited them in the back of the car, and returned some books to the library, where Arlene stopped her reorganization of the card file while we discussed Doris Lessing, the pitfalls of middle age, and the overpriced, unripe fruit and wilted vegetables being sold every day in spite of Bess Myerson. Then I drove home for a cheese-and-unripe-apple lunch, spent some time in the yard lapping up the fifty-degree sunshine and throwing a ball for George to chase, and finally, at a quarter to three, got back in the car with my tape recorder and headed for Sidonie Seberg's glassy house.

The South American woman in the white uniform admitted me to a foyer with flagstone floor and walls in which stood a six-foot metal sculpture which probably cost a fortune but looked like the result of a collaboration between the mechanic at Victor's Garage and one of those magazines Gordon had been talking about. From there we went to the room with the forty-foot window and the white leather sofa. In addition to these outstanding features, there was a zebra-striped rug, a very low seating arrangement upholstered in a fabric splattered with one of the currently popular African designs, two huge, belligerent paintings of what looked like technical illustrations of the gastrointestinal tract, a coffee table made of some purple mineral, and a glass-and-chrome cabinet through which one could see Steuben's entire collection of stemware and the contents of several liquor stores. Homey.

On the coffee table lay a manuscript in a red vinyl cover. I chose to assume that it wouldn't have been left there if she didn't want me to see it. A label on the cover read "*One Soda, Two Straws,* a novel by Elaine Jaynes." Well, well, I thought. A female *Summer of Forty-Two.* I opened it and read a paragraph. I might have been wider of the mark if I'd predicted *Rebecca of Sunnybrook Farm,* but not much. Evidently Elaine Jaynes was one of those female authors who, if times were bad, could always earn a living doing complicated acrobatics in a rented room on Eighth Avenue. Or she could teach sixth-grade English, if she didn't mind being on the same literacy level as her pupils.

The South American woman showed up for a minute to say that Mrs. Seberg was on a long-distance call and apologized, but she would have to keep me waiting a little longer. I continued reading.

I skipped from chapter to chapter, but they were all different camera angles of essentially the same scene. It was clear that Elaine Jaynes belonged to that growing number of novelists for whom the Alps, the Nile, the rain forests, the ceiling of the Sistine Chapel, Brahms's Third, _King Lear_, Chaplin, Plato, the French Revolution, and so forth might never have existed. They have somehow succeeded in reducing the entire experience of living to the varieties of sensation possible between the nose and the knees.

I put down the manuscript and wondered where the family was. There weren't even any sounds of human habitation. Had she tidied away the husband and child the way I got rid of scattered newspapers and dropped clothing when company was coming? Were they lying behind some closet door?

There was a faint scent of musky perfume and she drifted into the room. She was small and slender and wore a black cashmere jump suit with a belt of gold links fastened by a gold arrow pointing downward. Her mouse-colored hair was cut like a mushroom cap and she wore sea-green eyeshadow over her large mouse-colored eyes. Her mouth was wide and soft and painted a kind of brownish pink. She extended one arm in its gold bangles toward me, and there was a very sincere smile on her moist lips. The voice was half honey, half smoke.

"I'm so sorry. I'm having a little trouble with an author's agent on the coast. What can I get you?" She half turned toward the cabinet.

"Nothing, thanks."

"Are you sure?" The wide, sincere eyes urged me to accept aid and comfort. I shook my head, she lifted a hand in defeat, moved to the cabinet, poured herself some white wine, returned to a low seat opposite me,

and melted into it. I had already depressed the tab on
the tape recorder.

"I gather your work week doesn't end on Friday," I
began in my best Hollywood-reporter voice (for me
these profile interviews always smacked of amateur
theatricals). "Do you find it a strain, juggling the two
parts of your life—I mean, home and job?"

She sipped at the wine and gave me a look of enormous candor. "I worry about Jennifer," she confided
huskily, "my daughter. She's seven. Very precocious.
Has antennae all over the place, you know? Well, it's
the kind of situation where you're damned if you do
and damned if you don't. One kind of problem if
mother has to spend a good deal of time away from
home, another kind if mother stays home, frustrated,
and takes it out on the child." She leaned forward and
took a cigarette from a glass-and-gilt cigarette box, lit
it from a black matchbook engraved "Sidonie," and
sank back against the African upholstery, glass in one
hand, cigarette in the other. A great girl for props.
"We didn't want to stay in the city," she went on, "for
obvious reasons. So there's the commute to contend
with. But I make it a rule to be home at least half an
hour before she goes to bed, no matter how difficult it
is. And some days it's *very* difficult. But"—she gave a
short, low laugh, inviting me to amuse myself at the
folly of her extreme dedication—"if you're sensitive to
a child's needs, you can't do any less."

"I appreciate the problem. A seven-year-old goes to
bed rather early."

"Eight-thirty."

Which brings Mommy home around eight o'clock.
"You have a long day at the office."

A sweet, superior smile. "It's not a nine-to-five job."

"Tell me about the job."

She told me—very sober now on the sacred subject
of Profession. She reviewed her rise to eminence, from
editorial assistant to executive editor. She talked about
the man she had replaced, who was evidently an old
dodo "living back in the fifties" who kept rejecting
manuscripts which were "tuned in to the contemporary
scene." She said that trade books are a tough commod-

ity to move, that a publisher's top priority is to stay in business, that she had been promoted because she could recognize a "winner" or a "loser" after reading three paragraphs, and that, in fact, she had a success record of seventy-five percent. She named the last ten books she had chosen and they made a nice little shelf of popular erotica.

"Do these books," I asked, "reflect your personal taste, or only your professional instinct in regard to winners?"

"Both, I don't recommend books that don't appeal to me."

"Then you have a personal bias toward the erotic?"

"I think sensuality is important, yes. I think we've finally emerged from the dark ages where sex is concerned. We're finally being liberated from all the hang-ups—the euphemism of romantic love—"

"Have you never experienced romantic love?" She looked at me blankly. "There's never been a man who—? Well, when you first met your husband, for instance—wasn't there an element of romance?"

"You're putting me on."

She sipped her wine and looked at me over the rim of her glass, then lowered it. "Humphrey Bogart and Ingrid Bergman? The fairy tales of the forties? I hope we've gone beyond that!"

"To what?"

She smiled patiently. "To the truth about what we are and what we need. Romantic love was a concept invented to perpetuate the family as a social unit. It's a hoax. An outmoded con game."

(You hear that, Cleopatra? Beatrice? Elizabeth Browning?)

"Good, satisfying, imaginative sex is what really makes the world go round. Sex"—she'd stopped smiling, to indicate that what she was about to reveal was profound—"is self-realization. And self-realization is the answer to everything."

Good. She'd solved the Middle East problem. That was a load off my mind.

"This manuscript"—she picked up the masterpiece in the red vinyl cover—"is probably the most courageous exploration of female sexuality ever written. This will be as historic, in its way, as the exploration of space." (One giant step for orgasm?) "And I guarantee"—she put it down and patted it gently—"it will go into a fifth printing."

"I suppose a book like this is likely to make the best-seller list?"

"Oh, God, yes. The book clubs will fight over it, we'll have our choice of the paperbacks, we'll probably have a prepublication movie sale—but those are the fringe benefits. The real joy is bringing out something worthwhile. That's what makes this job so rewarding—the opportunity to discover a real, rare talent."

"Sort of like Maxwell Perkins stumbling on Thomas Wolfe," I said with a straight face.

"Exactly."

"Except that a book like this will prabably make a lot more money than Wolfe did?"

"The money," she said seriously, "is unbelievable." She took another sip of white wine and moistened her lips.

"Do you think you could put your philosophy of publishing into one sentence?"

"One sentence. Well. Let's see. Yes, I think so. My philosophy would be: 'One chapter in the bedroom is worth a hundred anywhere else.' "

I moved so abruptly that I knocked my hand against the edge of the coffee table, but I hardly noticed the pain. Julian Trager was popping up like a new word. (Twenty years earlier, when I first came across *symbiotic,* I thought, That's an interesting word, wonder why I've never seen it before, and for six months afterward it suddenly appeared in every newspaper, book, and magazine I picked up. So with Julian, only more so.)

"That's a nice succinct philosophy," I said. "It must have made the rounds of the industry offices in about five minutes."

"It couldn't have. I just thought of it."

"Just now, you mean? As a result of my question?"

She gave a throaty laugh. "You sound surprised."

"Well—it's so nice and cryptic—not easy to do, off the cuff."

She made a modest gesture.

"What—uh—" I floundered—"do you—I think people would be interested to know—uh—which authors you handle. Could you name some of the better-known ones?"

She mentioned about six or seven. I'd only heard of two, and neither of them was Trager. I tried again.

"Did you know we have a few authors living in the area? Have you met any of them?"

"I've only been here a few months." She gazed at me sweetly and sincerely, her head tilted a little to one side.

"Julian Trager?"

The head didn't move by so much as a hair, the half smile didn't waver, the candid gaze never faltered. But I knew as sure as apples make applesauce that she was about to tell me a lie.

"I've never met him."

"Oh. I assumed you would have. I guess the publishing world is bigger than I thought it was."

She swam right by the bait, lifted a large round gold watch from her cleavage, where it hung on a chain, consulted it, and murmured, "Are you sure I can't get you a drink?"

I declined again and shut off the tape recorder. She rose from the depths of the upholstery. "When you've written it up," she said, "just drop it off anytime. But give me more than a few hours to look it over." It took longer to judge biography, evidently, than fiction.

I followed her to the foyer. She gestured to the metal sculpture.

"That's an original Kling if you want to mention it."

"What's it called?" I asked, thinking "Coitus," no doubt.

"Coitus," she said.

On the way home I had a thought, turned back the way I had come, and drove to the library.

"Twice in one day!" Arlene greeted me. "The poor thing must be lonely!"

"I am researching. An honor I seldom confer on this

lowly branch of the library system, so enjoy it while you may." I went to the shelves without much hope of finding what I was after, since Sloan's Ford boasts something less than a comprehensive collection, but there between Trachtenberg and Tryon was a copy of Trager's last book, *The Brooklyn Brahmin*. The date of publication succeeded by eights months the date of Sidonie Seberg's first move toward Chief Erotica Editor and the publisher was . . . Curtin-Driscoll.

Never met him? She'd have to prove it to me with documentation. But why would she deny knowing him? Simply because she had plagiarized his motto? Or had he taken it from her? Or had they both borrowed it from a third party? Anyway, why lay claim to a high school senior brand of wit? And what was there about Trager that brought out the best in everyone?

That evening at Parsely and Sage, while we ate our way through artichoke soup and baked trout in mustard sauce, I told Barbara about the interview, and she had no difficulty analyzing Sidonie Seberg's reaction.

"She must be bedding him," Barbara said.

"Then why the reticence? Considering the way she proselytizes for sexual liberation, I'd think she'd advertise it in all available media."

"The husband," Barbara explained, "has this archaic notion that having your wife disrobing for one strange man or another every couple of weeks tends to disrupt family life. That's why he made her move out of the city. He figured the commute wouldn't give her time. But evidently she was managing, because after the last one he gave her an ultimatum, with graphic details of what he'd do to her *and* the man if it happened again—according to a neighbor's maid, who got it from the Sebergs' maid."

"Why doesn't he just leave her? Or she him?"

"Well, I think he's like the little kid who sees another kid with a red truck and wants it. You can offer him six hundred identical red trucks, but the only one he wants is the one in the other kid's hand. As for her—well, you spent thirty minutes with her, didn't you detect an aura of Marjorie Morningstar?"

"There *was* the engraved matchbook," I admitted, "and it's easy to see her as a girl who wants to have her cake and eat it, and decorate it, and call it something exotic."

"Speaking of cake—" Barbara said, eyeing the pastry cart.

She had chocolate mousse and I had an almond tart, and then I persuaded her that it would addle her brain if she went back to her books and papers on a Saturday night, and we stopped in to see a movie. This movie had been touted as the work of a new young director of blazing originality. It proved to be one of those hand-held camera jobs which make you feel as though you're viewing the action while riding on a lopsided camel. It also had a sound track which specialized in suspense; whenever there was the slightest danger that any of the dialogue would give you a clue as to what was going on, it was promptly drowned out by the background noises of traffic or poolroom or whatever was handy. However, in the car going home we finally decided what it was about—it was a simple message by, of, and for the men of the world: Happiness is letting your wife pay the bills and take care of the kids while you lurch from pillar to post with your arms around each other's shoulders recalling the basketball victories of your adolescence.

George was asleep inside the front door when I got home, and barely opened one eye when I stepped over him. Great watchdog. As I started up the stairs to the bedroom, the telephone rang.

Telephones ringing after midnight send me into a blind panic. Within four seconds I had covered the possibilities from Matt and Alan having been found at the bottom of a ravine to Elliot having run off with a movie actress in California. With my pulse rate about one thousand, I grabbed up the receiver.

It was Greenfield, with one of his cute tricks, picking up a previous discussion without preamble, as though he expected me to spend the intervening hours between our conversations waiting breathlessly for his next words.

"If you're really concerned about preserving your self-confidence," he began, "I may be able to help."

"Good God! Do you know what I went through between the time the phone rang and I heard your voice?"

"I didn't realize you were waiting so anxiously for my call."

I took a deep breath. "You'd better have something important to say—"

"I have. If you'll stop interrupting." He paused to let the admonishment sink in, then continued, in his most infuriatingly maundering fashion. "Gordon is right, of course, about those magazines. They're an insult to just about every living species on earth. They can probably do some damage to the psyche, if consumed by impressionable youngsters. That place is also dirty, I wouldn't be surprised if he's spreading physical disease as well."

"*Who* is?"

"That man. The place you sent me to."

"*I* sent you?"

"I see you weren't joking when you said your faculties diminish after a certain hour. Do you deny advising me to go there over the weekend because that's when 'the action' takes place?"

"You went to Dodie's?"

"What," he said wearily, "have I been saying?"

"You found the teenager who was driving someone else's car without a night driving license?"

"No, I did not. Half of the vehicles there were motorcycles without a scratch on them, and ninety percent of the cars had dents and scratches and worse. Besides, I spoke to Walchek at headquarters this morning and they had several kids with previous license and speeding violations—they'd already checked them out; they were all elsewhere at the time. He said they would check Pinecliff, Chester, and Gorham, but his feeling is that a Tuesday night in February, when there's no school vacation or holiday, is an unlikely time for that kind of trouble."

It was then I realized that all this had been the usual

flimflam to avoid leading up to what he had really called to request.

"I don't see," I said, "how even you can make a connection between this and preserving my self-confidence, but do me a favor, Charlie, don't try. It's late. Just tell me what you want."

"I want you to think up a plausible excuse to go to the farm tomorrow."

I stretched out on my bed. "There is no excuse, plausible or implausible," I whined, and immediately thought of a reasonably plausible one. "Why should I?"

"I need to know if Mr. Trager took the train into the city last Tuesday."

I laughed. What else was there to do?

"I'm offering you," he said with hauteur, "an alternative to Victoria Hollis."

I sat up. "What did you find out?"

"Will you find out if Mr. Trager took the train?"

"Certainly. It's simple. I'll just call him and ask him. 'Mr. Trager? This is Mrs. Rome. You may remember, we met in your living room last Wednesday and you hated me on sight. By the way, did you take the train into the city last Tuesday?' I don't see why he shouldn't answer an innocent question like that."

"Don't be whimsical."

"How do you expect me to find out such a thing? I can't think of a single way to do it without appearing either schizoid or crude."

"I have faith in your powers of invention."

"Besides, Julian Trager could not be involved in what happened Tuesday night. I told you, he was in the city."

"You saw him there?"

"Oh, come on. What's this all about, anyway? What did you—? Ah-ha! You found out something at Victor's Garage this morning. What did you find out?"

"How do you know I was there?"

"I saw you. Right after I left Andrew—"

Ah, Maggie. So unathletic, yet you have no trouble putting your foot in your mouth.

"Andrew who?"

"Mmm," I said airily. "He's the hired hand from the Hollis farm. He was in Farnham's complaining he'd been shortchanged on his angle irons, and I went in to get a new—"

"The . . . hired . . . hand?"

"Oh, the man who takes care of the horses and chops down the trees and so on. I told you about him."

"No. You did not."

"Oh, well. So what did you find out at the garage?"

"Tell me. About him."

I told him. Briefly. Just facts, no commentary. There was a silence, to indicate extreme displeasure, before he deigned to speak again.

"And what else have you been keeping from me?"

"I had dinner with Barbara. Would you like a run-down of the menu?"

"Relevant to the matter in hand."

"Well, I'm not certain this is relevant, and it's not even something I know for a fact, it's just something Barbara made a guess about. You wouldn't be interested in Barbara's guesses."

"Tell me."

"She thinks this lady editor I interviewed today may be having an affair with Julian Trager. Because when I asked her—the editor—if she knew Trager, she lied, said she'd never met him. However, his last book was published by the publisher she works for, at a time when she was in a position to meet every author in the stable, and she is not the type to pass up an opportunity to meet anyone of even the slightest importance."

He considered the relevance of the information and discarded it.

"This is coffee-klatch material. What I want to know is whether or not Trager took a train on Tuesday."

Two weeks later I reminded him of the juxtaposition of those two sentences and he refused to admit he'd said anything of the sort.

"Let me know when you get the information," he added.

"Tomorrow is my day off," I said coldly, still smarting from the "coffee-klatch" implication.

This time the silence was a long one, and the voice, when it finally returned, was soft, dignified, and lethal.

"In that case . . . I'll simply have to go there myself."

I choked back a laugh at the thought of Greenfield driving solemnly up to that cozy little fortress and trying to explain his presence to Victoria Hollis. Then I realized there was more folly than humor in the situation. There was no telling what the chemical reaction might be between Greenfield and that family, or what explosions might follow.

"All right. If I can find a decent reason for going"—I sighed—"I'll call you in the morning."

"I'll give you until noon."

◙ 9

I woke to the sound of rain pattering down in that quiet, steady drizzle that means it will last all day. Wet Sunday. A reading-the-Sunday-*Times* day, a television day, a straightening-out-the-closets day, a keeping-George-in-the-house-and-having-to-walk-him-morning-and-night day.

Sunday breakfast was lots of orange juice and French toast with marmalade and several cups of Sanka. Before I got to the third cup, and while I was still trying to find the Ninas in the Hirschfeld cartoon on the front page of the theatre section, the phone rang, and Alan's world-weary drawl reached over the miles to caress my ear.

"Mother?"

"Well, hello there! How are you, chick?"

"Oh—well—you know—it's the pits."

"What is?"

"Everything." Sigh. "Frankly I don't think the academic standards in this place are much good. I'll probably flunk, because I just can't get interested. The professors are boring as hell."

"You've been saying more or less the same thing since first grade."

"Don't put me down, will you please?"

"I'm doing the opposite. I'm pointing out that in spite of everything, somehow you've managed to make it to your junior year at college, and you'll probably go on making it, so relax."

"That's sophistry, Mother."

"Couldn't you call me something else? The way you say 'Mother' sounds so decadent."

"I am decadent. I think I was born out of my time. I

95

should have been one of those Edwardian fops, squandering my youth in the pubs around Oxford or one of those places."

It went on like that for a while, until he finally revealed the source of his low spirits. He was having jealousy problems; one of his girls was jealous of the other. He concluded his cheery phone call with the complaint that Matt always seemed to have enough money whereas he kept running short, and left it to my conscience to correct that unjust state of affairs.

I cleared away the remains of breakfast while mentally composing a treatise on living beyond one's means, to be enclosed with the money order. Then I bundled up in two sweaters, a slicker, and rubber boots, and ran George up the street and back, and had just started on the bedroom closet when the phone rang again.

"Mrs. Rome! This is Catherine Trager! I hope I'm not disturbing you! I didn't wake you, did I? People often sleep late on Sunday and I never seem to remember that. I'm always up at the crack of dawn, I don't know why, I suppose I'm a morning person!"

"Don't worry about it, I've been up for hours. And I wish you'd call me Maggie."

"Oh! Thank you! Maggie!" she laughed uneasily. "Well! That makes it easier to—to ask a favor! You see—this is a terrible imposition, I know, but since you were kind enough—about the photographs—for the appointment with Mr. Drexler—I was wondering if you could spare some time to go over them with me! Help me choose what to take! I can't seem to make any decisions—this is the first time I've ever—I know it's a lot to ask—"

"I don't think my opinion's worth very much. Why don't you take all of them?"

"Oh, no! I think—it's like putting too many articles in a shop window, you know? They tend to cancel each other out!"

"I really don't think I'd be much help—"

"Oh, you would! You're such a decisive person! But of course I don't want to put you to any trouble—"

Me? Decisive?

"I'll be glad to help, I just don't want to ruin it for you. Remember, I don't know the first thing about photography—"

"Oh, you can't imagine how relieved I am! This is really very good of you! When would you like to come? Any time is fine for me! I am at your disposal—is that the phrase?"

I wondered for a moment about the nature of Greenfield's influence with the forces of destiny. "I could make it this afternoon."

"Why don't you come for lunch! I could make another—"

"No! No, thanks, I—wouldn't be able to get there before three or so."

"It's terrible to drag you out on such a wet day! It's so gloomy out there—some rainy days are comfortable, and in the summer, of course, it can be lovely in the rain, but this is just dreary! Dreary!" Her voice had an edge to it I hadn't heard before, "You're certain you don't mind coming out in the wet? Would it be better if I brought them over to you?"

"No, it's fine." Catherine alone was too slim a chance—I needed alternate sources of information, in case. "I'll be there about three."

I finally managed to cut through another profession of gratitude and replace the receiver, only to pick it up again and dial Greenfield's number. I heard the stereo in the background as he answered the ring: Rampal playing Telemann.

"You can stay cuddled up with your music," I said, "I'm going to the farm. I was asked."

"By whom?"

"Mrs. Trager. Now you tell me what brilliant plan you had for introducing the subject of trains."

"Plan? I don't have a plan."

"You mean you were going to leave it to sudden inspiration?"

"All that's required," he assured me, "is the reasonable ability to seize an opportunity and make the most of it."

"I see. How likely do you think it is that an opportunity will present itself, in the natural course of things?"

"If none does, make one. Obviously. And since you're taking over that piece of research, I'll probably go to visit one of my girls. I should be home this evening, if you want to reach me."

Greenfield would walk away with first prize in any contest for the most oblique way of saying thank-you.

Catherine was right, the farm looked gloomy under the drizzle. In the sulfurous light the naked wet mahogany branches of tree and bush glimmered darkly, and the stones of the long fence were slock and gunmetal gray. I climbed reluctantly out of the car to open the gate and climbed back in to drive through, when a figure in a red slicker and black boots appeared on the track ahead of me.

Elizabeth waved briefly as she jogged down to the gate and shut it behind me. I let down the window just enough to yell, "Get in." and she trotted around to the far side and climbed in beside me, water dripping from every square inch. From her expression it was quite possible that the moisture on her cheeks was not unadulterated rain, but her manners, as usual, were impeccable. She forced a smile and said, "Hello, Mrs. Rome. Sorry I'm making your car so wet."

"It'll dry. I hope you didn't come out in all this just to take care of the gate."

"No, I just had to get out of the house—" She broke off, and watched the windshield wipers in silence while I continued up the road.

"Rainy Sundays," I said finally, "can be very difficult with everyone trapped in the house."

She didn't say anything immediately. Then she cleared her throat and asked, "Do you think people fight more often in bad weather?"

I put on the brakes. "Look, if there's something wrong up at the house, it might be a good idea if I didn't come in."

She turned and looked at me with unconcealed disappointment. "Well, if you'd rather not—"

"I mean it might be better for everyone else."

"I don't think so. I think it would probably be a relief to have someone else around."

"Not if it's serious trouble."

"It's all over now. Andrew's gone."

"Gone!" I was surprised by a small internal upheaval. "You mean for good?" She nodded miserably. "What happened?"

"My father—um—accused him of stealing."

"Good God!" I caught myself and added, in a lighter tone, "Is that all? I wouldn't worry too much. It sounds like a typical Sunday tantrum. Your father will find whatever it is and Andrew'll be back in a few days."

She didn't contradict me, but her silence said I was making a molehill out of a good-sized mountain. I realized that uncomfortable as it might be for an outsider stepping into an atmosphere of family discord, Catherine was probably counting on my appearance to justify an escape to the studio. So I took my foot off the brake and continued up the drive and parked near the shed, and Elizabeth and I made a dash past the old stone well to the back porch, where she disposed of her boots and we tried to shake off as much rain as possible before entering the house.

Julian Trager was standing on the sun porch, pipe in his mouth, hands thrust deep in his pockets, a green wool turtleneck shortening his short neck. I half expected a confrontation: "Who asked you to come around here giving my wife notions about her talent?" That kind of thing. But he ignored us, both of us, and stood gazing out the big windows, past the barn and the pasture and the orchard, to where the thin thread of the Sloan River would be visible if it weren't raining. I remembered Victoria, that first day, scanning that same horizon with an equal, but different, intensity.

Elizabeth hurried past him, her head down. I glanced at his face, ready to say hello, but received the distinct impression that it would be intrusive, not to say dangerous. He looked like a man who'd just been told that while he was vacationing in the Caribbean vandals had destroyed his home. Strange—I'd expect Andrew to look that way, not Trager.

I followed Elizabeth down the hallway and heard Catherine coming quickly down the stairway to meet us. We reached the foot of the stairs simultaneously, and Catherine made a U turn and faced me, with a fixed smile, a pale face, and red-rimmed eyes.

"You're so good to come sloshing out in this weather! I feel terribly selfish! I'm going to give you some hot tea! A cuppa, as the British say, guaranteed to take the chill out of your bones! I'll bring it upstairs, why don't you go on up, I won't be a minute, Elizabeth you'd better have some too, you've been out in that drizzle for an hour, but dry your hair first, that rainhat is useless!"

She disappeared in the direction of the kitchen and Elizabeth and I went dutifully upstairs, out of the way of any possible aftertremors, and parted at the landing, me to the studio, she to her room. Victoria was nowhere in sight.

I sat down on a high stool by the worktable laden with photographs and began picking through them. A third of the way through the pile I came upon a shot of Andrew I hadn't seen before. He was looking straight into the camera, which of course meant straight at the photographer, and I had to conclude that Catherine was either careless or too innocent for this world. That face was sending an unmistakable message. On second thought I didn't believe Catherine would be careless about something like that, nor could I believe in that much naiveté. If she didn't recognize the look in those eyes it was because she'd been so programmed by Julian to think of herself as inferior material that if a man threw himself at her feet, her immediate reaction would be to call an ambulance.

For Julian, on the other hand, its meaning would be as clear as the sound of a fire alarm. Was sexual jealousy, I wondered, the basis for that trumped-up charge of stealing? Because trumped up I knew in my bones it was.

Catherine came in with a tray supporting a teapot, teacups, sugar bowl, cream pitcher, a dish of lemon slices, hot buttered corn muffins, and a pot of jam.

"Elizabeth is taking hers down to the piano. She always goes to the piano when she's . . . when she's out of sorts. Have you been looking at them? I thought I might divide them according to subject matter—a few still lifes, a few landscapes with figures, a few portraits . . . lemon or cream?"

A faint sound of Scarlatti drifted up from below, carefully played. "Out of sorts" was a nice, innocuous, old-fashioned way of sweeping the trouble under the carpet. Evidently Catherine, for once, was not going to unburden herself of all that was going on, and that was all right with me.

I held up the portrait of Andrew. "Do you like this one?"

She immediately looked doubtful. "Oh—don't you? I thought the chiaroscuro was interesting—if one can use that term for photography—but of course if you think—"

Maybe she *was* Little Red Riding Hood, walking through the woods with her basketful of Japanese film and a telescopic lens.

"I don't think you should keep this lying around," I said.

"Is it that bad?"

"It's marvelous." She looked bewildered. "Catherine, look at that man's face. And he was looking at *you*."

Frowning, she picked up the photograph and studied it carefully, and slowly the vertical lines between her brows disappeared and she looked up at me with wide, startled gray eyes.

"What are you thinking!" she exclaimed. "Oh, that's impossible, you know! I mean, it's fantastic! I would *never* do a thing like that!'

It hadn't occurred to me that she would take it as automatic proof of her complicity. Her face flushed, she dropped the photograph, and got up and sat down and got up again.

"I couldn't *conceive* of it!" she went on. "I think fidelity is one of the most vital—one of the most *crucial* precepts of marriage! I know people are doing all kinds of things these days, but that's not what I understand by marriage, that's not the way I'm made! I've never even *thought* of Andrew as a—as a—"

"I'm sure you haven't. But I'm not so sure about Andrew."

"I can't believe it! You must be mistaken!" She glanced at the photograph again. "But he's—he must be ten years younger! Why would he—well, in any case, it would have been totally one-sided, I assure you! I don't see the point of being married if you're going to—going to—sneak around!"

"Nevertheless, the history of marriage is littered with the smudged handkerchief and the incriminating letter."

"That may be," she picked up her teacup and put it down again, "but it won't happen to me!" Suddenly she looked like Victoria. "Julian will never find an incriminating letter in my pocket—and if I ever found a smudged handkerchief in his—I won't, but if I did—that would be the end of it!"

I smiled and said lightly, "Catherine, you belong to an endangered species."

She turned away from me and fiddled with the enlarger, and when she spoke it was not in her usual exclamatory fashion.

"I could never stay married to a man who betrayed me. That's what it is, betrayal. It's taking someone's faith and trust and throwing them on a garbage heap. It's a violation of someone's spirit. That's not permissible."

I picked up the photograph of Andrew and put it to one side.

"I shouldn't have said anything," I murmured, "it really was none of my business."

She turned back, and the old exclamatory style came back with her. "Oh, no! I'm glad you felt free to say it! It was a personal thing, the kind of thing only friends can say to each other! We've become friends!" She smiled and I smiled back, and we got down to the business at hand.

At the end of an hour, with very little help from me, and Catherine, whether she knew it or not, doing all the deciding, we had whittled the two hundred photographs down to twenty. Catherine stood regarding the selection thoughtfully.

"Yes!" she said. "Absolutely! This is the best possible choice! I knew I was right to ask you, I could never have done it alone!"

Oh, yes you could, Mrs. Trager, company is all you need.

She put the twenty photographs carefully into a carrying case, chattering about the appointment and her nervousness. I heard the sound of a car driving up to the house and stopping, and wondered if by some miracle Andrew was back, and then suddenly remembered my mission for Greenfield and realized I had probably let a hundred opportunities go by without seizing a one. When Catherine mentioned Victoria's pleasure at the prospect that something might come of her photography, I seized.

"How did she enjoy her day in the city?"

"My mother never enjoys the city, she suffers it! She only goes in when what she has to do can't possibly be done locally! I don't even know what she went in for, she wouldn't say, it was probably something to do with Elizabeth's birthday next week! Fifteen! I can't believe it!"

"I suppose I wouldn't enjoy going into the city either, if I had to depend on those trains. They're always too cold or too hot or too crowded."

"Oh, it isn't the trains. She loves trains! She's a train addict! She's read *The Great Railway Bazaar* by Paul Theroux at least four times!"

"It's interesting about trains. People seem to have strong feelings about them. I've never heard anyone say they can take them or leave them. They're either for or against. My husband is definitely against. He'll do anything to avoid getting on a train." (Forgive me, Elliot, I lie in a good cause.)

"Isn't that odd! Julian's like that. Do you know, in all these years he's never once taken the train to the city?"

I took a deep breath. "Never?"

"It's a phobia. I think that's the word. He doesn't believe they'll stay on the tracks, or something of the sort. Yet he'll fly anywhere and it never occurs to him there's nothing underneath the plane but thousands of miles of empty space."

I decided I was not going to let Greenfield know how easy it had been.

The soothing sound of Scarlatti had long ceased, and going down the stairs we heard voices in the living room. One was Victoria's, the other belonged to a male, but it was soft and hesitant, definitely not Trager's.

"Ah! Mr. Kittell must be here!" Catherine said.

I missed a tread and clutched the bannister.

"He's giving us an estimate. We decided to have some painting done and Elizabeth said that was Mr. Kittell's line of work and it would be a good idea to give him the work because . . . because of what happened. Come in and say hello!"

I shook my head. "I don't want to interrupt. Remember me to your mother. Say goodbye to Elizabeth for me."

I left her in the doorway still calling thanks after me.

Near the shed, next to my Honda, was a dark blue van with white lettering announcing KITTEL PAINTING & DECORATING, and below a telephone number.

I drove home through a diminished drizzle, wondering what Catherine would actually do if her puritan code were put to the test. If, for instance, Trager and Sidonie had been kicking up their heels and she somehow discovered it. I wondered, too, if there were really a woman with soul so dead who never to herself had said, "This Andrew here is a force beyond the bounds of human discipline."

I spent a couple of hours with the tape recorder and the typewriter trying to create an objective verbal portrait of Sidonie Seberg, and that evening, before settling happily against my pillows to watch "Masterpiece Theatre," I called Greenfield.

"Did you have a nice day?" I cooed, my tone a nicely judged mixture of syrup and sarcasm.

He considered the day he had had and summed it up. "I'd be obliged if you'd teach Deborah what to do with an eggplant. Did you find out if Trager took a train?"

"He did not. Has not. Never has. Never will. Absolutely refuses to. In fact, has a phobia against."

"Ahhhhh!" He sounded like Lawrence of Arabia after a long drink of water.

"*Now* will you tell me why you want to know?"

"Yes." A long pause while he savored the choice morsel he was about to share. "It neems that last Tuesday . . . Mr. Trager left his Mercedes at Victor's garage . . . to be inspected." He took a deep breath. "The bov there drove it back . . . in the evening . . . and parked it in Trager's garage, or shed . . . the building you described to me."

I sat up from my pillows, all my relaxed muscles back on the job.

"How did you discover that?"

"Given the circumstance," he said, launching on one of his circumlocutory spiels, "that I would have *preferred* it to be Trager driving that Volkswagen . . . and the premise that he wouldn't be likely to exchange the Mercedes voluntarily for it . . . I had to postulate a situation . . . in which he was unable to *use* the Mercedes. . . ."

"Such as it was in for repairs, and that would mean Victor's Garage, and you inquired, and it wasn't there for repairs, but it *was* there for inspection."

"Interruption," he said sternly, "is a form of contempt."

"Not with me. Just a form of avoiding death from impatience. Sorry. Go on."

He waited awhile, to punish me, and finally said, "It's obvious. You remember the photograph. The station wagon was covered with snow, so he didn't avail himself of that. There was no other car on the premises. It's unlikely he would hire a taxi to drive him to the city when the Volkswagen was available. It *was* used, as witness the lack of snow on the windshield and so forth. I find it very difficult to believe he *wasn't* driving the Volkswagen that day—and evening."

"All right. Let's say he was driving it. But he still wasn't home when I called the farm, and that was long after the accident."

"It's possible that even someone as thick skinned and domineering as Mr. Trager wouldn't want to face his family immediately after committing a crime. He probably continued driving until his emotions were under control."

"Mmm." I tried to visualize Julian Trager in the situation, but there was something wrong with the picture.

"There's just one thing," I said. "Julian Trager may be a bully and a coward and all the other things you called him, but he's also no dummy, and if he ran down a boy on a bicycle, he would never leave him lying there. Granted it would be unpleasant to face the consequences of an accident, but even the best people can have an accident—he could survive that. What he could never survive is a charge of hit-and-run. Apart from the criminal aspect, can you imagine what the *Times* would do with that? 'Celebrated Novelist Leaves Child Unconscious in Ditch.' End of career."

"You're assuming he anticipated being found out."

"He could never be sure. What if Peter saw him and regained consciousness and described him, or the car. It was too big a risk. Bigger for him than for most people."

There was another pause while Greenfield mulled. Finally he conceded the point. "I admit that would be a very compelling reason for him not to *run*."

"Thank you."

"So there must have been an even *more* compelling reason for him not to *stay*."

◙ 10

I had a dentist appointment at eight o'clock on Monday morning. The reason I make dental appointments that early is that if I ever come awake enough to realize where I'm going I'll never go.

My dentist, an excellent dentist, one of the best, and a nice man who could make me very happy by saying I would never see him again, had his office in Gorham. I got the Honda out of the garage and drove up Chatham Drive, turned left onto Hawthorn and down through the village center, over the bridge that spanned the Sloan River, and turned right onto the Gorham road.

It was not a bad morning, chilly but clear and sunny. The sky looked newly washed after the rain and wore its small puffy white clouds with an air of having just dressed up for a party. It was the kind of morning that transmuted the mysteries of the night before into lighthearted fantasies and the fears into foolishness. I began to doubt the significance of the circumstantial evidence piling up against Julian Trager. I began to suspect that Greenfield's sinister speculations were part of a middle-aged-male syndrome: a wistful return to the sensation of being violently engaged.

I turned on the radio and listened to a trumpet voluntary. Untamed landscape flashed by on my left, the dead-grass banks of the Sloan on my right, I whipped along the sparsely trafficked road until something anomalous in the scenery up ahead alerted me.

Blinking lights. A patrol car—two of them—pulled off the road onto the riverbank. People moving and pointing and gesturing. Policemen. Other people. Other cars. A dove-gray Mercedes! Two-seater! Twenty thousand dollars' worth of automobile!

I slowed to a crawl and pulled off the road, a pulse beating heavily in my throat. A young policeman came toward me. He looked familiar. It was the officer from the scene of Peter's accident.

"Please move along," he said crisply, "just keep going—"

"But what's wrong?"

"Just move along, please—" He kept waving his arm to the north.

"But I know that car! I mean, I think—"

He gave me a sharp, quick look. "You know the owner of that car?"

"I'm pretty sure—" It was clear we were both talking about the same car, the one in the spotlight, the star, the Mercedes.

"Shut off your motor, please."

I turned the key and got out of the car while the stern young man produced a notebook and pen. The ground was soggy, I sank into it. Stupidly I wondered if the water-repellent spray would save my boots.

"Your name, please."

I told him and he gave me another searching glance. I expected the next question would have to do with my propensity for showing up at scenes of accidents, and I tried to forestall it.

"Could you just tell me what happened? Is anyone hurt?"

"We don't know, ma'am, can't find the owner of the car."

"Can't find—?"

"You want to come talk to the sergeant, please?"

He steered me over toward the group standing at a distance from the Mercedes on the far side of it, and it was then I saw, past the patrol car, the dark blue van with the lettering: KITTELL PAINTING & DECORATING. By some stroke of luck I had the presence of mind not to blurt out, "Oh God, not the Kittells again!" But I was thinking it, furiously.

The officer guided me away from the area immediately around the Mercedes and words popped into my head—television words. "Evidence." "Scene of the crime." "Footprints." (Although from what I could see, the entire area, including the ground around the Mercedes, was such a trampled mess that the footprints of a giant would be indistinguishable.) I began to feel unreal, part of a melodrama. The Mercedes was parked nose toward the river, and on the shining clean hood was what looked like an open wallet.

We approached the group and I saw Sergeant Walchek, looking solid, handsome, and faintly unintelligent, standing next to a tall, burly man in a gray overcoat, Mr. and Mrs. Kittell standing a little to one side, he looking wary and she feverish, and a small dapper man in a Burberry facing the sergeant, explaining something to him with crisp little motions of his hands. By some unspoken consent the Kittells and I ignored each other.

"And I saw this gentlemen and this lady here—" the dapper little man was saying, pointing to the Kittells, "waving to me to stop, so I pulled up and it was just as you see it now—just the car—and this gentleman's van over there, and no one else anywhere in sight. And they said there seemed to be something funny going on, they had seen this car standing there and they stopped to see if anyone was in trouble, just what they told you, sergeant, that they'd gone down to the edge of the river and looked in both directions, and they'd seen the wallet on the ground, and come back to the car and—and saw—that."

He pointed to something the man in the gray overcoat was holding in one gloved hand, and I looked, and my stomach heaved.

It was a black angle iron and one end of it was wetter and shinier than the rest.

"So—" the little man went on, "they flagged me down and explained the situation, as I just told you, and asked me to call the police, and said they would stay and wait for them—you—to come. And I drove on to the motel up the road, and called, and came back here thinking you might want my—uh—my testimony."

"Did you walk around anywhere while you were here?"

"No, sir. No. I just took right off to make the call."

"Okay. Thank you." The sergeant turned to look at me.

"This lady says she knows the owner of the car," my officer said. Sergeant Walchek knew my face, if not my name—we'd seen each other often enough over the past ten years—but there wasn't the slightest flicker of recognition. He waited for me to talk.

"I *think* I do," I said hoarsely, and cleared my throat. "At any rate I know someone who has an identical Mercedes, and they're not that common. The name is Trager. Julian Trager."

Walchek nodded. "That's the identification we found in the wallet."

"Was the—what was the wallet doing on the ground?"

"No way we could know that. Could have been a holdup. There was no money in it. How well do you know this party?"

"I don't really—just casually." He waited again and I explained the circumstances of my meeting with Julian Trager, and the officer took down my address—for the second time in a week. I felt more like a suspect than a reporter, but my need to know was greater than Walchek's power to intimidate, and besides, I knew he wasn't averse to seeing his name in print. "Could I get a little information," I asked, "for the paper?"

"Don't have any to give you," he said, "except what you just heard." Note, he didn't ask what paper, so he recognized me.

"Well, for instance, what—" I pointed at the angle iron—"what's that all about?"

"Some kind of fence post," he said, "for a wire fence or something. It was lying on the ground near the car."

"And that stuff on the—on the end of it. Is that—?"

"That's blood—yes, ma'am. We don't know whose, we don't know how come, we don't know anything yet."

At that point Mrs. Kittell muttered something I

didn't catch, and I saw Mr. Kittell put a hand on her arm to silence her.

"Have you found anything else? Other than the wallet and the—the fence post?" I felt foolish as I added, "Any signs of a struggle?"

Walchek glanced at the man in the gray overcoat and said, "It looks like something heavy was dragged from the car down to the river, but we don't know what." He looked around at the cars and the river and the people, and raised his voice. "Well, we're going to have to do some work around here, so I'd appreciate it if you people would go on home and keep yourselves available.

The dapper little man stepped forward briskly, personification of the good citizen. "I'm going to be out of town for a day or two, but I can give you an address in Albany if you—"

"Take it down, Ernie," Walchek said, and the young officer pulled out his notebook with a flourish, and wrote, and the dapper man got into his Chrysler and drove away, and the Kittells got into their dark blue van and pulled slowly off the verge onto the road and headed north.

I looked at the Mercedes and thought of Catherine and remembered that this was the day of her appointment with Bob Drexler. I glanced at my watch, satisfied myself that by the time the police got up there she would be on her way, then realized that would leave Victoria alone to face this news.

"I suppose you'll be going up to the farm?" I asked. Walchek looked at me as though I had suggested a weekend retreat. "Where Mr. Trager lives," I added.

"Traprock Road," the young officer promptly supplied.

Walchek nodded. "We'll be sending somebody up there."

"It might be a good idea to wait awhile. I mean— there might be a simple explanation. No need to alarm anyone yet. Is there?"

"The car might have been stolen."

"With the wallet in it?" Walchek flushed and I went on quickly. "But in that case Mr. Trager would report it. Or you could call up and ask for Mr. Trager, if he's there you could tell him what you found if not—if not, you could ask when they expect him back. If they know where he is, you could—well, there's plenty of time, isn't there? The thing is, Mrs. Hollis will probably be there all alone. His mother-in-law. She's seventy—"

Walchek's empty pale blue eyes finally stopped me.

"There's a procedure to follow. We have to follow the procedure." He walked over to the Mercedes, opened the door, and stuck his head inside. I was dismissed.

The man in the gray overcoat was watching me through his heavy-lidded eyes. I didn't like the look of him. One of those men who had concluded that the only way to deal with the sleazy side of humanity was to turn into a six-foot callus. I carried my anxieties back to the Honda and drove on to my dentist appointment, trying to think of rational reasons for Trager's car to be found on the riverbank with Trager's wallet on the ground, a bloody angle iron in the vicinity, and the whole mess discovered by the Kittells. The event was staggering in its complexity. Far from activating my brain cells, it left me numb. I told Dr. Solkin I probably didn't need Novocaine as I was already anesthetized, but he gave it to me anyway, and such was my preoccupation that I, who normally sit gripping the chair arms with whitened knuckles from the initial hand-washing to the final spraying of mouthwash, had to be told twice that the deed had been done, the tooth filled, don't chew on it for an hour or so, see you in six months.

I headed back down the Gorham road in the southbound lane wondering if there would still be activity at the site. Very little. Two policemen sitting in a patrol car looking at the Mercedes was all. Walchek and the gray overcoat were gone. When I was out of sight of the patrol car I put my foot down on the accelerator. The sooner I passed this development on to Greenfield and we agreed on what and what not to tell the police, the easier I'd feel. It was entirely possible that the police, knowing I'd gone to the farm in the first place at the behest of my boss, would send someone to ask him what he knew about the family, and there was no telling what Greenfield's stand on civic duty might currently be. He certainly knew things about the Tragers which could cause them grief and make me a blood relative of Judas.

At the office Helen gave me her usual scout-leader greeting, and I handed her the envelope containing my six hundred words on the Hollis farm.

"I don't know what we're going to do about this," I said. "It may turn out to be about as pertinent as a story on that nice new ship the *Titanic*. But you'd better have it ready, I guess,"

"That's a lot of typing if we're not going to use it—"

"All right, let me ask Greenfield."

"He's not in yet."

Oh, Lord, where was he scavenging now?

Calli came in from the hallway on her way back from the john.

"Maggie, how are you! Your mouth is crooked."

"I've just been Novocained."

"Ugh! Dentists! That is the worst hell in the world. Do you know, since I caught this cold I'm running to the bathroom ten times a day, I wonder if something is wrong with my liver?"

"Kidneys," Helen said. "It's your kidneys, not your liver."

Calli's eyes went wide with drama. "You think so?"

"She means it *would* be your kidneys. Not your liver. If it were anything." I went to the alcove and made myself some Sanka while Calli went back to work in the layout room and held forth in a resounding voice on the possible significance of her frequent trips to the bathroom. (It really was a bathroom, with a bathtub and all.) I joined her. I was tense with the bottled-up knowledge of the incident on the Gorham road. Trust Greenfield not to be there when I needed him most.

Calli was standing with a layout sheet in one hand and an institutional ad in the other, scowling.

"*Sto Diabolo!* I have a space left over not big enough for anything!" She went to the large wide file cabinet with the shallow drawers marked "Standing Headlines," "Letters to Editor," "Little League," "Christmas drawer," and so on. She pulled out the drawer marked "Overset," which contained various nontopical leftover items, and riffled through them looking for something small enough. I sipped my Sanka.

"Something peculiar just happened on the Gorham road," I said, without meaning to.

"Yes? What," she asked indifferently, still searching.

I told her, leaving the Kittells out of it.

She straightened. "And you recognized this car! You know the guy?"

"I've met him. He's a writer. He lives just off Cliff Road."

"Crazy," she observed. "Every day the world gets a little more crazy. What is a man like that doing driving around so early in the morning anyway? A businessman has to get up early. Or a truck driver. But writers get up whenever they want, true? Unless he was still up from last night." She gave me an arch look. "Maybe he was coming home from a big night at that crummy motel they have up there. Don't look at me like that, Maggie! You don't know the half of what goes on!"

"It was the wrong side of the road for that. This happened beside the northbound lane."

"So he was going to meet somebody. Early-morning party. A new kind of kinky."

"You're obsessed—" I said, and the front door opened and she and I heard Greenfield mutter a greeting to Helen and start up the stairs. I ran out to the hall and started up after him, and he stopped halfway to see who was following.

"New development," I said.

He looked carefully at my face, said "Your mouth is crooked," and continued up.

When he was seated and leaning back in the noisy swivel chair and I'd cleared a place for myself on one of the old armchairs, I took a good-sized breath and said, "Julian Trager's Mercedes was found standing on the grass beside the Gorham road facing the river with no one inside it or outside it, and his wallet was on the ground with no money in it and"—I swallowed—"and there was an iron fence post nearby with blood on one end."

He continued staring at me, tilting slightly backward and forward, and said nary a word. I gave him the punch line.

"And the people who raised the alarm," I said, "were Mr. and Mrs. Kittell."

He came down with a thud on the forward tilt. "Kittell! Are you certain?"

"I saw them there. They were standing there with Walchek and some other cops and a little man who said the Kittells stopped him as he was driving by and told him to call the police."

"And what were *you* doing there?"

"Driving by on my way to the dentist. And they're going to go up to the farm and I think Victoria Hollis is there alone and maybe I'd better get up there in case she needs any—" I stopped.

"Any what?"

"I don't know. Someone to talk to, or be with. But first I think we should decide what we're going to say if and when they start asking us about the Tragers. Don't you? Charlie?"

He was still looking at me, but he was tuned to a different drummer.

"The Kittells," he mumbled, "what the devil were the Kittells doing there?"

"They could have been on their way to the hospital—"

He thought about that, and nodded half-heartedly. "Why would they stop?"

"Abandoned car—"

"Could you tell from the road that it was abandoned?"

"Well—no, I guess not. But a car pulled off the road usually means trouble of some kind—"

"Do you stop to investigate every car you see in trouble?"

"I'm selfish."

"Even supposing you were a model of altruism. The Kittells were not taking a Sunday afternoon pleasure jaunt, they were on their way to the hospital. Why would they stop?" He swiveled around and stared out the window. I took a sip of lukewarm Sanka. He swiveled back. "Is it possible they knew the car "

"I don't see . . . wait a minute. I suppose it's possible. Mr. Kittell was up at the farm yesterday giving them an estimate on a painting job." Greenfield's eyebrows climbed upward. "Mea culpa. I forgot to tell you. Anyway, about what we're going to say to the police when they ask us—"

"Ask *us?* Why should they ask *us* anything?"

"They *might*. I'm already down in their little notebook, and I had to tell them I was doing a story on the farm to explain how I knew Trager's car, and that could lead them to you, and they just might ask us for any information we have that might throw some light on the—"

"Throw some light! You sound like one of those television series."

"I feel like one."

"What do you *want* to tell them?"

"Nothing! Well—just the bare facts. He's a writer, his wife does photography, they live on this farm with their daughter and Mrs. Hollis—"

"And a hired hand who recently bought angle irons, which is what I suppose you mean by a 'fence post'?"

"You see, that's what I mean! Why do we have to tell them that?"

Greenfield's sigh begged the world to witness my simplemindedness. "Why," he said, "is going to depend on what happens. If Trager is found alive and well, that's one thing. If not—"

I sank back against a pile of old magazines. "That man is the human equivalent of an ancient city. All roads lead to him. The VW with a scratch on it, Gordon, and his antiporn fever. Sidonie Seberg and her philosophy of publishing, Andrew leaving the farm in a huff— Oh, God! All right, that's another thing I forgot to mention—"

But before I could tell him the telephone rang and he got into a hassle with some local politician on the other end who was looking for free publicity, and when he finally ended the call he said to me, "I have to go to work," and turned to his desk.

I stared at his back in its shapeless blue cardigan. My, my, how the winds do shift.

"You're no longer interested in Julian Trager?"

"It's not my move," he said without moving. "When the police find out what happened—*if* they find out— I'll decide whether or not I'm interested."

And that was that. He'd put Trager in the same category as last week's issue of the *Reporter*. What had been an obsession was now an irrelevance. It was almost as though he knew Trager was dead and Peter had been avenged.

For one wild moment I wondered if Greenfield had appointed himself executioner! But no—quick vengeance wasn't his style. He'd want to torture the man, pile up the evidence, drag him into court, expose him before the world. Besides, where would he get an angle iron?

"Can we use the farm story?" I asked his back. "Helen won't start typing until you say so."

"Better hold off until tomorrow. Tell Dohanis to dig out an alternative and show it to me."

I went down the stairs, told Helen to hold off, gave Calli the message, which elicited an indelicate gesture from her to the ceiling, went out to the Honda, and drove to the farm.

It lay under the sunshine and the innocent blue sky like a newborn babe, soft and clean and purring in its sleep. Hawkeye and Radar moved dreamily around their pasture (who would care for them now that Andrew was gone?), but otherwise it was a motionless landscape, bathed in tranquillity. There was no patrol car parked near the shed, and no station wagon—only the infamous VW. I pulled up beside it and went to the front door, and had my hand raised to the brass knocker when I heard the sound of a viola.

I shivered, not with the cold. I mean, one doesn't usually sit down to play a little solitary music in the face of one's son-in-law's strange disappearance. Or did this mean he'd been found having breakfast somewhere, with a perfectly plausible explanation? Somehow I didn't think so. I remembered Greenfield contending that Victoria Hollis had given up music because of Trager's possible ridicule. And here she was, alone in her house, opening the sacred, thermostatically controlled cabinet, removing the precious instrument, and—apparently for the first time in years—sitting down to play. As though Trager was gone for good, *and she knew it.*

I told myself I was becoming, as they say in Old English novels, fanciful. But I stood holding my breath, listening to the sweet, pure note of a Schumann theme, and wondered if I should leave. What was I doing there, after all? Wasn't I being presumptuous, thrusting my unsolicited concern at a group of relative strangers? This was a private family matter. If Mrs. Hollis wanted to respond to the news of the discovery on the Gorham road by playing her viola, it was really not my affair. It was even possible she *preferred* to be alone at a time like this. Not to mention that she might even be secretly relieved at this turn of events: Who knew just how much she had suffered from Trager's presence? He was undoubtedly a man who spread sunshine by his absence.

I realized suddenly that the music had stopped, and a moment later the door opened and Victoria Hollis stood there with her white hair and her straight back and a pair of bifocals in one hand.

"I thought I'd heard a car drive up. I was waiting for someone to knock. How are you, Mrs. Rome? Come in." She shut the door behind me. "I was just trying out some Schumann. I'm very rusty. It offends my ears, some of the sounds I make."

She'd gone ahead into the living room and I followed. A music stand was set up near the begonias on the windowsill, with a straight-backed chair facing it, and the viola and bow rested on the piano top.

"I'm sorry I interrupted," I said. "I only came by because I—happened to be driving on the Gorham road this morning and I saw—I saw the car." The terrible thought struck me that possibly the police hadn't been here yet, and she didn't know. But no, there was no perplexity in her expression, she didn't ask me what

I was talking about, she merely picked up several books lying on a table and went with them to the bookcase and replaced them.

"Yes," she said, "the police were here. It's very disturbing. They don't know what to make of it."

She sounded—what?—annoyed?

"Then you don't know where he is?"

"I have no idea. He was at home last night. In his study, with the door closed. The rest of us went to bed early. When Catherine woke up this morning, he was gone. Apparently he hadn't been to bed. As I told the police, we had a disagreeable episode yesterday. It isn't unusual for Julian to—absent himself from an unpleasant situation. Please sit down."'

I sat, and she sat opposite me, her cheekbones a little more pronounced than usual, her lips more firmly closed, her eyes glinting with some barely contained emotion. She looked, in fact, angry.

"So you think he might just be—absenting himself somewhere?"

She didn't answer immediately, and I wondered if she'd heard me. Then her eyes came back to me and she said, "Ordinarily I would say that was more than likely, but in the face of what the police described . . . how did it look to you?"

". . . Unusual."

"Unusual. Yes."

"Does Catherine know—?"

"No. She'd gone off to the city before they called." She gave me a brief, mechanical smile. "It was very good of you to make that appointment for her." She looked toward the window and her voice took on the flat, ambiguous tone of those who talk to themselves. "Catherine needs some sense of herself as a person. She has always defined herself in terms of someone else—as a daughter, a mother, a wife. Always thought of herself as completing someone else's life. And of course she picked the one man made to order for that role."

There was a silence, and I sat very still, surprised into immobility by this unexpected confidence from someone who normally made a British diplomat's wife look like Runyon's Adelaide. She went on, in the same uninflected voice.

"Julian is not a bad man. Not corrupt, or evil. He's merely a middle-aged adolescent. With all the qualities which are relatively harmless in youth—the extravagance of emotion, the intemperate greed and lust and self-centeredness. Unfortunately, in a middle-aged man those qualities are rendered harmful by the power implicit in being chronologically adult. He is destructive. He destroys. And now it's come to this."

She raised her eyes and noticed me sitting there.

"I suppose your going to write this up for your paper."

"No! I mean—that's not why I came!" I protested, realizing suddenly how it must look.

"I didn't think it was. You don't strike me as one of those people to whom everything is grist for the mill."

"I'd probably be a better reporter if I were."

"We each have our priorities. That's what determines our virtue or lack of it. We can't take credit either way."

"I just want you to understand that if and when the paper prints an account of this, nothing you've said will—well, I won't repeat it to anyone."

She leaned over, gave my hand a single pat, went to the window, and stood there rubbing two fingers against her forehead. "Catherine should be home in an hour or two. And then Elizabeth. This is not going to be an easy day."

"Maybe the police will know something before then. Or Jul . . . Mr. Trager will turn up."

"I doubt it," she said shortly, then came back and sat down again, and the look of annoyance or anger or whatever it was had returned. "The situation does not look promising. An abandoned car, a bloody iron post, an empty wallet—and the river, to which, according to the police, something 'heavy' had been dragged. There seem to be a great many deranged people wandering around these days, prepared to do anything for a few dollars."

I opened my mouth to say that if Trager had been robbed, the villain must certainly be deranged, to take a few dollars and leave a twenty-thousand-dollar automobile standing there, but I shut it again because the fact that the car had not been taken could point in uncomfortable directions. My subconscious, though, as usual made its own little jump.

"How will you be able to manage here without Andrew?"

She looked at me thoughtfully. "Andrew has come back."

Andrew back! I stared at her. Trager gone and Andrew back! The coast is clear!

"Oh, I'm glad," I said lamely, "for Elizabeth's sake, too. She seemed upset—"

"He came back this morning. I was sure he would." She paused and added, "He's an eminently rational young man."

There were a hundred things I wanted to know, such as was Andrew here when the police arrived, and if so did they question him, and did the subject of angle irons come up, and did they know he'd told Farnham there was one missing, and was there really one missing or had he wanted an extra one for use other than as a fence post—But I had no right to ask Victoria Hollis any of these questions.

Instead I asked, "Is there anything I can do for you, or Catherine or Elizabeth?"

She shook her head. "We could use a little extra patience. And strength of character. But no one else can supply that. Thank you." She reached over idly and turned a page of the music. We had a brief conversation about the Schumann she'd been playing and by the end of it I was on my way out.

As the front door closed behind me I had a feeling she would be back at the music stand before I reached the car.

I looked around for a sign of Andrew. None.

My brain teemed with questions as I drove home to spend the afternoon finishing off the Sidonie Seberg profile, a project which became less absorbing with every passing minute. I typed, and listened for the ring of the telephone that would bring Sergeant Walchek's mellifluous voice to my ear. When it finally rang, I jumped, and then lifted the receiver warily, but the voice on the other end was not Walchek's. It was a voice both familiar and strange. Catherine Trager's voice, minus its high-voltage generator. Catherine as she might sound after several years of Eastern-type meditation.

"I just wanted to thank you again," she said, "and tell you that the meeting with Mr. Drexler was very encouraging. He thinks I have . . . have some options open to me in terms of how to go on from here."

"That's great," I said, in total bewilderment. I would have been ready for either hysteria or catatonia, but this calm disregard of what might prove to be a major crisis in her life left me disoriented.

"Mother told me you came to see her this morning."

"Well—yes—it was—I hope she didn't mind—"

"It was very thoughtful of you. But I don't think there's anything to worry about. I just have a feeling that Julian is all right."

"Do you have any idea where he might be?"

"Well, no," she said placidly. Placidly! "We've tried his office in the city, of course, and his friend Ziggy. He wasn't at either place. But there are any number of places he could be."

Including the bottom of the river.

"Would he be likely to leave the Mercedes that way—just abandon it?"

"I don't understand why he did that," she admitted, "but Julian does behave compulsively from time to time."

That was an understatement if I ever heard one. However, abandoning a Mercedes on a riverbank was, to my knowledge, a new high in compulsive behavior.

"At any rate," she continued, "I'm feeling quite wonderful. And I'm in your debt, Maggie. I'd like to do something for you."

"Please. I'm not good at being thanked."

"You'll have to learn." She laughed and said goodbye and hung up.

I went back to my typewriter and stared at it, and wondered if Victoria had slipped a tranquilizer into Catherine's tea. I decided that a woman who spoke about strength of character would have no truck with such things as tranquilizers, that Catherine was on a high that had nothing to do with any chemicals but her own. But even granting the euphoria induced by professional recognition of her worth, it was damned bloody deucedly funny that the collection of objects on the Gorham road should leave her not only undisturbed, but positively sanguine!

When at last I completed the intensely dull piece on Sidonie, I put the cover on the typewriter, the carbon copy in an envelope with a note bearing both home and office numbers and saying I would be very grateful if Mrs. Seberg could give me a verdict by noon tomorrow, fed George and myself, and drove over to Dunstan Hill to deliver the copy.

There was a cold half-moon in a cold black sky sitting over the Seberg's suburban version of Xanadu. I went up the steps of multicolored slate. They were lined on either side by head-high laurel bushes which continued right up to the front door and effectively screened anyone approaching the house from the view of those inside. an arrangement with which I wouldn't have cared to live.

As I reached the door a thin, nasal male voice cut through the night with such venom that I peered through the bushes at the forty feet of glassed-in living room. There, captured as on a giant screen, was such a tableau of marital tension as would satisfy even Ingmar Bergman.

Sidonie, in satin pants of a leopard design and a loose gold fishnet top, stood in the living-room doorway, one arm thrust behind her, pointing to something unseen, the other curled into a fist and clutching a cigarette in a holder as though it were a club. Facing her, backed into the room in retreat from her onslaught, a man in his mid-thirties with receding brown hair, narrow shoulders encased in a midnight-blue pinstriped suit. lavender shirt, and maroon print tie strained forward from the waist, his insignificant chin jutting as far as possible out from his budding dewlaps, the whiskey glass in his hand raised in threatening reprisal against the puny attack of the cigarette holder.

This, I decided, could be none other than the redoubtable Marshall Seberg, creative talent agent, crusader for female monogamy, and, from what I could see and hear, a likely candidate for least charismatic man of the year.

"—on your stinking career!" he shrieked. "You get your ass home at a decent hour! Then you can talk!"

"I'll talk right now, mister!" Sidonie's velvet voice had fallen into a gravel pit. "Leaving me alone all night with a sick child! You knew it was what's-her-name's day off, you crud! And I had to get up and go to work, you bastard! Where were you all night, you scum!"

"Not so much fun when the shoe's on the other foot, is it?"

"I come home every single night."

"But not from work!"

"Where were you?"

"I visited a hangout of yours! Okav? A place where you show up at least once a week—with a friend! You rotten—"

CRASH!

From Sidonie's primal scream one would have supposed the Michelangelo David had been vandalized.

"That was *Steuben!*"

I withdrew. Silence. I wondered what to do. If I rang the bell at this point, would I be regarded as having been a witness to their battle and risk having my story refused the seal of approval? If I tucked the envelope into the mailbox and went home and called and told her it was there, would she suspect anyway and be just as likely to vent her spleen on me? I decided the odds were fifty-fifty no matter what course I took, and maybe if I waited awhile nothing else would happen and I could conceivably have arrived after the fact. A great deal of time passed. I was beginning to feel the cold. There was nothing but silence. Finally I rang the bell.

After a count of about two hundred, the door opened and Marshall Seberg's round, babyish, apoplectic face appeared.

"This is for Mrs. Seberg," I said quickly, and handed it to him, and left.

It was only 6 P.M. in California. When I got home I put in a call to California to the hotel where Elliot was staying. He had just come in from a meeting in Palo Alto. He said he was fine and still unseduced either by San Francisco weather or any of its female inhabitants, and would be home sometime over the weekend, and what about the mortgage payment and the Chevy. I lied and said both had been taken care of, and before sitting down with my Graham Greene I wrote out a check for the mortgage.

▣ 11

By nine thirty the next morning my fingers had twice
strayed to the telephone dial to call headquarters and
ask if they'd found out anything new, but I didn't want
to remind them of my existence and risk being invited
to come in and answer a few more questions. Finally I
dressed and went down to the office to see if Greenfield
had heard from the officers of the law.

Calli was coming down the stairs in three-inch heels,
an emerald-green pantsuit, and a Gauginish scarf
around her hair. When she saw me she tried to run the
rest of the way down, but of course she was hobbled.

"Maggie! Maggie! A miracle! You won't believe it!
Peter! He's out of the coma!"

My heart leaped. "Are you sure?"

"Sure I'm sure! What do you mean am I sure? Mrs.
Kittell just called Charlie! Is that terrific?"

"Terrific!" I agreed, and suddenly felt a good five
years younger.

Callie went screaming her good news to Helen and I
ran up to see Greenfield. For a man who had just been
told something so uplifting he was a grim spectacle—
long face, eyes fastened on a hole in the carpet, shoulders sagging under his dark-green corduroy jacket, one
brown-socked ankle resting wearily on the opposite
knee, its attached foot dangling limply. When I realized
he was not going to acknowledge my presense, I spoke
up.

"There seems to have been a breakdown in communication," I said. "According to Calli the news was
good."

He nodded. "The boy seems to be out of danger."

"There's something she didn't tell me?"

"There's something I didn't tell her." He leaned back in the swivel chair—it complained loudly—raised his martyred eyes to mine and said, "They suspect the Kittells of doing away with Trager."

I dropped into a chair full of reference books. "They—*What?* You're kidding!"

"You can easily check with the police. Detective Pratt or Bratt or Hornblower or some damn thing, the fellow who replaced Galloway."

"A gray man. Shifty. Then they— What makes them think Trager was done away with?"

"His jacket was washed ashore a few hundred yards downstream from the car. This Pratt or Bratt came to see me—not because of your presence at the farm, as you predicted, but because the Kittells, when questioned at length, mentioned my name. Mentioned that the boy had been here just before his accident."

"His accident? You mean *Peter's* accident? Why were they questioning the Kittells about *that?* Why did they assume there was any connection between Peter and . . . wait a minute! You don't mean they found out about the VW!"

Greenfield sighed deeply. "No. It seems that yesterday, when the police arrived at the abandoned Mercedes, one of the cops said it looked as though Trager had ended up in the river. Whereupon Mrs. Kittell cried out, 'God has punished him for what he did to my boy!' "

"Key-ryste!" I collapsed further into the chair, causing my coccyx to collide with the hardcover spine of a looseleaf note-book. As I rearranged myself I had a mental picture of Mrs. Kittell standing on the verge of the Gorham road, her arm raised in righteous wrath, uttering those fateful words, and suddenly the significance of that was borne in on me.

"But how did *she* know? Mrs. Kittell? How did *she* make the connection between Peter and Trager? How did *she* know about the VW?"

"That," Greenfield said heavily, "is precisely what I've been pondering. According to the police, she said that when the boy came out of the coma he named Julian as the driver of the car which ran him down—

his sister knew Elizabeth, after all, it's conceivable. No doubt Mrs. Kittell will coach him to repeat this when the police come to question him. But that was obviously a lie on her part, to protect me, because she told *me* that Peter remembered nothing, it all happened too quickly."

"Protect you? From what?"

He uncrossed his legs, stood up, went over to the record cabinet, and stood regarding the albums resting there. "Last Friday"—he removed an album, looked at it, and put it back—"she came here to see me about something. As she left, you arrived. There is no door to this room. You and I were discussing Trager and the Volkswagen. Then you found a glove on the floor, belonging to her. It's possible she went downstairs, discovered the glove was missing, started back up again to retrieve it, overheard enough of our conversation to draw her own conclusions, didn't want us to know she'd heard, and left without the glove."

He withdrew a César Franck album and put the record on the player. I found I was nodding to myself like some old Talmudic sage. It all came back to me.

"That's why it took so long for the front door to open and close," I said. "I thought Helen had stopped her, but that's what it was. She started back up the stairs and heard us. That's where she got the idea."

"And that," he said bitterly, "makes me responsible for the fact that she is now under suspicion."

I was about to reply that it was her own silly tongue that had landed her in this mess, but it was useless to point that out. He *wanted* to be responsible.

A sudden spurt of purposeful energy took him to the stairs, where he somehow projected his voice to Helen without raising it. "No calls," he said, and went back to the desk, where he grabbed a note pad and a pen, one in each hand, dropped into the swivel chair, and sent a look of pained but determined efficiency in my direction.

"Yesterday," he said, "you made some remark to the effect that all roads lead to Trager—Peter, Gordon, that woman you interviewed, the woodchopper at the farm. I'm sure they don't constitute even a fraction of the people who might be glad to see the end of Trager, but they're the only ones we know and their grievances are recent—"

"I never said Sidonie had a grievance against him. In fact—"

"Yes, I know, but that kind of relationship is always fraught with possibilities. *If* the relationship exists. Now"—he lifted his pen and pointed it at me as though I were a dart board—"you are going to recall for me every single incident of the past week. Inch by inch, we're going to cover every one of those roads leading to Trager, including your random thoughts and impressions and any stray word or sign which set off a train of thought connected with him."

"Charlie, you have really gone off the deep end. Do you know how long that would take? I have a husband coming home in four days. I have two sons I would like to see again before they're middle-aged. It's only ten months to Christmas and I haven't done my shopping!"

"You'll be amazed how quickly the time goes."

"Besides, it's ludicrous. If anything *did* happen to him, it was probably a total stranger—Trager probably gave somebody a lift and they mugged him."

"Possible. But statistics prove that most victims are assaulted by someone they know."

"And anyway, who says anything happend to Trager? You know what Walchek is—he'd decide there was a Russian submarine in the river if it would make him the center of attraction."

"The sooner you begin, the sooner we'll finish."

I put my elbow on the arm of the chair and my forehead into the palm of my hand and shut my eyes. Now that Peter was going to be all right I could have kicked him for starting this endlessly unrolling imbroglio.

"If I'm not stepping out of line," I said with my eyes still shut, "just being an employee here and all that— could I ask you to decide once and for all which line of business we're in? I'm beginning to sympathize with Clark Kent, changing his clothes every five minutes."

I opened my eyes and glared at him.

He looked at me with one of his most put-upon expressions. "I . . . am . . . trapped . . ." he said, biting off each word, "in an obligation . . . which I cannot fulfill . . . short of cutting my way . . . through this jungle-growth . . . of suspicious circumstances . . . to wherever the truth of the matter . . . is hiding!"

So, for the next three hours I went slowly and painfully over every hour of every day in the past week, and just to get even, I spared him nothing. I made him listen to all of it, including the gossip in the beauty parlor and a description of the movie I had seen with Barbara. He sat there without complaint or interruption, scribbling occasionally on his note pad and getting up only once to change from César Franck to Elgar. Finally, when I was recounting the scene of the evening before at the Sebergs', he stopped me.

"Those were his exact words? 'I visited a hangout of yours—a place where you show up at least once a week—with a friend'?"

"That's what the man said. There was an extremely nasty tone of voice attached to it, but I can't reproduce that."

He sat staring at the note pad for a while, then got up and went to the head of the stairs. "Dohanis!" he shouted quietly, and went back to his chair, swiveled away from me, and stared out the window. There was a clatter of heels on the stairs and Calli brought her Gauguin and emerald-green into the sepia-colored room.

"You think I can do my work when I have to answer the phone all day, Charlie? Then why don't you pay me double if I'm a secretary? You take advantage, you know that? Here!" She slapped a number of messages onto the desk top. "And Maggie, some Seberg called you, she said okay you can print the story only she doesn't like one part—here—I wrote it down—she made me copy *exactly* how you should write it, she spelled every word for me! I said, 'Lady, I know how to spell, the Greeks were educated before you even had *Indians* here!' "

"Good for you. Only you shouldn't have called her a lady, that could have blown the whole thing for me."

Calli guffawed in her hoarse voice and clattered

back down the stairs, and Greenfield sat with his messages in one hand and the pen in the other, which he began to tap slowly and repeatedly on the edge of the desk. *Tap . . . tap . . . tap . . . tap . . . tap . . .*

"Ask not for whom the pen taps," I murmured.

He came out of his reverie, reached in his pocket, and held out two ten-dollar bills. "Take this—" he said, and explained what they were for.

My first reaction was that he had a very quick mind, my second that he was adding two and two and getting at least one hundred and forty, my third that if we were going to do it at all we might as well go whole hog. I took the twenty dollars and headed for the stairs.

There I stopped, remembering unfinished business. "What are we going to do about the piece on the farm?"

"Run it."

"And what about this—this business on the Gorham road? Are we going to write it up as a separate news item?"

"There's nothing to write up. A man's car was found, apparently abandoned. That's not a news item."

No, not if you leave out all the interesting details. "Police blotter?" I suggested. "The wallet, the—mm—weapon?"

"We don't know it's a weapon. We don't know anything yet. Frankly—well, never mind. One problem at a time. Get that other information."

And don't fool with the master plan. Okay. I went down to the workroom and told Helen to go ahead and type the piece on the farm. She was glowing with the news of Peter's recovery, which she somehow attributed to her own powers of positive thinking, and while she explained this to me I checked Sidonie Seberg's rewrite of my paragraph, taped it over its opposite number in my script, left it on Helen's desk, declined the cup of tea Calli was offering me from the alcove, and left.

Feeling the need for a little exercise I walked the quarter mile to Francine's Beauty Parlor. They were having a quiet morning; the customers consisted of two small, ancient, and fragile ladies, translucent and bony as chicken feet, from the Senior Citizens Home in Pinecliff. One was sleeping under the dryer, her sparse white hair curled, strand by strand, around rollers. The other was sleeping in the chair under Anthony's gentle ministrations, and her hair was even sparser—in fact I couldn't see it at all—and watching Anthony's fingers stroking and winding at thin air, I reflected that he had remarkable sense-memory. Anthony was full of admiration for these old ladies who came every week, driven there and back by a social worker, holding on to what pride and dignity was left to them by having their hair "done."

Janice was in the far corner with the green poster board and crepe paper, making her St. Patrick's Day decorations. I made my way to her side, leaned against a stand bearing wigs and wiglets, and engaged her in conversation, in the course of which I recalled her reference to the motel on Sixty-four and Carl, the night clerk who worked there.

"Oh, sure," she said. "Carl Hauser, I know him for years. The families were neighbors."

"I need a favor, Janice."

"Yeah, what?"

I stepped closer, looked conspirational, and lowered my voice.

"I have a friend," I said, borrowing freely from one of Janice's own soap operas, "who is separated from her husband and wants a divorce, which he will not give her. She also wants custody of the children, and if she can prove that he's—you know—fooling around—"

"Hey! That sounds just like 'Light in the Window'!"

"What's that?" I asked innocently.

"On television! A soap opera! How do you like that. And people say real life isn't like what they do on TV." She threw Anthony a dirty look—wasted, since his back was turned and he couldn't hear us.

"Well," I hurried on, "she has reason to believe he's been meeting someone at that motel, but she has no proof. And"—I hastened to add, "she can't afford to hire a detective. So I said I'd try to help." Janice's eyes were glued to my face, a streamer of green crepe paper hanging from one forgotten hand; at last she was inhabiting one of those glossy dramas from which her dreams were spun. I pressed the advantage. "If you could introduce me to your friend Carl—of course, all this has to be completely confidential, you understand. You can't tell him my real name. You could call me—Mrs. Lester."

"Lester," she said. "Yeah, I could do that. Sure." Then her sense of self-importance asserted itself. "Of course, I don't know how much information he's allowed to give out—he couldn't do anything that would get him in trouble—like he'd have to testify in court or something—"

"No, no! *I'm* going to be the witness," I said, throwing logic to the winds. "That is, if it comes to that. Probably all she'll have to do is threaten him with my testimony, and he won't contest anything."

Janice nodded. She knew all about this kind of machination.

"So you want me to call Carl and tell him I got this friend who has a friend who—"

"No. No, don't go into any details. Just ask if I could meet him somewhere later today—anytime after five, say. Just tell him this is a personal favor for a friend of yours who—um—who needs some confidential information—and his name will never be mentioned by me—not to anyone."

"Okay, I know what to tell him, don't you worry."

"Good. And I'll call you about four o'clock to see if you've managed to reach him. And Janice—I don't have to tell you how important it is to keep this strictly between you and me. And Carl, of course."

She nodded, her lips pursed with the gravity of the situation. "I just hope she gets plenty of alimony from that creep."

"Thanks." I had faith in her silence because I knew she would be willing to wait years for the eventual triumph of revealing her trusted role in this drama. I took one of Greenfield's ten-dollar bills from my bag and slid it into the pocket of her white smock.

"Oh, listen," she said in mild protest, but I held up

my hand and left, telling Anthony I'd see him on Friday. He was putting the second little old lady under a dryer, and she was smiling at him flirtatiously. Some habits die hard, and in this case more power to them.

My next errand was a bit more touchy, because it involved seeing Catherine and Victoria and possibly Elizabeth in the aftermath of Trager's jacket being found.

I was not going to call them in advance to ask if it was convenient for me to come over, because it was just possible they'd say it was *not* convenient, and that would throw the whole operation out the window.

I stopped at home, gave George a short lecture on the futility of trying to catch squirrels when you are on the ground and they are leaping from bough to bough, and picked up the mail. I opened it as I lunched on tuna fish and a pear. There was a bank statement, which for once agreed with the addition and subtraction in our checkbook. Also a letter from my mother who seemed put out by the fact that winter in Boston took so long to go away, and said there was no justice in a country where all the warm states were reserved for nonintellectuals. She had once driven the southern route from Palm Beach to Palm Springs and reported that except for the Santa Fe Opera, it was desert from coast to coast—three thousand miles of supposedly grown-up people who made a lifetime goal of preserving their suntans.

There was a strong wind blowing as I got back into the Honda, and the sky was growing sullen. Along Cliff Road I felt the wind buffeting the car, and when I turned in at the farm the entire orchard was inclining to the south, like a ballet company completing an ensemble arabesque. The oaks and maples around the house were tossing their empty branches restlessly and the dead grass rippled. With all this turbulence the place seemed alive with activity, but actually there was nothing going on; the horses were not even in their pasture.

I drove up to my accustomed space near the shed and parked. This time, around the corner of the barn, I saw the tail end of the gray, slat-sided truck. I scanned the area around the barn, but saw no sign of Andrew. Mr. Chanin, though, suddenly appeared, a small, distant figure, leaning into the wind, scarves flying. That crazy old man was battling a near gale, tottering back two steps for every one he took forward. Walking was all very well and good, I thought, important to the continued functioning of aging arteries and all that, but there are times when staying inside by the fire is more beneficial to an eighty-two-year-old man than—And even as I thought it, he collapsed in a heap on the ground.

I covered the distance between us at a speed that amazed me, but when I got there he was simply sitting on the cold ground, huffing and puffing and looking annoyed.

"Almost made it, damn it!" he gasped. "Only had a half mile to go!"

I stood between him and the wind. "You shouldn't do this!" I reprimanded, "in this kind of weather! That wind could blow down a *tree*, let alone—" I bent over and got hold of him as he struggled to get up.

"I'm perfectly fine!" he said crossly. "Perfectly fine! I walk in all kinds of weather. Always have. Got to get home now."

"You're going to come over to the house with me, and sit down for a while!" I steered him toward the house.

"No, No, I never imposed on that lady and I'm not going to do it now!"

I kept going, taking him with me. "Listen, you've given her enough trouble as it is. All winter she worries about you slipping and falling. If I go in there and tell her I let you go off home after you got knocked down by the wind—"

"I didn't get knocked down! I *sat* down! I was tired fighting that wind and I sat down! What do you mean, she worries about me?"

"She does, I tell you. That you'll have an accident one of these days, or get frostbite or something."

"She's a fine woman. Fine family. I like them all. Well—I don't know *him* too well—"

"Him?"

"The daughter's husband. Don't see him much. Saw him a few days ago, though. Practicing his golf."

"His *what?*"

"Looked like that to me. Behind the barn, practicing his golf shots."

"Behind the *barn?*"

"Swinging a club, anyway. Probably got a new club and he was trying it out, getting used to the weight of it. Must have been Saturday. He's not around during the week, so it must have been Saturday or Sunday. No, Sunday was raining, so it must have been Saturday." He stopped suddenly. "I'm not going in there. It wouldn't be right."

It took a lot of gentle and not-so-gentle persuasion before I finally got him to the back porch, where I knocked loudly on the door with my knuckles, there being nothing else available for the purpose. Catherine opened the door and stood there looking mildly astonished to see me, especially in the company of Mr. Chanin. I explained what had happened and she bundled Mr. Chanin into the living room and onto the sofa while he protested that he was perfectly fine and could only stay a minute. Victoria appeared and looked at him sternly and ordered him to put his feet up, and Catherine went to make him a cup of tea. I followed Catherine into the kitchen, which was small and had a brick floor and walls covered in lovely old delft tile, with a square scrubbed wooden worktable under a casement window. I sat on a rocker beside the table and watched Catherine. Yesterday's euphoria was gone, but she was still very calm for a woman whose husband's jacket had been washed ashore.

"I suppose you've heard—" she said, measuring tea into the teapot.

"Yes."

"I don't understand it. I just can't believe anything's happened to Julian. I know I'm flying in the face of reason, but I think I would *know* if something had happened, don't you. I always knew when something happened to Elizabeth. Once she fell in the playground at school and fractured her wrist. I was out in the woods, taking photographs, and I suddenly knew something was wrong. I ran home, and just as I came in the phone rang, and it was the school calling to tell me. Once she was at a summer camp in New Hampshire and I suddenly felt nervous and called up there, and she was in the infirmary with a fever. I always knew. And I don't feel anything now, so it's hard for me to believe—"

"Did anything unusual happen on Sunday? Did he get any strange calls—or visitors?"

"No. Well—there was that trouble with Andrew. It was all nonsense. Julian and Andrew don't get along, and I'm afraid Julian's always looking for reasons to get rid of him. He had a rather expensive notebook— Julian had—tooled Florentine leather—it was very old and beautiful—he had it fitted with notepaper and he used it sometimes to write down ideas that came to him. Well, it disappeared and he claimed Andrew had taken it—ridiculous, of course, what would Andrew want with a notebook?"

"Other than that, nothing happened over the weekend?"

"Nothing at all." She put the tea things on a tray and started out of the kitchen.

"Catherine—" She turned and looked at me inquiringly. There was no way to ask for what I wanted except to ask for it. "Could I have a picture of Julian?"

She looked at me for a long moment, with a small puzzled smile on her face. "Yes," she said uneasily, "but why?"

"It's just an idea I have, it probably won't come to anything—"

"An idea about Julian? How could you possibly know—?" She looked confused and anxious and I wished there'd been some way to take one of the photographs from her studio without her knowing about it. As it was, I had to wriggle out of the situation as best I could.

"You said you were in my debt," I reminded her, "which I don't believe for a minute, but I'm going to take advantage of it anyway and ask you to do me this favor without asking any questions."

"Well, of course, I'll—give you the picture."

She went back to the front room with the tea tray and left me with Victoria and Mr. Chanin while she went upstairs. Mr. Chanin was enjoying himself enormously, complaining about being treated like an invalid, insisting that he could outwalk an army of people twenty years his junior. Victoria paid no attention and plied him with tea and sugar and cream.

When Catherine came down she handed me a manila envelope. "That's the most useful one I have," she said. "It's full-length and full-face." I said thanks, thinking it was shrewd of her to guess the requirements, and wondered what speculations were going on behind the gray eyes. Victoria glanced at us with curiosity, but said nothing and was told nothing.

I was offered tea, of course, but pleaded an imminent appointment. At the door I asked about Elizabeth.

"She's at school," Catherine said. "She's anxious but she doesn't seem terribly upset." For the first time there was a dry, knowing tone to her voice. "Having Andrew back seems to eclipse all the rest."

The wind was howling across the fields as I made for the car, and the wood was alive with tossing trees. I drove away from the farm down Cliff Road and turned left for Dunstan Hill, and it occurred to me that if you went into the wood where it bordered the farm and continued eastward, you would eventually emerge in Dunstan Hill. Birnam Wood. Dunsinane. Ah. Will, how endlessly your imagery lends itself. I must tell Barbara.

I pulled up at the Seberg house, climbed the slate steps, and rang the doorbell fearlessly, knowing that at this hour only the South American lady would be there. She opened the door a crack, on the chain, a smooth, round Italian mask peering out through opaque black eyes.

"Jess?"

"I'm Mrs. Rome—from the newspaper—I was here the other day—"

"Ah. jess." She recognized me. took off the chain, and held the door open. "Mrs. Seberg not here now. She working in the city."

"Yes, I know. And I forgot to get a picture of her to print with the story. Is there a picture I could borrow? I'll bring it back tonight. A picture of the family would be nice. Mr. and Mrs. Seberg and the little girl?"

"Is some pictures, jess," she said hesitantly, then, reassured by my trustworthy countenance, led me past the living room and down a spiral stairway to what, in a less pretentious house, would be called a playroom. It was floored with terrazzo, sprinkled with polka-dotted couches, and boasted six stereo speakers, a pair of sliding glass doors, looking onto a patio, and an enormous bar backed by a three-paneled mirror, the center panel of which as my South American guide was only too pleased to show me, slid open to reveal the largest possible television screen. On the bar top, along with the decanters, were three framed photographs, one of an elderly couple looking very tanned, affluent, and discontented, one of young Jennifer taken in a studio, with all but a halo around her head, and, happily, one of Sidonie and her husband taken in a nightclub—Sidonie exuding languor and importance, her husband full of false bonhomie.

I asked permission to slide this last photograph out of its frame, assured her again that I would return it that evening, and put it in the envelope with the picture of Trager.

It was almost four by the time I got home. I called Francine's and Janice answered.

"Hel-lo-oh," she said, hitting a G, a C, and an A all in one word.

"It's Mrs. Rome, Janice."

"Oh. Yeah." Her voice dropped to the conspiratorial level. "I—uh—spoke to the person we were talking about—and-uh—he says okay, only he starts working six o'clock, so he'll meet you up there five-thirty."

"Up where?"

"At the . . . at the place. Where he works."

"At the motel."

"Right. He says in the coffee shop there."

"What does he look like?"

"Mm—well, he's kind of blond—well, dirty blond. And skinny."

"Tall? Short?"

"Medium. And he wears tinted glasses—not sunglasses, just tinted. That's because he has this eye condition, ever since he was a kid. First they kept giving him all these different drops to—"

"I see. Good. Thanks again, Janice. My friend is very grateful to you. Remember—you don't know anything about this."

"Oh, listen, don't worry about that," she said.

I had just over an hour before I had to set out for the motel, and I could either spend it running the vacuum cleaner around the house or tackling the last movement of the Beethoven. I set my preference aside in favor of a little exercise, assembled the various parts of the vacuum cleaner, and went to work.

At five ten I left the house, if not spic and span, at least span, and drove out of Sloan's Ford and up the Gorham road. The wind had blown the sky clear and the last disappearing edge of sun streaked the horizon. After about five minutes the northbound traffic began to slow perceptibly, and the reason soon became evident.

There was a small crowd gathered on the riverbank where the Mercedes had stood. No Mercedes now, only patrol cars and police uniforms, and a man in a gray overcoat. One of the cops was standing at the edge of the road furiously and vainly trying to get the gawkers and gapers to keep moving. We crawled by at such a tortoise pace that I had ample time to figure out what they were doing. They were dragging the river.

Dragging the river.

Much as I could have lived contentedly without ever again setting eyes on Julian Trager, I desperately did not wish him at the bottom of that river in the cold wet mud. The light was beginning to fade and I peered intently at the group on the riverbank, trying to reassure myself that they hadn't come up with anything. I saw the man in the gray overcoat (Pratt? Bratt?) turn wearily away from the river, and in answer to some question from an officer closer to the road, shake his head.

At the same time the group began to disperse, and the men handling the equipment seemed to be packing it up. Nothing. They'd found nothing. I let out my breath, and only then realized I'd been holding it.

I arrived at the Wayside Motel, obviously named by a man with unlimited imagination, at five twenty-eight, parked in the parking lot, and went in search of the coffee shop. The motel was a dreary establishment, everything about it looking a little grimy and soiled, including the coffee shop with its flyblown Danish pastries on smudged glass shelves, and stools on which the leatherette was cracking. There was a sulky young waitress behind the counter slapping halfheartedly at the sandwich board with a wet rag, and a stout middle-aged man on one of the stools eating Boston cream pie. A tense couple in jeans were holding a muttered conversation in one of the booths, and in another—ah! I would have known him anywhere. Skinny, with dirty blond hair, tinted glasses. My hero.

I went up to the booth. "Mr. Hauser?" It always pays to treat younger people with respect.

He half stood up and cleared his throat nervously.

"Mrs.—Mrs." He'd forgotten the name and for a minute I couldn't remember what I'd told Janice, then it came to me.

"Lester," I said, and slid into the seat opposite him.

"Hi," he said lamely, and sat down again.

I smiled encouragingly into his tinted glasses and then an awful thought crossed my mind. "Those are nice glasses," I said. "Those tinted glasses are becoming quite popular now."

"He reached up nervously and pulled them off. Naked, his eyes looked normal, if undistinguished. "I don't really need them when it gets dark."

"Oh, I thought they were just ordinary glasses. Are they special?"

"Yes. I mean no, the glasses aren't. But I have to wear them in the daylight. I have sensitive eyes."

"Oh, I'm sorry. Does it affect your vision?"

"No, no. No. it doesn't. I have good vision. As long as I'm not in a strong light."

"It's lucky you're on the night shift."

"What? Oh. Yes. Um—would you like some coffee or something?"

"No thanks. Car—Mr. Hauser, I need some information. It's terriby important, and if you can help me, I give you my word your name will never be mentioned."

"Yes. Okay. Janice said it was okay." He looked around nervously. No one was paying the slightest attention to us. The glum waitress was yawning, the middle-aged man was belching politely, the tense couple in the booth were still tense. "What—what kind of information?"

I took the picture of Julian Trager from the envelope.

"Have you ever seen this man?"

He looked at the picture and his answer came promptly. "Yes," he said, and put it down.

I wasn't really ready for that. Somehow I'd expected this to be just an impersonal exercise in investigation, nothing real involving answers which might have repercussions. I was prepared only for negative results which would serve the purpose of eliminating another of Greenfield's theories. But here I was, after only two minutes, with positive identification. Now what?

"Um—when—when was the last time you saw him?"

"Last week. I think it was last week. Yes, about a week ago."

"He came into the motel?"

"Yes. To register."

"Was anyone with him?"

"No. There usually isn't, in these—they wait in the car."

"Who does?"

He cleared his throat again and said, "The women."

Terrific. It was almost pointless to show him a picture of Sidonie, but since she wasn't the only one in the picture, I pulled it out.

"How about these people?"

He studied it for a moment. "This one," he said finally. "I've seen this one. But not that one."

The one he'd seen was Sidonie!

"You saw *her?* I thought you said—" No, no leading questions. "Where did you see her?"

"She came into the lobby to get cigarettes from the machine. She needed change."

"When was this?"

"I don't know—last week sometime."

"The same night the other man came in to register?"

He thought about it and then he nodded and smiled reminiscently. He had very bad teeth. "That's right. It was the same night. Because the cashier was out sick and when he paid the bill I had to take care of it, and when she needed change I had to give it to her, and I don't usually handle the money."

It was becoming a little stuffy in the coffee shop. Harder to breathe.

"If the cashier was out sick, you could check and find out exactly which night it was?"

"That's right. That's right. I didn't think of that. Sure. I don't have to check. If I'd remembered about the cashier I could have told you right off the bat. It was last Tuesday night."

Last Tuesday night! I could hardly breathe at all. I grabbed his glass of water and took a swallow.

"What time? Do you remember what time?"

"Well, it was right after I came on the desk that *he* showed up. So it must have been six ten, six fifteen."

"And the woman? What time did she come in for the cigarettes?"

"About—well, about an hour later."

"What did she do after she got the cigarettes?"

"Went out to the car, I guess. I heard a car start up outside the front door and drive away."

"What kind of car?"

"I didn't see."

One hour. Quick and efficient. When there's no love involved, time is of the essence.

"But you never saw this other man?"

"No."

"You're sure."

"He could've been here sometime when I wasn't on the desk."

"When do you go off?"

"Two A.M."

Well, it was possible, I supposed, that Marshall Seberg had arrived after two and left at seven to meet Trager—or intercept him—on the Gorham road. But possible and provable are worlds apart. There was no point in looking at the register, no one ever signs his own name in a motel such as this. There was one other possible explanation.

"Which is your day off?"

"Usually Monday. But once a month I get a Saturday or Sunday. My last one was Sunday."

Goodbye and good luck. I reached in my bag, took out Greenfield's second ten-dollar bill, added another ten to it because Greenfield had not kept up with inflation, and handed them to Carl Hauser.

"Mr. Hauser, I'm very grateful to you."

"Oh, thanks very much." He looked quickly around to make sure no one had seen him taking the money.

"And please don't worry, you won't get into any trouble over this—you can just forget all about it."

"Yes. Sure. That's okay."

I put the pictures back into the envelope, slid out of the seat, gave him a smile and a wave of the hand, and left, past the waitress who was leaning her elbows on the counter, her chin cupped in her hands, as she listened empty-eyed to something the middle-aged man was telling. In the booth, the tense couple were no longer talking. She was looking out the darkened window at nothing, and he was looking down at the ashtray into which he was shredding a cigarette.

I drove back to Dunstan Hill. Jennifer opened the door with one hand; the thumb of the other was in her mouth. She was an odd little girl with a narrow face, large restless eyes, a runny nose, and a furtive air. I smiled at her and said hello, but she only stared, breathing quickly and shallowly. Unexpectedly I felt tears pricking my eyes. It was a relief when the South American woman came bustling up. I handed her the photograph.

"Please apologize to Mrs. Seberg for me. I was too late to get the picture into the paper."

"Too late, Jess." She looked at me with disapproval.

"And thank you. I'm sorry I put you to so much trouble."

"Thass all right."

To my horror, Jennifer suddenly screamed. A long, wailing scream. The woman quickly shut the door.

I stumbled down the stairs, feeling a little sick. I hate to admit it, but under stress, like most people, I tend to think in clichés. Dear God, I thought, where are we going? How will it all end? And I wasn't thinking only of Sidonie and Trager and Peter and the events of the past week. I was thinking of the whole bloody mess.

◙ 12

I noticed, next morning, that quite a few people rolling the carts up and down the aisles in the supermarket had smudges on their foreheads. It was Ash Wednesday. The beginning of Lent. A time of sacrifice. I wondered just who and what, in my circle of acquaintance, was going to be sacrificed.

I hadn't called Greenfield the night before to give him the results of my inquiry, since the Tuesday-night deadline was enough of a headache for him without an additional problem to contemplate. In fact, I didn't intend to tell him about it until he arrived for dinner that night. If he called and asked, fine, otherwise I had work to do. A meeting of the Ad Hoc Citizens' Committee was scheduled for that afternoon, and I was supposed to cover it. I was also planning paella for that night's dinner, and that took time to prepare.

I had just deposited my grocery bag of chicken, shrimp, olives, pimientos and assorted accessories on the kitchen table, when the doorbell rang. There was a short, trim little woman standing there with a practiced smile on her face and an armful of leaflets.

"Hello, I'm Harriet Fraser," she announced. "I'm running for the school board and I'd like to leave some literature with you."

"The school board! I almost forgot about it! Isn't there some kind of meeting next week? Come in, come in."

She stepped daintily over the threshold and I shut the door.

"Yes, we're having the usual meet-the-candidates meeting next Tuesday night," she said. "Coffee and cake."

"Tuesday night, right. I have it written down somewhere. I'm supposed to cover it for the *Reporter*. Stewart Klein usually does it, but he's got theatre tickets and I volunteered. I was going to call someone about it, but you can fill me in." I picked up pen and pad from beside the telephone. "The names of the other candidates, first of all. I know Miles and Russell still have a year to go and there are two seats vacated. Who else is running?"

"Jean Otis, Gordon Oliver—"

"Gordon!" I said delightedly. "He didn't tell me!"

"—and there was someone else, but he seems to be out of the picture now. Julian Trager."

I stared down at the pad over which my pen was poised, and sighed deeply and wearily. Was there no end to Trager's tentacles?

"The committee tried to get in touch with him," Mrs. Fraser went on, "but they were told he was out of town and there was no way of telling when he'd be back. It wasn't very considerate of him not to let the committee know he was going away. But then, he's a bit of a boor. I probably shouldn't say that, but it's not exactly a secret. Someone told me that Gordon Oliver tried to have Trager's name struck from the voting list."

"Is that so," I murmured.

"Anyway, the problem solved itself, because he seems to have gone away for an indefinite period."

"Mmm."

"What else can I help you with?"

I struggled back to the present, asked a few more questions made a few notes, and ushered Harriet Fraser out. promising to read every word of the literature she'd left me.

While I unpacked the groceries and made the initial preparations for the paella, and later while I partook of sardines on toast and an apple, I thought about Gordon's probable reaction to the idea that Trager might be elected to the school board. I imagined his cold fury at the thought that Trager might be in a position to influence the reading habits of schoolchildren, his calm, implacable determination to keep it from happening. I imagined him calling Trager to arrange a meeting. (On what pretext? Never mind, he'd fine one.) I imagined his rational, perfectly planned handling of the whole project, including arranging for it to look like a mugging, even including leaving the car there to attract police attention. It was not in the least unbelievable. Except for one thing—the angle iron. I just could not see Gordon wielding an angle iron.

All through the meeting of the Ad Hoc Citizens' Committee, while I listened with one ear and made notes which I could not later remember having heard or taken, I worried at bits and pieces of the puzzle: Victoria's reaction to the disappearance, and Catherine's, the jacket being washed up, the wallet on the ground, the Kittells just happening to come along, Andrew returning to the farm, round and round. . . . When I finally wrote up the article on the committee meeting, it was, to take a very tolerant view, sketchy. The paella, however, was pretty good.

It wasn't until I had dished it out that I had the opportunity to bring Greenfield up to date on the Trager affair. He had arrived more or less on time, but with a large, flat package which he unwrapped silently, standing next to the record changer, where he removed my stack of Haydn, Chopin, and Victoria de los Angeles's *Songs of the Auvergne*, and substituted the contents of the package. Then, with our respective bourbon and sherry in hand, and a monitory gesture from Greenfield, we listened, in silence.

The music that filled the room was classic, graceful nineteenth-century lyricism alternating with long-drawn-out crescendos of staggering suspense in which what sounded like a zillion strings of the Amsterdam Concertgebouw, playing as one, soared and soared and kept soaring into the air like a musical version of one gigantic layered fountain, while you held your breath waiting and wondering if it would ever subside. It was pretty exciting. When it was over, Greenfield stood up, with a complacent smirk.

"That," he said, "is the Bruckner Opus Zero." He

took the disc from the machine, returned it to its jacket, and handed it to me. "For you."

And we went in to dinner.

As we ate I told him about Janice and my improvised soap opera, my visit to the farm, my rescue of Mr. Chanin, Catherine's stubborn refusal to believe that anything had "happened" to her husband, my acquisition of Trager's and Mr. and Mrs. Seberg's photographs, and finally, for both literal and figurative dessert, my meeting with Carl Hauser.

"So," I concluded, "you were on target. Yet again. Sidonie and Trager were there Tuesday evening. And the times are right. But it still doesn't prove any of the other things I assume you're thinking. And if you want evidence that Marshall Seberg was at that motel checking on his wife sometime between midnight and dawn, Sunday to Monday, I'll have to wangle an introduction to the deskman who replaced Carl Hauser that night, and do the whole thing over again."

"He had to be there," Greenfield said, helping himself to more apple crisp. "Unless he was making a stab in the dark, or unless we're talking about the kind of woman who has these little rendezvous at a different spot each day on her lunch break—and from what you tell me I don't think she has the panache for that—then this is the 'hangout' he was referring to. She'd probably also been there with Trager at sometime when Mr. Hauser's replacement was on duty."

"That's possible. What I don't see as possible is Seberg's arriving at Trager as the villain in the first place."

"Conceivably he bribed the man for a description of his wife's partner, and recognized the description."

"That's what I mean—how could he do that? Trager doesn't have a saber scar across his cheek. His description could fit half a million men."

Greenfield held out his cup for more coffee with a certain smugness. "It's possible he already suspected it was Trager, having seen the attraction blossoming. Seberg is Trager's agent."

I opened my mouth and it stayed open.

"It was an idea," he said modestly. "I confirmed it by calling Creative Talent International."

I closed my mouth, watched Greenfield enjoying his apple crisp, and wondered if there was a course you could take to overcome slow-wittedness. His agent. Of course.

"And she had the bloody chutzpah to say she'd never met him!" I sipped too-hot coffee and burned my tongue. "Okay, so he calls Trager from the motel and says—what? 'I just sold your new book to United Artists, sight unseen, come to the Wayside Motel immediately and sign the contract'? And then he lies in wait on the verge of the Gorham road, knowing, naturally, that Trager drives a pale gray Mercedes, and flags him down—?"

"You have a tendency, at times," Greenfield murmured, leaning back in his chair, replete, "to be frivolous. I don't know how—or even if—he lured Trager to the Gorham road. But if I were asked to hazard a guess, I'd try to come up with something a little more plausible."

"Such as?"

"Sending a note, signed with his wife's name, indicating there was a matter of great urgency to discuss—"

"At dawn?"

"She'd want to be in her office at the usual time. A careful woman, Mrs. Seberg, and her husband would be aware of that, and use it."

"And what could be so urgent that a self-centered, self-indulgent misogynist—" Greenfield raised his beetling brows—"Of *course* he is, Charlie. The more he sleeps around the more he proves it. What could be so critical that such a man would jump when she said jump, and speed to her side in the early dark?"

"If you haven't worked that out," Greenfield sighed, getting up, "you don't deserve to know." He picked up his coffee cup and moved at a leisurely pace to the living room. I followed.

"Oh, fine," I said, "that makes all this extracurricular intrigue really worthwhile, being treated with such respect and consideration."

Greenfield helped himself to a pistachio from the pewter bowl on the lamp table and settled comfortably into the big armchair.

"I think I've adequately demonstrated my respect for you," he said, "in innumerable ways." I tried to think of one and couldn't. "This is for your own good. If I go on spoon-feeding you, how are you ever going to learn to think for yourself?"

"There's a school of thought that considers benevolent paternalism a little sick. Anyway, nothing we've found out proves anything."

"True."

"That's all you have to say? No new schemes, plots, stratagems, conspiracies—?"

"I'm waiting."

"For what?"

"Oh, that's right. You haven't read the paper."

There was only one "the paper" in our world. "How could I? You're the one who brings me my copy."

He got up, went to the hallway, took a copy of the paper from his coat pocket and brought it back.

"I took the liberty," he said, handing it to me, "of adding a postscript to your profile piece."

I found the page, and the postscript, which was signed "Editor." It read: "Mrs. Seberg's husband, Marshall Seberg, is the literary agent for the noted author Julian Trager, resident of Sloan's Ford. The Sloan's Ford police have been investigating Mr. Trager's disappearance since Monday morning. By an odd coincidence, as this paper recently ascertained, Mr. Seberg was also missing from his home for the ten hours preceding the discovery of Mr. Trager's abandoned automobile. By Monday night Mr. Seberg had returned. Mr. Trager, however, remains undiscovered."

I looked up at Greenfield. "I don't believe you did this! I don't—you *know* you can't print a thing like this. How could you do it? It's practically libelous!"

"Not a word of a lie."

"You know what I mean—insinuation—innuendo—whatever you call it! And nowhere in the paper is there any other mention of Trager. You drop this little bomb in a corner at the bottom of page four, with no explanation, no story—my God, how could you do this to those people at the farm! And the police will be—"

"And you," Greenfield interrupted taking a deep breath and shaking his head, "talk about lack of respect. There are exactly three copies of that. One was delivered to the Sebergs. Mine is at home. That one is yours. Barney yelled, of course—overtime, and so on—but he finally did it for me." I subsided. He leaned back and looked at me through half-shut eyes. "I don't have that many tools to work with. I have to use what's at hand. I'm not the police. I could go to them—and probably should—but you wouldn't want Pratt or Bratt walking all over Mrs. Trager's sensibilities with his big feet."

"When the Sebergs read this," I said, "they'll probably go running to the police anyway."

"More likely Mr. Seberg will come running to me, irate and vengeful. And, with luck, say something incriminating."

George suddenly got up and ran to the door, his radar working, and sure enough, the doorbell rang. Greenfield and I stared at each other, neither of us moving. A good half-minute ticked away and the doorbell rang again. George barked. I got up and went out to the hallway and opened the door.

It was Barbara.

"I'm escaping," she said, stumbling in, clutching her coat around her, face drawn, nose pink with cold, hair every which way under a wool scarf. "All hell is going on at the house. Stereo, rock, telephone ringing, doors slamming, Greg and Amy arguing over the dish—"

She saw Greenfield and stopped.

"Give me your coat."

"I forgot," she whispered, "I forgot it was Wednesday."

"Come on, I'll get you some coffee."

"No. No, I don't want to barge in, it's—"

"Give me your coat or the whole friendship is off."

"I can't! Look at me! Are you kidding?" She protested, but I got the coat and prodded her into the living room.

She and Greenfield exchanged amenities. I searched vainly for a spark between them; to my mind they couldn't do much better than each other, but then, chemistry was never my strong point. I often wondered what solution, if any, Greenfield had found for his solitary bed, and assumed that somewhere he had a quiet little woman with whom he found physical comfort, but if so, she was apparently a small and separate part of his life and not the type to share his major interests. Where he and Barbara were concerned, I was beginning to resign myself to failure.

I brought in a fresh pot of coffee and some biscuits while Barbara conscientiously made conversation about her courses at law school and Greenfield politely asked the right questions.

"Then there's the real property course—" she was saying.

"*Real* property?" I put in. "As opposed to what? Imagined."

"Real property relates to land as opposed to—I don't know—jewelry or things like that. The land, what grows on the land, what's built on the land—anything you can't move around. Also—wait a minute, I think I actually remember a definition, would you believe it? 'Property which, on the death of the owner intestate, passes to the heir.' Maybe. If I remembered it right."

Greenfield was listening to her with that glazed expression people get when suppressing a yawn. I could have kicked him. Barbara sighed, took a sip of coffee, and continued bravely.

"I can't believe this is *law* I'm studying. I always thought law had to do with justice and wisdom. All it has to do with is *winning*. Beating the other guy to the draw. We might as well be back in the Dodge City saloons."

"A lawyer's relationship to justice and wisdom," Greenfield observed, "is on a par with a piano tuner's relationship to a concert. He neither composes the music, nor interprets it—he merely keeps the machinery running."

We went on for a while discussing the deficiencies of the judicial system until Barbara suddenly jumped up and said, "I just had an intuition the kids are setting the house on fire," and insisted on leaving. When I'd seen her out and gone back to the living room. Greenfield was at the cabinet examining my collection of recordings.

"You're a real charmer," I told him, gathering up the coffee things. "You really make an effort."

He looked at me, injured. "I thought I behaved in a civilized manner."

The telephone rang.

I carried the tray out to the hall and picked up the receiver. Sidonie's voice was so bass-baritone I thought at first it was Orson Welles.

"What is *this* all about?" she spat. "What are you, some kind of slimy little *spy*?"

"If you mean the editor's note, you'll have to ask the editor. I had nothing to do with that."

"And where do I reach this stinking little editor? Give me his number!"

I hesitated. "Hold on a minute." I went back to the living room. "There's a contract out on you," I said. "Madam Capo wants to know where she can find you."

Greenfield looked as pleased as he ever could. "Tell her."

I went back to the phone. "He happens to be here. Do you want me to put him on?"

"You're damn right I—" A background voice interrupted. Tenor. There were a few moments of acrimonious bickering, then she demanded, "Where do you live?"

I gave her the address.

"You keep him there!" she hissed, and hung up.

For the next ten minutes, while I cleaned up the remains of dinner and tried not to be nervous, Greenfield sat calmly in the big armchair, pulling at George's ears and listening to some pieces by Satie. I was stacking the dishwasher when the doorbell rang, and a fork dropped from my fingers down between the rubber grating and into the machine—another black mark against the Sebergs.

It was Marshall, solo, red in the face and carrying a copy of the *Reporter*. He marched past me and into the living room as though my house were a public building, and confronted Greenfield, who looked up at him mildly from the depths of the armchair.

"You the editor of this dishrag?" he squeaked. Greenfield nodded. "You looking to be sued?"

"What for?"

"Invasion of privacy, for one thing! Character assassination! Defamatory—"

"Please sit down," Greenfield commanded.

Seberg glared at him, and then, surprisingly, sat.

"Was I mistaken in printing that you are Mr. Trager's literary agent?"

"Certainly I am! That doesn't make me responsible for his behavior! If he decides to walk out on his wife—"

"*What*?" That was me.

"Why do you assume anything! From this garbage you printed it sounds like he was kidnapped or murdered or God knows what, and it strongly insinuates that *I* am somehow involved! If you—"

"You're very concerned about yourself, Mr. Seberg, but remarkably sanguine about your client. Perhaps you know something the police don't."

"I don't even know the police are *concerned* except that you say so!"

"They are."

"All I know is his wife called the office on Monday and again yesterday, to see if he'd been there. When a wife starts calling around to find her husband—"

"*Had* Mr. Trager been there?"

"I'm not here to answer questions! I'm—"

"Then you *had* seen him?"

"How the hell could I have seen him! I was in Washington! I have a goddamn playwright in big trouble down there! They're threatening to close the show on the road! I had to massage his goddamn ego from Sunday afternoon to Monday afternoon with no sleep!"

Greenfield looked long and carefully at Seberg and Seberg pugnaciously stared back.

"I'm sorry to hear that," Greenfield said, ambiguously. "What play is this?"

"*The Gaming Table!* The playwright is Michael Zandra! It's at the Kennedy Center! I took a four-thirty flight out of LaGuardia on Sunday and a two-thirty flight out of Dulles on Monday! I was in my office all day yesterday and today, and I have not seen Trager! Anything else you want to check up on? Who the hell are you, anyway? What's all this about Trager, and why should *you* be interested? And what are you going to do about *this*?" He rattled the paper at Greenfield.

"You can forget about that." Greenfield stood up. "No one else has seen that paragraph and they won't. It was a very limited edition." He shrugged. "A ploy, and it worked. I apologize."

"A *ploy*? A ploy, that's just fine! What gives you the right—"

"I apologize, Mr. Seberg. Please, I think we've imposed long enough on Mrs. Rome's hospitality."

Seberg aimed his vindictive chinless face at me. "If that's all Mrs. Rome pays for her snooping, she's getting off easy! I want some answers! I want to know—"

"I can't tell you anything more, Mr. Seberg. It wouldn't be in my interest, or yours. If Mr. Trager has been in serious trouble, you'll hear about it soon enough. In the meantime, if you resent being questioned by me, think what it would be like with the police, and keep this episode to yourself." Greenfield's gentle voice and bland expression managed to suggest a variety of unpleasant consequences, should Marshall Seberg decide to blab it around.

Suddenly Seberg's manner changed. He slipped without effort into the smooth, hollow sincerity of the archagent.

"No, seriously, if something's happened to Trager, naturally I'm deeply concerned—"

"Good night, Mr. Seberg. Thank you for coming."

Seberg continued to stare at Greenfield, drawing in such a long, deep breath that I thought he would rise into the air like a balloon and get stuck to the ceiling.

But he turned abruptly, without another word, and marched out. When he slammed the door behind him, he nearly caught George's nose in it, and George, through the closed door, gave him a good piece of his mind.

Greenfield slowly picked up another pistachio. "He's too shrewd to tell me anything I couldn't verify," he grumbled.

"Ah, well, another day, another perfectly good suspect down the drain. Now what?"

He wandered disconsolately to the hallway and took his coat from the hanger. "We'll just have to look elsewhere."

I thought about the alternatives and said, reluctantly, "Oh, yes, there's something I forgot to tell you."

He stopped with one coat sleeve on and the other arm raised.

I told him about Mrs. Fraser's visit and the school board election and Gordon Oliver's attempt to have Trager's name struck from the voting list.

"I knew that," he said shortly, pushing his arm through the second sleeve, then looked at me again. "I very sincerely hope you're not suggesting Gordon as a suspect."

I summoned all the defiance I could muster, which wasn't much, and said, "Why not?"

He looked grim. *"Need . . . you . . . ask!"*

"I take it your answer is the same one I gave you when you asked me why I refused to be suspicious of Victoria Hollis."

"Ha!" He went to the door. "Do you know how many *years* I've known Gordon? And since you mention Mrs. Hollis—there are a good many questions still unanswered in that direction!"

But he looked nervous, and I was beginning to wonder what kind of toll this investigation was taking.

"Look," I ventured, "since you know in your heart—or wherever you keep your convictions—that the Kittells are blameless, why don't we just let time take care of it? They can't charge the Kittells without evidence, and there isn't any of that, and sooner or later the truth will come out, so why don't we just wait?"

In the time-honored tradition, he answered my question with a question.

"Have you ever been under suspicion?"

And let himself out.

◨ 13

Thursday was a dark, glowering, gusty day, the sky like a purple bruise, leafless trees tossing and creaking, a day reminiscent of the Bronte moors, Wuthering Heights, Heathcliff. And that day there were several events of considerable interest.

The first was that the police had learned from Farnham about Andrew's purchase of fence posts, and Pratt or Bratt had finally found time to go up to the farm and question him, throwing everyone there into a state of restrained anxiety. This I learned from Catherine, who appeared on my doorstep, a windtorn waif against the sullen sky, to ask if I thought it was possible that Andrew could have struck Julian with a fence post and dropped him in the river. (She didn't put it quite that graphically.)

The reason she was asking my opinion, I gathered, was that I was the one who'd suggested Andrew was harboring a secret desire for her, and she assumed I had a key to his character that no one else had. The best I could do was to assure her that it would send me into a severe depression to think Andrew would do a thing like that, and since I was clearly not depressed, that was a good sign.

I noticed she was no longer rejecting the idea that something had happened to Julian. On a day like this, I thought, all terrible things were possible.

I asked her if Andrew had told the police where he'd been between Sunday and Monday, and she said, yes, he'd gone to the Wayside Motel on the Gorham road and stayed there overnight.

At which point I went immediately into the kitchen

to brew some tea and keep her from seeing my face, which I'm sure spelled DISMAY in foot-high letters.

By the time she left, I'd gone into the aforementioned depression.

The second event was Greenfield's visit to the farm.

I'd called him, of course, to report the latest development, which he received in a silence so full of mental activity that I all but heard the vibrations over the phone.

Then he said, "I have to speak to this Andrew. Call Mrs. Hollis and arrange it."

I shook my head in awe at this bland assumption of monarchial privilege. Henry the Eighth couldn't have done it better.

"I'll do that, Charlie, and while I'm at it, I'll get us an invitation to share the balcony with the Pope on Easter Sunday."

"No cheap sarcasm, please, this is imperative."

"They've had a rough few days up there, you know. Don't you think it's a little gauche to suggest a social visit?"

"Why suggest that? Tell her the truth. I'm trying to clear the Kittells of suspicion and I need information."

"Great. And she'll say why are the Kittells suspected, and I'll say because Mrs. Kittell thinks Julian was the hit-and-run driver who knocked down her boy, and she'll say how did she get *that* idea, and—"

"Yes, yes, all right."

Another silence. Then, "You, as a friend of the family, are greatly disturbed by the strain to which they are being subjected, particularly now that a man they trust and depend on has come under suspicion. You are convinced of Andrew's innocence and I respect your judgment and have, to a certain extent, the ear of the police. And since I was responsible for sending you to the farm in the first place, I'd like to help clear Andrew. That should do it."

"If," I said, "Victoria is so upset that she's not thinking straight."

Evidently she was upset, because an hour later we were on our way. Greenfield drove, in his usual imperial fashion, down River Road, up the hill, and along

Cliff Road, with the wind buffeting the car from all directions.

"You're not going to see this place in its best light," I told him. "To get the full impact it really should be viewed in serene sunlight."

"It's meant to be a painting?" he suggested dryly. "Or one of Catherine's photographs, caught like a fly in amber, fixed in time, impervious to the brutal onslaughts of real life?"

"See? It's got to you already. Just anticipating it has got you waxing poetic. Turn to the right by those evergreens."

He turned and the farm came into view, crouching under the bruised sky, the orchard groaning, the trees in the wood dark and restless, the meadows cobalt in the lurid light, a brooding, Mephistophelian landscape.

"Night on Bald Mountain," Greenfield muttered.

I opened the gate for him to drive through and it whined on its hinges—it had never whined before. When he was through I closed it and got back into the car, having come to a decision about something I'd been debating all the way to the farm.

"There's something I didn't tell you—" I began.

"There usually is." He was a man resigned to duplicity in his hirelings.

"About Andrew. It was a very private matter. And anyway only conjecture. And I wasn't sure I had the right to pass it on. But now—"

"If you put it off much longer, we'll *be* there."

I told him about the camera portrait Catherine had done of Andrew in which he seemed to display more than a passing interest in the photographer. "Evidently," I added, "Catherine was oblivious. She had no idea what I was talking about, and when I explained she just about exploded with indignation. She has very firm convictions about the sanctity of marriage. If she found out about Sidonie at two P.M. she'd start divorce proceedings at two-oh-five."

"Or find some other solution?"

I flashed a baleful look in his direction. "She doesn't know about it. I'd know if she did."

"Mmm. So it's possible Andrew had more than one score to settle with Trager."

"Possible," I agreed, "but far from proven."

We reached the house and parked the car, Greenfield's eyes darting hither and yon, taking in all the details of VW and station wagon and shed and barn, and we went to the front door and used the brass knocker.

Catherine opened the door. She gave me a wan smile, greeted Greenfield with a mixture of nervousness, courtesy, and abstraction, took us into the apple-green room, and left us there while she went to get Victoria. Greenfield was very busy taking in the room, and then he saw the cabinet with the viola in it and made for it like a homing pigeon. I remembered I'd brought with me the photograph of Trager I'd borrowed from Catherine, ran upstairs to give it to her, didn't see her, left it in the studio, and went down again. Greenfield was still standing there, staring at the cabinet, deeply in love, when Victoria came in.

The meeting between Victoria Hollis and Greenfield should someday take its place alongside such historic encounters as those between Churchill and Roosevelt or Caesar and Cleopatra; two champion persuaders, each taking the other's measure while exchanging amenities, recognizing each other's expertise, eyeing each other with respect, and jockeying for strategically advantageous ground.

"I admire your newspaper."

"Thank you. I admire your house. In particular that cabinet. I'm thinking of having one built for my cello."

"I can give you the name of a very good man."

"I'd appreciate that."

"You wanted to see Andrew. You didn't need my permission for that."

"I don't like to trespass, Mrs. Hollis. This is your house and Andrew is in your employ."

"He also lives here. Or rather, over the barn. We don't issue passes to his visitors."

"Does he have many?"

"He's never had *any*, until today."

"The police were here."

"They were." The tone said everything. "I hadn't

known about the business of Andrew buying the fence posts. The bill doesn't come until the first of the month—and naturally I didn't know there was one missing. But Andrew wouldn't normally come to me about something like that. He simply took care of the problem. That's what he's paid for, and he does it very well." She looked at Greenfield as though daring him to take her next words lightly. "Andrew is a rare young man. He has both integrity and common sense."

"And you can't imagine him compromising either of those qualities."

"Judge for yourself. You'll find him over at the barn. I've told him to expect you."

She came with us to the back porch and stood there while we crossed the stretch of ground to the barn. Passing the old stone well I had a feeling there was something different about it, but I couldn't think what. Greenfield stopped, intrigued, examined it, and inserted two fingers in the hole of the wooden cover to lift it.

"Mr. Greenfield!" Victoria's voice cut through the wind. We looked at the back porch and she shook her head. "Please don't touch it," she called, "the wood is rotten."

Greenfield nodded and we continued on. We found Andrew working on some bridle leather with rags and a tin of saddle soap. When he looked up and gave me his crooked smile I wanted to grab Greenfield's sleeve and hustle him out of there and tell him I didn't care if Andrew *had* done something to Trager, I didn't want to know about it, just leave him alone and let him adorn the world. Instead, I introduced them and stood by while Greenfield engaged him in a discussion of horse-breeding, horse genealogy, the mythical beauty of Arabian horses, and so on, until, in his own devious fashion, he arrived at the purpose of our visit.

"I understand you and Mr. Trager had an altercation over the horses."

Andrew suddenly looked sleepy. "Mr. Trager doesn't care for animals." Then a fleeting smile. "Likes to tell people he has horses, though. Country gentleman, you know."

"I thought the horses belonged to Mrs. Hollis."

"He treats the place as though he owns it."

"You don't like him."

"No reason to. He's a *small* man. I don't mean his size."

"He accused you of stealing something."

Andrew shook his head, not to deny it, simply amazed. "A notebook. Can you see me stealing his notebook? I don't like what he writes—why should I want to see his notes?"

"You've read his books?"

"One of them." One eyebrow rose in disdain.

"The notebook was valuable. An antique."

Andrew looked faintly amused, as though at a naïve observation by a child. "What would I do with it?"

"What did the police ask you?"

"Where I went when I left here on Sunday. I told them—I asked Mrs. Hollis if I could borrow the truck, I packed a few things, and I started out for Syracuse."

"Why Syracuse?"

"My sister lives there. She married a man from Syracuse. I was driving up the Gorham road, thinking about what happened here, and I began to feel I'd acted like a kid. It's true, he'd been getting to me for a long time, but even so I shouldn't have walked out on Mrs. Hollis until she'd found someone else to do the work around here. I decided I'd wait until he was gone to work the next day, and I'd come back and just stay out of his way and do my work until she found someone to replace me. So I pulled into that motel up there—"

"Any particular reason for choosing that one?"

Andrew pondered the question. "No," he said quietly, "just it was there."

"And you stayed the night?"

He nodded and smiled a rueful smile. "Didn't get much sleep. Some little—waitress—from the coffee shop—kept scratching at the door, asking to be let in."

I'll bet she did.

"And you let her in? I ask only because it could be helpful."

Andrew raised his dark eyes to Greenfield in surprise. "A silly, sloppy girl with dirty hair. I'm not that hard up."

"Did anyone see you leave in the morning?"

"The police asked me that. I don't know. Maybe. I paid in advance, so I didn't go back to the office. Didn't go back to that coffee shop either."

"What time did you leave?"

"About nine. I slept late—the scratching and whining kept me up until two or three."

"And coming back down the Gorham road, you didn't notice Mr. Trager's car on the riverbank?"

"I didn't come back that way. I went north, to get some breakfast in Gorham, then I cut across Eighty-seven and took the parkway down to the exit just south of the village and came up that way."

"What else did the police ask you about?"

"They asked about the angle iron, of course. I told them I bought two dozen, tied with a cord, left them in the barn. Saturday I cut the cord, counted them, and there were only twenty-three, so I went back to Farnham and told him. . . . Then they asked me something else." Andrew looked thoughtful and puzzled. "They asked if I knew a Mrs. Kittell."

Greenfield lowered his eyes to the barn floor and caught his upper lip in his teeth. Then, "And do you?"

"Nope. Do you?"

"Yes," Greenfield mumbled, "I know a Mrs. Kittell." He looked up. "Andrew, I'm sorry to have put you through this again. I don't know how much help I can be. I'd like to be able to get the police out of your hair, but I can't promise."

Andrew gave a minimal shrug. "I don't see what they can do to me. I haven't done anything."

When we emerged from the barn, we met Catherine heading for the meadow with her camera. She looked intent, but not particularly eager.

"I want to get that sky," she said without visible enthusiasm.

Greenfield asked her to convey his farewells to her mother, she thanked Greenfield for taking the trouble to come, I told her I would call her, and we went to the car, Greenfield mumbling about the thick-headed Pratt or Bratt trying to make out a case that Mrs. Kittell had enlisted Andrew's muscles for the job.

Getting into the car I looked back at the barn, and the field beyond it, where Catherine was struggling against the wind. It reminded me of Mr. Chanin, breasting the gale and falling to the ground. The scene came back to me vividly, and the dialogue that went with it. I slid quickly into the seat beside Greenfield.

"Out there," I said, pointing, "is where I picked up Mr. Chanin, and on the way to the house he said something about seeing Trager behind the barn on Saturday, swinging a golf club!" I waited for the significance of this to sink in. It took about two seconds.

"Oh, yes? A golf club? On that terrain? In February?"

"It's a good bet Mr. Chanin does not have all his vision."

"No doubt. Yes. It's possible."

"But why would Trager take the angle iron? And if he took it, how did it end up beside his car, with blood on it?"

Greenfield stared through the windshield at the barn, the field, Catherine focusing her camera in the distance, and said reflectively, "It's lunchtime."

At my suggestion we stopped at the Napoli for their exceptionally thick, chewy pizza and coffee. Crowded into a small booth, with the restaurant noises insulting his educated ears, Greenfield was physically and mentally restless.

"I need room to think," he complained. "There are too many arrows pointing in too many directions. Too many people with too many motives. We have to organize our information." And he went on, about separating the chaff from the wheat and the dross from the gold and so on, while we contended with our gooey shreds of mozzarella.

"To our knowledge," he ruminated, "there are seven people who have had—or thought they should have—confrontations with Trager in the past few weeks. Seberg, who certainly had a grievance, though there's no proof he knew about it. Mrs. Hollis, who had ample reason to dislike the man. Catherine, who has been a victim of his contemptuous bullying—oh, I know, she defends him against all comers, but in her secret heart she could very well—" He dropped that. "Elizabeth, who held him responsible for driving Andrew away. Andrew, of course, who evidently had more than one quarrel with Trager. Gordon—as you see, I'm being painfully objective—Gordon, who all but came to blows with him. And Mrs. Kittell, who believed he was responsible for what happened to her son. All of them but one could have been on the Gorham road in the early hours of Monday. Elizabeth can't drive a car, so unless she was an accomplice, it's difficult to place her at the scene . . ."

"Charlie! Elizabeth? Going at her father with a . . . you really are becoming—"

He ignored me. "The Kittells obviously were there, but not necessarily at the crucial time. Andrew was within a stone's throw of the place. Victoria claims that she and Catherine were asleep, but either one could have been there. Seberg has an alibi, which remains to be confirmed—and probably can be—though his own words about visiting his wife's 'hangout' are suggestive. We know where every one of them was—or says he or she was—except—" He paused and finished the last of his coffee.

"Except Gordon," I supplied.

He nodded funereally, picked up the check, and we made our way out to the car. As he unlocked the door on the passenger side (*never* did he leave the car unlocked), he said, "We might as well get it over with," and then remained silent all the way to Dunstan Hill and up the tortuous drive to the Olivers' house.

I don't know if he had any plan for finding out where Gordon had been at dawn on Monday without jeopardizing the friendship. *I* certainly didn't have one. As it turned out, the answer was only too clear.

Shirley came to the door looking somewhat less spectacular than usual. It's difficult for her not to be beautiful, but I had to admit she was not up to form. She seemed harried, her face drawn, her eyes a little puffy, her jeans and shirt slightly rumpled.

Her greeting, too, was considerably lacking in joie de vivre.

"I should've known," she said, "even if you don't tell a *soul* about it, Charlie Greenfield will sniff it out. Come on in."

Greenfield's eyes examined her face intently. "Is something wrong?"

"Is something wrong!" She shut the door behind us. "If there was nothing wrong you wouldn't be here, right? Gordon's in the workroom . . . working. He'd go on working if Gabriel was sounding the last trumpet." She threw up her hands. "You can go in. He can't hide forever."

She started for the workroom, but Greenfield stopped her, his face stiff with self-control.

"One minute. Before I go in there. Tell me about it."

"What's to tell? He went to inspect the work going on at the site of the new building, couldn't afford to waste any time getting from one point to another, jumped off some goddamn low girder or something, and fractured a tibia!"

There was a silence as of the whole world having stopped.

"When did this happen?"

"Saturday."

You could see relief flooding Greenfield like a tidal wave. I felt pretty good myself.

Greenfield actually put an arm around Shirley's shoulders and squeezed a little.

"Damn idiot blew the whole Boston trip!" she grumbled.

We went in to see Gordon. He sat awkwardly by the ebony table making sketches on a pad on his lap. His right leg rested on a stool and was encased from toe to thigh in a plaster cast. A pair of crutches leaned against his chair.

No way that man could have driven to the Gorham road in the early hours of Monday.

"How did you find out about this?" Gordon asked.

"You know I don't reveal my sources," Greenfield replied smoothly, and suggested that since Gordon couldn't go to Boston for the weekend, we might play a little Beethoven the following night.

Half an hour later I was walking down the hospital corridor to Peter Kittell's room, bearing a letter from Greenfield. He had dropped me off at home, and when he suggested I take Peter a letter from him, I agreed, because I'd been meaning to pay a visit in any case. I knew Greenfield could never force himself to go. I knew he had a horror of hospitals, and I never asked him why.

I knocked softly on the door and in a moment it was opened by Mrs. Kittell. Her face looked tired, but no longer hard and strained. She even smiled a little and told me to come in.

The top half of Peter's hospital bed had been raised so that he was almost sitting, but I hardly recognized the robust boy I had known; he looked frail, his face without animation, his arms resting limply on the cover.

I gave him Greenfield's letter and a book of crossword puzzles I'd bought, knowing he was an addict, and told him that Mr. Greenfield was going to come himself but there was a crisis at the newspaper and he had to take care of it.

Peter thanked me for the book, then opened Greenfield's letter, and as he read it I watched a faint pink flush come to his cheeks. When he'd finished reading he looked at his mother and his eyes were almost lively.

"I'm getting another bike," he said. "Mr. Greenfield said, so I don't have to wait till I save up the money again, he ordered it already and I can have it as soon as I'm better and pay it off working for the paper."

Mrs. Kittell looked as though the idea of Peter riding a bike again was no thrill for her, but she was wise enough to say that was very nice and Peter must write Mr. Greenfield and thank him.

I was shown the cards and candy and fruit sent by Helen and Calli, and various games and books contributed by his brothers, sisters, and classmates, and after the usual exchange about the hospital routine, the nurses and the food, Mrs. Kittell said it was time for a

nap, and I left. I glanced back from the doorway and
was reminded of a picture I'd once seen in a *National
Geographic* of a tigress licking a cub.

It was about seven thirty that night—I was washing
up my single dinner dish and coffee cup—when the
phone rang and Greenfield's voice announced that he
would be pleased to see me in half an hour, if not
sooner. I drove to the office, left the car in the driveway leading to the garage in the rear that housed
Greenfield's Plymouth, and went in the back way, up
the stairs to the top of the house and into Greenfield's
living room.

It was a Rembrandt room: lustrous browns and
deep rich burgundys, lamplit brandy-colored woods
and a rug the color of bronze chrysanthemums on a
floor like a satin chestnut. There were large, comfortable, and slightly worn armchairs, a nineteenth-century
music stand, an old armoire which held his recordings
and the turntable, three walls of books and one of
framed lithographs. Greenfield sat in a plum-colored
wingback chair, scribbling on a pad of yellow paper.
Scattered on the floor was a mess of yellow lined sheets
bearing his indefinable calligraphy, and three library
books.

I picked one up and read the cover. *Castles in
Schenectady* by Julian Trager. I picked up another.
Julian Trager—*Dover Soul*. The third was Trager's
Brooklyn Brahmin.

"Good evening," I said. "I'm tempted to ask if
you've ready any good books lately."

"I'll be with you in a minute," he said, scribbling
away.

I sat in the armchair opposite and began to open the
Brooklyn Brahmin, but decided I was in no mood for
Trager. Instead I picked up a copy of Boswell's *Lon-
don Journal* and opened it.

"*. . . I now received a card of invitation to the rout
on Tuesday the 7. This raised my spirits, gave me notions of my consequence, and filled me with grandeur.
Fain would I have got rich laced clothes, but I commanded my inclination and got just a plain suit of a*

pink color, with a gold button. . . ." Ah, Brooks Brothers, those were the days.

Greenfield got up, made a slow tour of the room, collecting all the yellow sheets, sat down again, and stared at me until I put down the book and gave him my attention.

"You were asking," he said, "about the books. When I committed myself to getting at the truth of this business about Trager, I realized I'd be forced to learn more about the man than I could get from hearsay. No one can create a body of work, whatever its shortcomings, without revealing something of the nature and quality of his mind. So I've been reading Trager, not in the hope of learning anything profound about the human condition—only in the hope of learning something about Trager."

"And did you?"

"It wasn't entirely unrewarding," he grunted, and without, of course, enlightening me further, went on. "I have some questions. First. Did you ever discover why Mrs. Hollis went to the city last Saturday?"

"No. Catherine thought she might have gone to get a present for Elizabeth's birthday, but Victoria never actually told her."

He made a note on his paper. "Second. Do you know if Trager was aware of his wife's inflexibility with regard to adultery?"

I thought about it. "I think he must have been. Her reaction wasn't matter-of-fact, it was almost violent, for her. No one could live with her for sixteen years and not know how she felt about that."

He made another note. "Tell me again what you saw in Trager's study at the farm. Close your eyes and remember details."

I did, and told him.

"And what would you say was the salient feature of Mrs. Hollis's behavior when you went up there on Monday—after you saw the Mercedes on the riverbank?"

"Her behavior? Impeccably courteous. It always is."

"I'm talking about her reaction to the incident on the Gorham road."

I closed my eyes and brought back her face again. "She was annoyed. No. Angry. Maybe somewhere between annoyed and angry."

He made notes again.

"The circle gets smaller and smaller," I objected, "Victoria and Trager. Trager and Victoria."

He nodded slowly, not looking at me. "That's how it's working out."

"Is there a slight possibility you could be prejudiced? Face it, Charlie, you'd do almost anything to get the Kittells off the hook. You latched onto Seberg like a limpet until he came up with a provable alibi, you grabbed at the possibility that it was Andrew, you were even willing to believe that Gordon might have—"

"*Willing!*"

"Yes, it was torture, but you conceded the possibility. But you concede *nothing* with the Kittells. Why not, for God's sake? What mysterious martyrdom are you indulging in?"

"The Kittells are inconceivable in that context. You don't understand their psychological makeup."

"I understand that Mrs. Kittell assured me, in so many words, when I saw her at the hospital that day, that not only would God take care of whoever hit Peter, but she herself would be glad to help Him out!"

"Yes, but not in the physical sense. The Kittells are unsophisticated and they really do believe in God's retribution. They could never put themselves in jeopardy by committing an act of violence."

"They could convince themselves they were God's vengeful instrument."

He shook his head. "I think I'm beginning to see where all this springs from." He stood up, stretched, took a deep breath, and slumped again. "Theres something I have to do," he said, "and it's going to be unpleasant."

I waited. He stared morosely at the armoire for the count of ten, and finally said, "I have to go back to the farm. I have to go very late at night. I have to see what's in that well."

I made a noise like a cat whose tail has been stepped on.

"There's something in that well. She didn't want me to look in. She followed us out of the house to make sure I didn't."

Two weeks earlier, I would have laughed. I would have said, "Charlie, you're bananas. You've been seeing too many of those California-bred horror movies." But too much had happened since that little boy's bicycle got smashed, and Greenfield's intuition about certain things had been too close to the mark. And furthermore, I had just realized what was different about the well when Greenfield stopped to look at it— the bucket was not resting on the well cover; it was on the ground.

So I swallowed and said, hoarsely, "When?"

"One A.M. Two A.M. That should be late enough."

"Tonight?"

He threw me an angry look, because he hated the whole thing.

"No," he said, "sometime in the spring when the weather's suitable."

▣ 14

It was cold, and dark, and a sallow half-moon spread a pallid light over the darkened house and fields. The trees were black brushstrokes on a gray wash, the edges blurred. We had left the car down on Traprock Road and made our way to the gate, climbing over it so as not to risk the creaking. We were dressed in dark jeans and black rubber boots. Greenfield in a heavy black turtleneck sweater under a dark green windbreaker, me in a navy peajacket, both of us looking like very amateur cat burglars.

Greenfield had made noises when I said I was going with him, but I persuaded him that lying awake in my house alone in the bleak hours of the night wondering what was going on, imagining scenes of ghastly confrontation, and waiting, helpless, while the minutes crawled by would have a more deleterious effect on my nervous system than actually taking part. So here we were, creeping stealthily through the trees carrying unlit flashlights, Greenfield's pockets bulging with screwdriver, pliers, a length of coiled wire and other objects, the purposes of which were clear only to him.

We moved slowly, cautiously, trying to avoid twigs and other things that might snap and crackle, stopping every few feet to look and listen. I figured we would probably reach the well by the Fourth of July. We'd gone about a thousand feet when a terrible thought struck me. I put a hand on Greenfield's sleeve, leaned close to his ear, and whispered.

"Do horses have a sixth sense? Can they tell when people are approaching?"

He put his mouth next to my ear.

"Supposing they could—why should they do anything about it?"

We continued creeping. Then I was struck by another and even more terrible thought. I stopped him again.

"My God! The dog!"

This made him uneasy. He leaned close.

"Where does he sleep?"

I turned up both palms to indicate ignorance, and whispered, "It's a she."

He took a deep breath and made a gesture I interpreted as meaning we'd just have to take our chances. We went on. And on. As we neared the well my throat closed and my teeth began to chatter. I clenched my jaw. I felt hot. Then cold. Then hot again. I could see the darkened windows of Andrew's rooms over the barn. We had already thought of that, remembering that the wide trunk of the monumental oak stood between those windows and the well, and judging it would screen us from his possible view. We would, of course, be entirely exposed to the back porch of the house and the sun porch beside it, but it was unlikely anyone would be inhabiting either of those, and on the floor above the only rooms on that side of the house were the darkroom, the bathroom, and Trager's study.

Suddenly we reached the well, and my immediate impulse was to turn and run. Greenfield put a finger to his lips and we stood still, waiting to see if any of the various animals was going to announce our presence. There was no sound, only the infinitesimal night noises.

Greenfield put his fingers into the opening of the well cover and tugged. It didn't budge. He reached carefully into his pocket for the long screwdriver, inserted it, and used it as a lever, slowly leaned his weight on it. There was a tiny screech as the wood complained. We froze. For a whole minute we stood immobile, scarcely breathing. Then Greenfield shifted the tool a fraction and leaned again. The cover lifted. I caught at the edge of it with my hands. Greenfield returned the screwdriver to his pocket and put his hands under the opposite edge. Together, with extravagant care, we jiggled the rest of the wooden disc free from the well opening and laid it on the ground.

Greenfield motioned to me to lean over the well and shine my flashlight into it. I felt nausea rising to my throat and stood without moving. He leaned close to me and stared furiously into my eyes. I took the two necessary quiet steps to the edge of the well, leaned over with my eyes shut while Greenfield peered over the opposite rim, and switched on the light. Hours passed. Slowly I opened my eyes and looked down—at nothing. An empty well.

No. Not completely empty. About eight feet down was a platform, and on the platform, close to one side of the well, was a small, shiny brown oblong. Greenfield motioned me to shut off the light.

He bent and picked up a twig, took the wire from his pocket, secured one end around the end of the twig, found another twig, secured that one to the first, then a third, a fourth, and a fifth, and wound the wire tightly around all of them, making a tiny raft. I watched him in a state of paralysis, waiting for the dog to bark, the horses to neigh, a voice to call sharply, "Who's there!" None of it happened. Greenfield took out his penknife, opened it, and wired it to one end of the object with the blade projecting over the edge, twisted the remaining wire off with the pliers, attached one end of that wire to one side of the contraption, the other end to the other side. Now it was a very small swing hanging at the end of six-foot wires.

He gestured to me to repeat my chore with the flashlight, and slowly and carefully lowered his invention down the well, a little at a time until it touched the platform. Then he guided it until the point of the penknife lifted the edge of the shiny object down there, and very, very slowly slid the seat of the swing under the package or whatever it was. I looked at him in awe. There was perspiration on his forehead.

Bringing the object up the well was the longest, most nerveracking process I can recall in forty-odd years of long nerveracking processes. At least six times the shiny thing threatened to slip off its insecure seat and Greenfield stopped, his hands trembling, and shifted it, one millimeter at a time, until it was back in position. At the end of a month or so, he had raised it high enough that by reaching down I could grab it with my hands, and I did, almost dropping it back down the well because it was slimy to the touch.

Neither of us had been doing what could really classify as breathing for the last ten minutes, and I was amazed we were still conscious. Even then, with the object in our hands, Greenfield moved at snail's pace, careful not to make a sound. He removed his contraption, winding the wire around it and stuffing it inside his windbreaker, picked up the well cover and with infinite patience replaced it without so much as a whisper of sound, looked around to make certain we'd left nothing on the ground, and indicated we could begin to creep back the way we had come. As I followed him, still holding the slimy thing in my hand and still not breathing, I thought. *Now. Now the dog will bark and the horses will raise hell and Andrew will come charging out of his rooms—this is when it always happens, with safety an inch away!* But no. We crept. We stopped. We listened. We crept. And I began to take in oxygen.

Getting back was as lengthy and agonizing a procedure as coming up had been, with one beautiful difference: with every step we were receding from danger, not approaching it. At long, long last we climbed over the gate, kept a slow pace until we rounded the evergreens, and then ran like hell, like escapees from Sing Sing, down Traprock Road.

"I—thought—" I gasped, running, "we were—going to find—*him*—in there!"

"Don't—be—an ass!"

We reached the car and Greenfield struggled with the keys (even for *this* he had locked it!) and finally we tumbled into it. I expected Greenfield to grab the brown object out of my hand and tear it open, but this, I discovered, was where you separated the Greenfields from the ordinary run of human creatures. He started the car without a further word, turned it around, drove sedately back down Traprock, onto Cliff Road, and back to my house, waited while I fished for the key with trembling fingers, stepped politely over George, took off his jacket, hung it up, walked into the living room, and only *then* held out his hand.

The thing I handed him was wrapped and scotch-taped in a brown plastic bag which had acquired a film of moisture down there in the well: hence the sliminess. I had wiped it dry with Kleenex as we drove, and now Greenfield ripped the plastic open to disclose a piece of heavy pink flannel. He unwound the flannel and held up what seemed to be a book. An antique, tooled-leather, Florentine book. Trager's notebook.

We looked at it, and at each other, and back at it for quite a while. Then I poured some bourbon for Greenfield and sherry for myself and we sat at the dining room table with the book between us, and opened it, and read.

It was writer's shorthand.

"Can make Leland look like fag? Then scenes with De Paulo come to life. . . . Does Fowles probe English domestication? That tidy countryside, like housewife's parlor. They go over it with a duster every day. Vacuum the hills. Sheep stand like porcelain figures in a china cabinet. . . . All that Vidal-type phony wit at Shepherd's. . . . Ervine in Senate: the intent of the bill is inimical to the competitive controls of free enterprise. . . ."

And so on. There was nothing in the first twenty pages that could possibly be construed as relevant to our problem. But then there began to be references which sent a few tingles down the spine.

"Saddle-smell. Leather obsession. Sexual banner. The groom thinks he has six balls but it's all bucolic bullshit. . . . Pattern Malvina on S. A rotten lay after all. Talk, talk, talk."

"Any fool could have predicted that," Greenfield snorted, "the woman's greatest passion is to be fashionable."

And finally, just before the notes ended and the pages became blank—

"Criminal. Define it. You are a criminal. You sweat. Your bowels back up. Your brain is sandpaper. The world is literally without light. You move in darkness. You watch people walking the streets and their clothes disappear, flesh disappears, they are skeletons. Skeletons ride the bus. Skeletons hail cabs. Skeletons carry shopping bags. A bicycle from nowhere. From hell. Materializes beside your wheel. The boy's face. To kill a boy. Remember Stephen at twelve. See Medea."

Each page was headed with a date, and the date of that last entry was Tuesday, the Tuesday I found Peter lying on the side of the road.

Greenfield closed the book thoughtfully and sat looking at it, running a finger over the tooled leather.

"He was going to use it," he said softly. "He was going to use the experience."

"What do you think it was doing in the well? You think Victoria was hiding the evidence?"

He shook his head. "No. Yes, hiding it, but not to protect anyone." He stood, picked up the book, went to the hall, and put on his windbreaker.

"What, then?"

"Blackmail."

"Blackmail?"

"Let's put this under lock and key," he said, wandering across the living room to an enclosed porch we used as a library. "Do you have such a place?"

I pointed to an old rolltop desk. "The top drawer locks. What do you mean, blackmail?"

"Where's the key?" he asked, having put the notebook in the drawer.

I reached into Alan's old baby mug full of pencils and showed him the key. "What kind of blackmail?"

He locked the drawer and pocketed the key. "It's very late," he said. "Get some sleep while you can. I want you back at the farm tomorrow—rather, later this morning."

"Back— Me? Why me? Whats wrong with *you?*"

"I'll be busy elsewhere. I want you to get the following information. . . ."

He told me what he wanted, I told him he was a sadist, sending me back to the scene of the crime I'd committed, he said never mind, just do it, and report to the office when you've successfully completed the assignment, and while I was still refusing, he left.

It was only as I put the chain on the door that I realized he'd managed to escape without explaining what he meant by "blackmail." I marched angrily upstairs, convinced I would spend the rest of the night frantically pondering the thousand and one nuances of that word. I woke to sunlight striping the bed where I lay peacefully on top of the covers in my jeans, jacket, and rubber boots. It was five minutes to ten. I ripped off the clothes, threw myself into the shower, dressed, poured myself a giant glass of orange juice, carried it to the phone, and dialed the farm.

"Sorry to bother you. I seem to have lost a silver fountain pen—my husband gave it to me—it's engraved—know I had it just before going to your place yesterday afternoon—possibly fell through a hole in my pocket—could I come and look?"

I let George out the back door, grabbed my coat and my car keys, and left the house, without breakfast, my eyes gritty, my mouth woolly, my knees wobbly. All this late-night escapading and early-morning tension was no way of life for a forty-two . . . allright, forty-five-year-old lover of leisurely living.

Going down the front walk, I hesitated. There was something peculiar about the day. A hint, or an echo. I stood still, breathed deeply, and realized what it was: spring. Not real spring, but that tantalizing advance notice. Earth smells, air that was soft and tender, an elusive ache that had to do with flowered dresses, grassy knolls, and lovely, lost lambent days of youth. For a moment I forgot what was happening—but only for a moment.

The farm was placid again, in the buttercup sunshine—pastoral, untroubled, innocent as a lamb. Remembering the wild, tree-tossed eeriness of the day before, and the stark black-and-gray terror of ten hours earlier, I could make no sensible connection between those and this. I only knew that I felt distinctly contemptible, coming back so innocently after the dead-of-night treachery

Victoria and Catherine helped me search the living

room, and then, taking Catherine with me so I could tactfully ply her with the assigned questions, I searched the barn and the ground between the barn and the house, passing the old well and shivering retroactively. All to no avail, naturally. Back in the house Victoria commiserated over my loss and Catherine excused herself, saying she had to change clothes as she was driving into the city to get some photographic supplies. I conveniently remembered having been upstairs the day before to return the photograph of Julian and followed her up, saying, "Don't bother with me, I'll just take a quick look." She went to her room and I immediately dodged into Julian's study, saw what I'd come for lying on the desk, slipped it into my bag, and went back downstairs, triumphantly displaying to Victoria the silver pen I'd never lost.

"Rolled into a corner," I said.

By a little past noon I was walking into the office, convinced that, feeling contemptible aside, I'd been cut out for a life of crime.

Calli greeted me with glee. "Maggie! Listen! I have found a *terrific* store, I'm not joking, cashmere sweaters *twelve dollars!* You believe that? Real cashmere—"

"Where's Greenfield?"

"He went out. Listen—"

"*Where?*"

"How should I know? He was making phone calls, then he went—" She raised her voice to a shriek, the better to reach Helen in the john. "Helen! Where did Charlie go?"

"To the County Court House."

The County Court House. What did that mean?

"Helen," I called, "did you say the County Court House?"

"Yes!"

The telephone rang and Calli clattered over to answer it.

"If that's Charlie—" I began, but at that moment the door opened and Greenfield walked in. "What were you doing at the County Court House?" I asked him.

"I was not at the Court House," he said, starting up

the stairs. "I was at the County Office Building in the Division of Land Records."

I followed him up and watched him remove his jacket and drape it over a month's accumulation of news magazines on the armchair.

"I retract any unkind remarks I may have made about your friend Barbara," he continued. "She has proved herself to be of value. Unintentionally, but nevertheless—"

"Barbara?"

He settled into the noisy swivel chair and said, "Report, please."

Too tired to pursue the non sequitur or protest his cavalier disregard of my comfort, I cleared a space on the arm of the chair, perched on it, and told him.

"I didn't find out much. Julian Trager's first wife is remarried and lives in California and there's been no communication between them for ten years. The son is studying marine biology out there and Trager has made sporadic attempts to establish a relationship but the son is hostile. Trager's parents have gone to their reward, or punishment, whichever is appropriate—the rest of the family seems to be living in Canada. Trager has one sister, in Ottawa, married to a man somehow involved in politics. There are some aunts, uncles, and cousins in various cities, including one male cousin who is a professor of anthropolgy at a university in Toronto. That's it." I reached in my bag and extracted what I had appropriated from Trager's desk. "Here's the letter."

Greenfield took the pale blue envelope, removed the contents, and sat reading it to himself—something I hadn't had time to do.

"Interesting?" I asked.

"Hmmm," he mumbled. And then, "Is Catherine at the farm?"

"She left when I did, to go to the city."

"Good. And Mrs. Hollis is going to be there?"

"Yes, but not for long. Catherine says she's leaving tonight to visit her sister in Massachusetts."

Greenfield erupted from the chair, setting it clanging and twanging and whining. "The hell she is," he breathed, and stood glaring over my head at the far wall. "When does Elizabeth get home?"

"Two-thirty. Three."

"All right." He fished in his pocket and handed me the key to the drawer in my rolltop desk. "Get the book and meet me at the farm in twenty minutes. If my car is there when you arrive, let yourself in. I don't want to be interrupted." He picked up his jacket and made for the stairs. I followed, stomping angrily down the stairs after him.

"Listen, Charlie, I've had it with being used as a combination audience, apprentice thief, and flashlight holder. I want to know what's going on! Now give!" He was through the front door. "Charlie!" By God, he could move fast when he wanted to!

"What's all the hellofaballoo?" Callie called.

I ignored her and went after him, in time to see him insert himself between the seat and the wheel of the Plymouth and take off.

I went home, got the notebook and a manila envelope from the drawer in the desk, put the one inside the other, and, for what seemed like the fortieth time in a week, drove in the direction of Traprock Road.

Getting out to open the gate, driving through, getting out to close it, and continuing up to the house, I felt as though I'd been doing this all my life. Greenfield's Plymouth was there, standing beside the VW near the shed. I looked toward the barn and thought I saw movement behind Andrew's windows. Was he one of the strands in this tangled skein Greenfield was unraveling? Was Catherine? Elizabeth? Seberg? Kittell?

Alice, the dog, appeared at my heels. I patted her affectionately for not betraying us the night before, went to the house, put my hand on the knob of the front door, turned slowly, and pushed. The door opened. There was no sound of voices. No sound at all. I looked into the living room, found no one there, went down the hall to the dining room and kitchen, also uninhabited, and went out onto the sun porch. Through the wide window the farm stretched out before me, and from this angle I could see figures dotting the landscape. In a distant field, a mere dot with flying ribbons moving at snail's pace across the horizon: Mr. Chanin. In the middle distance Hawkeye and Radar ambled around their pasture while Victoria Hollis, in her loden coat and shapeless slacks, walked the outside perimeter of the pasture, her head at an angle, examining the fence as she went. And prowling at her heels, hands in the pocket of his gaudy plaid hunting jacket, was Greenfield.

And he didn't want to be interrupted! Terrific. I had planned to slide unobtrusively into the shadowy corners of the living room and remain unheard and unseen. As it was, the best I could do was keep my mouth shut.

I went onto the back porch, down the steps, past the old well—I'd never again be able to pass that spot with ease—around the side of the barn and out toward the pasture, trying to pretend I wasn't there. By the time I reached them they had stopped walking and were leaning against the fence, Victoria presenting her profile to Greenfield, her chin up, face taut and wary, arms crossed. Greenfield was speaking.

". . . so you see, it was neither a whim, nor a ruthless professional interest, nor a desire to meddle that prompted me. I simply could not let those people shoulder the undeserved penalty of official investigation with all the social stigma that implies."

He looked at her for some sign of acknowledgment. She stood immobile, like one of Trager's "porcelain figures." No one paid the slightest attention to me. Finally Victoria spoke, in a tight, low voice.

"I had no idea the Kittells were under suspicion."

She still hadn't moved, she stood looking out to the orchard, waiting for the intruders to finish their business and leave.

"Where is Trager?" Greenfield murmured.

No reply.

"Well, of course you won't tell me. That's part of the bargain you made."

He reached out a hand in my direction without looking at me. I put the manila envelope into it.

"I've done something shameful, Mrs. Hollis. I did it for what I believe to be good and sufficient reason, nevertheless I did it. Apology would be ludicrous under the circumstances, but I want you to know it wasn't a callous or unrepented act."

He opened the envelope, removed the tooled-leather notebook, moved into her line of vision, and held it up.

Her eyes fell to the book, her jaw tightened, she seemed to stop breathing for a moment, but she said nothing.

Greenfield replaced the notebook in the envelope and handed it back to me, again without turning his head, as though I were a familiar mailbox.

"I've spent a great deal of time and thought," he said, "on this unhappy puzzle. I've juggled fact, deduction, and educated guesswork, and I've put together what I think is a fair approximation of what's taken place. But I prefer to hear it from you. I suggest we go back to the house, where we—"

"You came without invitation," Victoria said, still in the tight, low voice. "This is the time for my rounds. And much as I appreciate your concern for the boy's parents, it seems to me you're taking a great deal on yourself. None of this really concerns *you*." She turned then, with a look of stubborn defiance. "What possible difference can any of this make to your life?"

"Mrs. Hollis. You don't for a minute expect me to believe you subscribe to that code of behavior, or that you think *I* do. Neither your concern nor mine stops at the boundaries of our own personal content."

"Playing God, Mr. Greenfield?"

"No more than you."

Anger flared in her eyes and then went out like a match in a wind.

"If you won't come inside," Greenfield said, "where we can pursue this in comfort, I'll listen to it here."

Victoria gave him a look of cosmic obstinacy, put her chin in her collar, and walked off across the meadow in the opposite direction from the house. We followed.

"I won't be put off." Greenfield told her, but she kept walking, saying nothing. Greenfield sighed. "In that case," he said, "I'll prime the pump." He trudged along in the lugubrious fashion of someone being unjustly persecuted. "Sixteen years ago," he began, "your daughter met and became infatuated with Julian Trager. He was married at the time, had a young son, was fairly successful and a bit of a celebrity, and Catherine probably considered him something of a god, someone she could never hope to interest.

"But Trager was a greedy man and he saw an opportunity to add luster to his image, to become the squire of a twenty-acre estate—" he gestured to the surrounding countryside— "horses, a country house of historical interest—it would look good on a book jacket. And Catherine was young, a willing slave, and had the kind of breeding he publicly despised but privately lusted after. He divorced his wife and married Catherine. You—" he looked at Victoria—"I don't suppose you were happy about it." He paused for a reply. There was none. "Perhaps you rationalized. Took into account that your daughter was socially inept, already twenty-five years old, far from the belle of the ball—?"

As though the words were being forced out, like steam from a boiling kettle, Victoria said, "I knew it was wrong. I knew it the moment I saw him. But of course I wasn't consulted."

She kept walking.

"And then?" Greenfield prompted. No reply. "I'm listening, Mrs. Hollis."

"You won't hear anything, Mr. Greenfield."

"If you don't speak, I'll have to."

"I can't stop you."

He glared at a large chestnut tree that rose in our path and went around it. "All right, then, Trager. A man of shallow passions. And eventually the novelty of playing the country gentleman wore off. At the same time he found that his success and popularity had declined, drastically. He used Catherine—and, I'm sure, you and Elizabeth peripherally—as an outlet for his bitterness and frustration. He bullied, wounded, and humiliated Catherine until you would have done almost anything to be rid of him. Did you speak to Catherine about divorce? Probably. And discovered that her belief in the sanctity of marriage was unshakable. It would have taken proof of infidelity for her to seek a divorce—and Trager was very careful not to let her have that, because he needed her."

We had come to a chicken-wire fence supported by angle irons. Andrew's fence. The ground beyond it had been staked out in rows with two-by-fours strung together with wrapping cord. Victoria stopped. Greenfield abruptly sat down on a large boulder

"He needed her," he went on, "because over the years, what with paying alimony and child support to his first family, and with the taste for high living he'd developed, which his income no longer met, he was in debt." He scowled up at Victoria, who stood looking at the ground beyond the fence. "He was in debt," he repeated, "he needed money and he took the one . . . totally . . . unforgivable . . . step." He waited for a reaction but she stood there staring at the staked-out ground and said nothing. "He underestimated you," he added, and watched her.

"Mr. Greenfield," she said, in a cautionary tone, "no more!"

"I can't oblige you." Greenfield shifted uncomfortably on the boulder, picked up a stone, and turned it about with his fingers. "Trager learned," he went on, "as I learned this morning, that when your husband died, the house and the acre on which it stands became yours alone, while the rest of the property—the farm in fact—passed to Catherine. With the hope that she, in turn, would pass it on to her children. You ran the place, I imagine, because you are capable of it and she isn't, but legally it belonged to Catherine. And Trager began persuading her to sell it. She was holding out, but now he was threatening to leave her unless she sold. You overheard the arguments and the threats, and you knew it was only a matter of time before Trager got his way, as no doubt he always did, and the farm would be lost." He paused, dropped the stone, and sat there waiting.

When Victoria spoke, it was as though she were continuing an argument. "These are my gardening plots," she said, "for older people to grow things. And children. Tomatoes. Carrots. Daffodils. Hyacinths. Where are these things to grow, when all the land on earth

disappears under concrete slabs and aluminum siding?"
She thrust out an arm, fingers spread, and raked the
horizon, taking in the wood, the fields, the orchard.
"Did he think I would let them level these magnificent
old trees, bulldoze these fields . . . *violate* this repose,
this . . . grace? The world can go on without shopping
centers and high-rise apartments. It *can't* go on without
trees, without grass, without a single field of wild flowers to walk through."

She turned and headed for the wood. Greenfield
went after her and I after him. "If I were a character in
a Chekhov play," she went on, "I'd sit in my house and
cry, and listen to the sound of the axe demolishing the
orchard. But I'm not a dreamer I'm a fighter."

"That's why I'm here, Mrs. Hollis. Because you're a
fighter. It's the nature of your weapons that concerns
me."

It was chilly in the wood, and the ground squelched
a little underfoot. We followed a narrow path bordering
the stream.

"Let's go on," Greenfield said. "You knew Trager
was threatening to leave Catherine unless she agreed to
sell the farm. And you were determined the farm
would not be sold. A week ago Tuesday, circumstances
played into your hands. Trager had an assignation with
a woman—who lives locally but works in the city. He
had left his car at the garage for inspection and borrowed your Volkswagen. In the Volkswagen he drove
the woman from the city to a nearby motel and after a
short time—because she, for her own reasons, wanted
to be home by eight o'clock—drove her from there to
the train station to pick up her own car, where she had
left it in the morning before boarding the train. En-
route there was a collision between the Volkswagen
and a boy on a bicycle. Trager panicked and drove
away, leaving the boy unconscious."

Victoria stopped. A tree had fallen across the path
and the stream, its branches forming a kind of dam
over which the water gurgled in a small waterfall.

"I'll have to tell Andrew about that." Victoria murmured, and prepared to make her way over the tree
trunk.

"Mrs. Hollis!" Greenfield looked thunderous. Victoria turned to face him. "It's no idle intellectual curiosity that has me tramping through these woods—I am in dead earnest! I insist that you give this your undivided attention!"

Victoria drew in her breath, plunged her hands into her pockets, and looked away from him, but stood still. Greenfield made his way to the tree trunk, sat on it, glared at the damp leaves on the ground, and went on.

"The morning after the accident—Wednesday—the day Mrs. Rome first came to the farm—you went out to the woods to collect the brush. Being well aware of Trager's carelessness with other people's property, you made a casual inspection of your car and found the scratches. You were angry and confronted him, demanding an explanation. To your surprise his reaction was violent—unnecessarily defensive, hysterical—something out of proportion to the situation.

"Then, on Thursday, when Mrs. Rome was lunching with you and Catherine and Elizabeth, you learned of the accident the night before involving Peter Kittell, and—perhaps subconsciously looking for something to hold against Trager—your mind made the connection.

"On Friday you went to the hospital to see Peter Kittell, hoping to find out in more detail about his condition, so that you could act accordingly. If he had come out of the coma, you would try to discover from him whether or not he had seen the car that had knocked him down, or the man driving it. Whether he had or not, it would work to your advantage if you knew, and against you if you didn't. But he was still unconscious.

"You returned home. Catherine was out, Elizabeth at school, you were alone in the house. It occurred to you that there might be something in Trager's study that would help you—some slight evidence of where he'd been that Tuesday night. You searched, found the notebook, read it, wrapped it in flannel and plastic, and put it down the well.

"You knew you had him then. The entry was dated Tuesday, before anyone but the Kittell family, the police, Mrs. Rome, and myself knew about the accident.

And if it wasn't evidence, that, plus the scratches on the car and his probable inability to account for his whereabouts at that time—if you read the notebook you must have guessed he was philandering—would certainly be enough to start an investigation. But you didn't want Trager in jail, still married to Catherine, and Catherine waiting for him and suffering even more humiliation than she already had. What you wanted was something else entirely.

"On Saturday you went to the city, a thing you never do except for matters of extreme importance. I would imagine you went to see your stockbroker or your lawyer about converting some of your investments into cash.

"While you were gone, Trager, who had been missing his notebook and probably turning the house inside out looking for it, enraged and fearful, knowing what it contained, got into an argument with Andrew and accused him of stealing it.

"Sometime Saturday evening or Sunday morning you arranged to be alone with Trager long enough to tell him that you had the notebook, and that you proposed to hand it, and the information about the scratches on the car, over to the police, unless he did what you asked.

"I'm fairly certain what you asked, Mrs. Hollis. But I want you to tell me."

Victoria hadn't moved, and she didn't move now. She addressed the trees. "Mr. Greenfield, we've gone as far into this as we're going."

Greenfield stood up, "I'm afraid not. I have to know what went on between you and Trager."

"I don't agree."

Greenfield moved in front of her and stared into her face from under the gray foliage of his brows. "Apparently," he said quietly, "you refuse to face the reality of the situation. I tell you frankly, your alternative to speaking is not attractive."

Victoria looked faintly surprised. "You're threatening me."

"Yes, I am. I have information relating to a crime. Possibly two crimes. As a citizen I'm expected to turn it over to the police That action will have consequences." There was a minute change in Victoria's posture, as though the scaffolding of her back had settled, fractionally. "Now," Greenfield continued, "before proceeding, I would like to know what those consequences will be."

There was a brief, silent contest of will as they confronted each other in that chilly clearing, and then Victoria said, "Perhaps we'd better go back to the house," and turned to leave the wood.

We trudged in silence out of the wood, across the meadow, past the barn and the old well, onto the back porch and into the house. In the hall Victoria removed her coat and laid it on a bench. Greenfield and I followed suit, and she led the way into the living room.

She sat down in a chair by the window facing the chintz-covered sofa, sunlight touching her white hair, her back straight again, beleaguered but unconquered. Grace under pressure.

Greenfield dropped onto the sofa and slouched there, frowning, patient, merciless. I slid onto a chair in a shadowy corner. We waited. Victoria sat looking out the window for minutes, without moving or speaking. Then the words came.

"He was in Andrew's room, over the barn, looking for the notebook. I told Andrew to keep away. And Catherine and Elizabeth too. I said I would handle it. I went up there—" Her hands clenched into fists. "He vandalized that room! Drawers. Bedclothes. *Flowerpots* turned over! He was vicious. Snarling . . ." She lifted her hand to her mouth, held it there for a moment, and put it back in her lap.

"I told him I had read the notebook and hidden it where it couldn't be found. He didn't say anything at first. He just stood there looking . . . murderous. His face was very red. The veins were standing out in his neck. I thought for a minute that he might . . . that my life was in danger. But he knew I was strong. He's not the type to risk physical violence on anyone who might fight back.

"I had no compunction about what I was doing He was no father to Elizabeth—she was always uncomfortable with him, suffered at the way he treated her mother. And Catherine's married life . . . as you pointed out . . . was . . . a bed of nails.

"I said, 'Julian, you are finished. You are leaving my house, my farm, and my daughter.'

"He said, 'You had the gall to read my notebook? You went through my private papers?' He was trembling

"I said, 'I have not used up my only life working for this piece of land—caring for it—keeping it safe—only to stand back and watch you fling it to the jackals! I want you out!'

"He laughed. He has a high, thin laugh. Very unpleasant.

" 'You're sending me away?' he said. 'You're going to go back to that house and tell Catherine you're sending me away? I'd like to see you try it.'

" 'I want you to disappear,' I said, 'from the face of the earth. I want you officially dead. Otherwise I'll go to the police with the notebook, *and* show them the scratches on the Volkswagen, and tell them you borrowed the car that day.'

"He said, 'You're demented. You think you can just dispose of anyone who doesn't fit your concept of graceful living? You think you have that right? Divine Right of the Matriarch? You're a relic. A museum piece. An artifact from an ancient despotic civilization.' Or words to that effect."

"I said, "You can think what you like about me. The fact is I have the evidence, and if you refuse to do as I say, there will be a police investigation, a jail sentence, and I will personally see to it that the newspapers get the whole disgusting story."

"He was breathing very shallowly, he could hardly speak, but I think it was more anger than fear. He still didn't realize what was happening. He said, 'To hell with you. You won't go to the police. I know you. You wouldn't do that to Elizabeth. It would be a nightmare for her.'

" 'Yes,' I said, 'it would be very traumatic. But temporary. It's the long run I care about. I'd go to the police this minute if there weren't a better way. This is the better way, this way Catherine will be free. But make no mistake—this way or the other, I'll do whatever's necessary to keep this farm for Elizabeth!'

"I think he realized then that I wasn't bluffing, that I'd thought it all out, that the outcome was inevitable. He sat down on the bed and said, 'You can't get away with this. People of consequence don't simply disappear.'

"'You're of no consequence,' I said, 'no consequence at all, except to the police. And in any case, you're wrong, people disappear all the time. They abscond with millions of dollars. They arrange plane crashes in which they have presumably died. If people have learned nothing else from the last few decades of spy stories, they've learned how to disappear. A ten-year-old child can tell you how to disappear. You pour gasoline over your car and send it over a cliff, you dye your hair, grow a moustache, dress like a clergyman or a construction worker...'

"'And then what?' he said. 'It's all very well when you're absconding with millions of dollars. . . .' You see, for a moment he was beginning to accept the idea. Then he got up from the bed and began walking up and down, muttering about his life, his childhood, the war, injustices. . . . I said, 'You deserve this. You deserve worse than this. It's unspeakable, what you did. That child is going to die!'

"He sat down on the bed again, and put his head in his hands. I think—" Her voice held a world of contempt. "I think he was actually crying. He kept getting up and sitting down again. He kept saying I was deranged. He talked about his friends, his bank account, his insurance policy, his publisher, his royalties, the Internal Revenue Service, the Motor Vehicle Bureau . . . he was incoherent. Then suddenly he began to . . . to . . ." Indignation quivered in her face. ". . . to *negotiate!*

"He said, 'Where do you expect me to go? How am I supposed to live?'

"I told him I didn't care how he lived, or even *if* he lived. I said I would instruct his agent to deposit his royalties in his bank account, such as it was, and not that there would be much to deposit—the checks have been getting fewer and smaller over the years—and that at the time he was legally pronounced dead and his money was turned over to the estate and the Internal Revenue had received their share I would somehow see that he got the rest. He doesn't respect much about me but he knows I'll keep my word.

"He said that was a long way off and in the meantime he had no funds. I said I would subsidize his departure, giving him enough to see him through the next few months. He said I would be gaining a great deal by his disappearance and he would be losing a great deal. He thought there should be a more equitable arrangement. I told him there was a limit to the amount of money I could spare. We finally . . . we finally agreed on a sum. I had five hundred dollars with me—my attorney had it waiting for me when I went to the city—it was a loan. I told Julian it would take me a week or so to get the rest of it together, but I wanted him gone within twenty-four hours. . . . And I told him he had to straighten up Andrew's room before he went back to the house. Then I left."

She stood up slowly and wandered to the piano, where she carefully folded the open music on the rack. Greenfield was scowling at the fireplace like a Dickensian illustration of a man with dyspepsia.

"I was very relieved," Victoria said, "when the police came and told me they'd found the car. What a charade. Typical of him to cook up that Grand Guignol so that innocent people would be involved. But I was relieved. I was afraid, to the last, that he would change his mind, decide it was too big a price to pay . . ."

Greenfield turned and looked at her with incredulity. "Too big a price!" He stood up, went to the piano, and searched her face. "You mean you threatened him with exposure simply in the *hope* that he couldn't face it? You didn't *know* that he had no choice?"

"How can anyone know for certain—?"

"*I* knew! Anyone who read his books would know. The man had no choice in a situation like this. Trager invented himself. He doesn't exist in his world except

as the embodiment of that aggressively sentimental morality that pervades his books. Look at his characters:
the soldier who refuses to shoot at the enemy, the cop
who can't use a gun, the French Canadian who knocks
out the hunter aiming at the deer. He crusades against
the taking of life, he canonizes the innocent victims of
man's cruelty, he's a literary lifesaver. This is the
image that feeds all his public posturing. Without it
he's an empty suit of clothes walking the streets. For
Trager to be exposed as the man who ran down a child
and left him to die would be the equivalent, to him, of
what the Washington revelations were to our recent
President. Not only would Trager no longer exist, he
would be shown *never* to *have* existed! Better to 'die,'
and have once lived than never to have lived at all."
He paused and lifted an eyebrow at his own para-
phrase.

"Well"—Victoria made a small, weary gesture with
one hand—"it's all academic now. You said before it
was your duty to turn over evidence relevant to a
crime. You'd better do it."

Greenfield heaved a seismic sigh that would surely
have registered something on the Richter scale, walked
ponderously around the room, ended up at the cabinet
with the viola in it, and stood there gazing at it, his
back to the room, shaking his head.

"So that's why you're off to Massachusetts," he said
to the cabinet, "to give him the money. That's where
he is."

"That's the one thing you won't get out of me."

"Unimportant." He resumed his perambulation of
the room.

"Mr. Greenfield. Are you going to the police? Or
shall I?"

Greenfield ignored the question and continued his
promenade. "What you just described—was that the
whole of your exchange with Trager? Nothing left
out?"

"No, that's all that was said."

"So you didn't concern yourself with where he was
going or how he would live?"

"No, why should I?"

"I don't believe you."

"Mr. Greenfield, you've forced me to go through a long recital of painful events. I've had a trying week and I have a trip ahead of me. I'm tired. I asked you a question."

Greenfield returned to the sofa and dropped into it. "No, Mrs. Hollis, I don't think we've had the whole story."

"I've *told* you," Victoria said with exasperation, "absolutely . . . everything!"

"No. I still want to know about the relatives. And the letter."

Wearily, Victoria went to the sofa and stood looking down at him. "I truly don't know what you're talking about. Could we please . . ."

"No false modesty, Mrs. Hollis. You're clearly a woman of foresight and ingenuity. You knew it would be necessary to ensure that Trager had not only the means to disappear, but a practical plan for the future. Because otherwise"—he leaned his head back against the cushions and stared up at her—"otherwise, being a man unused to scanty living, he could easily pursue a money-making scheme that would cause him to surface. And he could be recognized, somewhere. And Catherine could hear about it."

Obviously taken aback, Victoria sank down on the sofa, a few dozen inches from Greenfield. "Surface . . ." she murmured.

"So of course you worked out a blueprint for the disappearance, using the relatives as a kind of underground railway, and the letter as the means of his future self-sufficiency."

"What relatives? What—?"

"Please. There's no longer any need to dissemble. I know that Trager has a sister in Canada. And the Canadian border can be crossed from the American side without so much as a driver's license."

"Yes . . ." she said thoughtfully, "it didn't occur to me. . ."

"Of course it did!" Greenfield snapped.

Victoria looked at him with honest puzzlement. I wondered what game he was playing now.

"If you were sending Trager far enough away." he said impatiently, "he'd need some way of getting a passport under an assumed name. There's that brother-in-law up there in Canada, with political influence—we know how that can be manipulated."

"Brother-in-law . . ." Victoria mused.

"And then, of course, there's the clincher. The cousin in Apia."

"Apia?"

"The letter, the letter," Greenfield said fretfully, "from Western Samoa. The letter you read when you were searching his study."

"I only read the notebook."

"I'll refresh your memory." Greenfield took the pale blue envelope from his sweater pocket, removed the letter and read aloud."

" 'I sometimes wonder if college professors could endure their life if it weren't for the occasional grant that allows them to spend large hunks of time in places like this. I'm doing a survey of outmigration, the change in island population, the young blood leaving the island, etc., and it's fascinating, the shades of cultural disparity between modern rural and urban families, the value systems, the multilinguistics. There is a total lack of tourism here, in fact they discourage it, but I am persona grata, having been brought in personally by my good friend the Government Secretary—and the sense of being completely away from the weary world is phenomenal. When time permits I lie for hours on the gorgeous white coral beach, or sit and listen to local stories over a Bloody Mary at Aggie Gray's hotel—which brings me to the fact that I have uncovered a sensational story that is crying to be written. It's part Michener, part Graham Greene, and someone could make a fortune with it. Best-seller list, movie, the works. I've tried getting it down on paper, but alas, as a writer I'm a great anthropologist. How would you like to collaborate? Just kidding. I'm not that presumptuous. Well, maybe someday I'll give you the story as a gift, in return for past favors rendered. . . .' " Greenfield slapped the letter down between them. "What more could you ask?"

Victoria picked it up carefully and looked at it.

"You can't expect me to believe," he went on, "that you didn't seize on this fortuitous combination of circumstances. A sundrenched island, virtually isolated from the rest of the world, a wealth of raw material for his pen, a close relative who would be willing to keep his identity secret for the privilege of being his front man and making his contacts with publishers, editors, agents, and so on. Not a bad life for a fugitive from justice."

"I wonder," said Victoria, fingering the letter, "if it already occurred to him."

"The important thing is that it occurred to you."

"I'm afraid it didn't. I—"

"*And,*" Greenfield all but shouted, "that you had the wit to use it as a means of keeping him tractable."

Victoria looked blank.

"*Merde!*" Greenfield exploded, and then, embarrassed, got to his feet and walked away, growling, "Do I have to spell it out for you? You saw a way of keeping a tight rein on him. Instead of merely sending him off with a single large sum of unproductive money, you . . . made an investment. 'Go to Samoa,' you said, 'write this book. I'll give you a portion of the money toward the writing of the book—a kind of advance against royalties. And when this one is published there'll be another advance, against the next book, and so on, made out to your pseudonym, sent by my lawyer if I'm not around.' As you say, he trusts your word. And the interest you receive on the money by this tactic is the knowledge that he will have to stay in Samoa and keep turning out books in order to receive it."

Victoria stood up and moved toward Greenfield, the bewilderment now replaced by a faint, wry smile. "So that's the procedure you recommend . . ."

"I recommend nothing!" Greenfield held up both hands in a cautionary gesture. "I am not an accomplice in this unlawful plot!"

"I apologize."

"I am merely reconstructing what already took place."

"Yes. Of course."

Greenfield turned and slouched out of the room. Victoria looked at me, acknowledging my presence for the first time.

"Remarkable man," she said, moved to the piano, spread the Samoan letter on its polished top, and gazed down upon it.

Greenfield returned wearing his plaid jacket and carrying mine. He handed it to me and said to Victoria, "If Mrs. Rome was a help to me in obtaining information, it was only under extreme duress. She consistently resisted my efforts to connect this household with either of these unsavory affairs. You might even call her a hindrance."

He left. Victoria and I exchanged enigmatic smiles, and I followed Greenfield out.

▣ 15

It was six weeks before I sat in Victoria's apple-green room again. When I did, it was a warm April evening, soft and moist, and the windows were open to the scent of a garden budding. There were six of us assembled there—Greenfield with his cello, Gordon with his violin, crutches, and no cast, Victoria with her viola, myself at the piano, and Elizabeth in a corner with Alice, listening.

Greenfield had finally gone to the police, but not with Victoria's blackmail scheme. He had, instead, unearthed the dapper little man the Kittells had flagged down on the Gorham road, established the exact time of that encounter, put that together with the exact time that Peter's sister had been dropped off by the Kittells on their way to the hospital, at the home of a friend with whom she walked to school, confirmed, via the older boy who had been awake with stomach flu all night, that his parents had been home all that time, and proved that it left the Kittells something less than four minutes to accomplish the mayhem of which they were suspected, at which time, even the police conceded, there was enough traffic on the road to make it impractical.

He then rooted around the Wayside Motel, discovered from Carl Hauser that the truck Andrew had been driving had been parked opposite the motel entrance in full view of the reception desk and had been there all night, and had found a chambermaid who verified that she had tried several times to get into Andrew's room to clean up and hadn't been able to until after 9 A.M., and the police conceded that all in all Andrew had a fairly good alibi.

Just to clinch it, Greenfield pointed out that if Andrew *had* taken the angle iron for nefarious reasons, it would be unlikely he'd broadcast it in Farnham's hardware store that one was missing, and suggested that Trager himself might have put the thing in his car to use as a tool for some purpose or other, and his unknown assailant, finding it available, used it as a weapon, and they conceded that.

The ultimate result of Greenfield's various disclosures to the police was that they began to suspect Greenfield. But since they couldn't come up with either motive or opportunity, let alone evidence, they turned their attention to greener pastures, of which, in terms of suburban crime, they had ample choice.

When we'd left the farmhouse on that final, climactic day, I'd said to Greenfield, "Okay, I worked it out for myself. The 'urgent matter' in Sidonie's hypothetical note to Trager that would have made him rush out in the middle of the night would have been: 'My husband is going to tell your wife about us.' And that's also why Trager panicked and left Peter on the road, because he had Sidonie in the car and if Catherine found out and divorced him, he'd lose all that money from the sale of the farm."

"It took you long enough," he said.

Now, on this tender April evening, I hit the A on the Baldwin and the room was filled with the sounds of stringed instruments tuning up. We were going to tackle a Mozart quartet. I heard the back door open and close, and Catherine's face appeared in the hall doorway. There'd been no transformation, she hadn't evolved into a radiant beauty, but I did think she looked ten years younger than when I'd first seen her. She smiled at me and disappeared, and Greenfield spoke.

Because, as should be quite obvious by now, he must always have the last word.

"All right," he said, "this is the tempo."

And thumped his foot on Victoria's rug.